AND *THE UNDEAD SITUATION*

"Eloise Knapp's sequel to *The Undead Situation* shows that surviving the apocalypse was not the hardest part... it's living it."

—Bricks of the Dead

"Knapp breathes new life into the walking dead with this harrowing, fast-paced sequel. Anti-hero Cyrus Sinclair is a character you won't soon forget!"

—Jim LaVigne, author of Plaguesville, USA

"*The Undead Situation* will please fans of classic zombie tales with familiar apocalyptic situations, but will also offer something for those looking for a twist to their zombie lore..."

—The Guilded Earlobe

"I implore you to buy a copy [of *The Undead Situation*], because if Robert Kirkman's got any sense, he'd buy the rights up to this pronto and somehow shimmy Cyrus V. Sinclair into *The Walking Dead*..."

—Snakebite Horror Reviews

"Brilliantly unusual characters are the reason that [*The Undead Situation*] stands out. Bluntly put... I've never so thoroughly enjoyed a book full of people that I can't stand."

—Jill McDole, Impact Online

Eloise J. Knapp

A PERMUTED PRESS book
published by arrangement with the author

ISBN (trade paperback): 978-1-61868-073-0
ISBN (eBook): 978-1-61868-074-7

Cover art by Eloise J. Knapp.

For Evan and Matt who have proven to be kickass fans through thick and thin.

Prologue

The mere thought Blaze could still be alive caused my newly developed—and much disliked—humanity to kick in. It didn't happen right away. No, weeks passed before that whisper of hesitation turned into full-blown doubt. Logic was gone and guilt, that infuriating, oppressive guilt, came to tell me I should leave the safety and perfection of Frank's fortress-like cabin and go find her.

Was she dead? It didn't matter. Blaze could be a shambling, festering zombie, but my need to know outweighed my inclination to keep quiet and safe.

Besides the feeling of remorse plaguing me, I grew increasingly sick of the still, deep forest I was in. Since I arrived, only two undead hikers that managed to wander this far northeast popped up outside my fence. I killed them, but not before tracking and studying them to amuse myself. It was the only excitement I experienced during the months I was there.

I disdained my solitude and craved danger and adventure. Prior to the apocalypse I lived a subdued life, but after spending weeks killing zombies and crazies, before ending up in the cabin, the taste for anarchy lingered in my mouth. It certainly suited me. Why not go charging back into it?

There were at least twenty solid reasons I used to justify loading a hiking pack with food, water, and other supplies. Justification flowed through me.

But why am I justifying it to you?

My name is Cyrus V. Sinclair, and I don't need a reason.

PART ONE

Chapter 1

A quick run to the gas station down the street should have been easy. It should have ended with a bag full of Sour Patch Kids and protein bars, but all I had was an empty stomach, an empty gun, and a massive headache.

I thought about Frank's cabin. It had been weeks since I left. I was nearly thirty miles away from it, still wondering if I made the right choice to abandon my home to find Blaze Wright. It felt like an eternity since I met her at the prison overrun with crazies in Monroe. I thought I was helping *her* escape, but by the time we got out of there she'd already saved my life once. The first woman I cared about also turned out to be more callous and sociopathic than I could ever dream of being.

Twenty rotbags shuffled over the pavement below me. Their gnarled hands clawed at the walls. It was too much to hope they'd just wander off. They hadn't forgotten about me, and I wasn't sure they ever would.

How many weeks had it been since they'd seen fresh prey?

I wiped a drip from my nose and leaned against the ventilation system on the roof. Twenty undead. I'd counted them twice in the past hour. Their numbers hadn't increased. Good. And they'd stopped groaning. Instead they walked the perimeter of the gas station, their necks craned upward.

Everett was a big town, but there weren't many zombies. Hell if I knew where they went, but I wasn't going to curse good fortune. It seemed safe enough a place to rest, so I had picked a house on the outskirts of town and settled in with Pickle for the night. I'd been feeling off. A couple nights of rest were in order. On the second morning, I locked Pickle in a bathroom and set off to find supplies. A mile down the road I found a gas station.

Then they came stumbling out of the forest like they'd been waiting for me. Only a handful at first, but more were behind them. I hadn't stepped five feet onto the lot when I had to break into a run. The gas station doors were locked.

And there I was. Cold, hungry, and desperate, wishing that I'd brought Pickle with me. I thought I'd be gone for an hour at most. Now she was alone at that house, trapped inside that room.

"Hey, Ricky! We got a bunch of 'em over here!"

I twitched. The voice was faint, but it might as well have been a shout. I hadn't heard another living person in weeks. I crawled to the side of the roof on my belly and peered over.

Three figures walked down the road. They all carried rifles. One of them held a walkie-talkie to his mouth. The slows below me moved en masse towards them.

As soon as the undead near the ladder cleared the area I shot down it, slipping on the bars, and booked it to the forest. People are bad news even if they have good intentions. Avoiding them was the only way I'd been able to survive the past couple months.

The frost-covered grass beneath my boots crunched. The edge of the forest was thirty feet away. Relief flooded through me.

Seconds later, roaring engines startled me. I glanced back just as two trucks pulled up near the gas station. One of them went off road and came straight towards me.

Automatic gunfire joined the sound of the trucks. I cleared the forest line as a bullet burrowed into the evergreen next to me.

What the hell had I done to deserve this? I risked another glance and saw figures trailing me. The truck that dropped them off was already circling back to the gas station.

My heart hammered in my chest. I didn't have enough bullets to take them out even if I hit each of them in the head. I wasn't sure where I was going or how long they'd pursue me

My boot hit a slimy, moss-covered log and I went down. My shin hit the log first, sending sharp pain up my leg. I tried to catch myself before the rest of me hit the ground, but it was too late. The side of my head smacked against a rock.

"Over there! Get 'im!"

Spots clouded my vision. Someone's boot was on my back and a hand pushed my face into the snow. My gun was snatched from my hands. I took a deep breath before it all went dark.

* * *

I woke up in a pile of people. I wasn't even at the top of the pile. Flesh pressed against me and I couldn't see faces. People whimpered all around me. I felt the edge of death surrounding us and wondered how long it would take until someone on the bottom died, came back, and ate their way out of the pile.

It was unpleasant.

My left arm went numb from being bent around my back. I tried to tug it forward, but aside from almost pulling a muscle, I accomplished nothing. I couldn't move. I was on my back, my head on someone's stomach, and it gave me an upside down view of foggy roadside.

I tried to take a calming breath, but the stench of fear and sweat and *people* made me gag. More than one person must've pissed themselves. The smell of warm urine was the strongest, and it saturated people's clothing.

Somewhere near me a man sobbed. The moans from everyone else were almost overshadowed by him. Whoever I was on top of was convulsing.

After another attempt at escaping the pile I had no choice but to give up. My legs were trapped. I had no control over my left arm. Taking calming breaths, even through my mouth, was difficult since my chest was crushed under the person above me.

I wasn't claustrophobic, but this was too much. I had no idea how many people were around me. How many crazies were guarding us?

"Where did that red haired one go, Bubba?"

"In the truck!"

"He ain't in the truck, stupid fucker. You put him with the rest of the meat?"

Two hulking redneck beasts moved closer to the pile from out of the mist.

"You know what boss says," one said. The pressure eased as he pulled a body off the pile. "Save the redheads 'cause they taste real good, ya know?"

"Well I left him in the truck, so I don't know who done took him out," Bubba said. "And no, ain't never eaten a redhead because they rare and any ones we come across get eaten by the boss."

Why me? I'm finding a box of hair dye if I make it out of here. Why the hell do people hate redheads so much?

I wanted to make a joke of it. Anything to lighten my mood, but it was proving difficult. I'd been around cannibals before. The prison in Monroe. The crazies in Startup likely ate people, also. Yet I'd never been so close to being eaten myself.

Do they kill you first? Burn you alive? Eat you raw?

They dropped one in front of me. The sobbing man. He got to his knees and started crawling away.

"Whadda we got here, Bubba?"

The rednecks surrounded the man. Watched as he crawled. It was pathetic.

"Looks like he tryin' to run, Bear. What do you say? We make it so he can't even crawl no more?"

Two hits later with the butt of his rifle and Bubba broke sobbing man's legs. The redneck's laughed at their cruelty.

"You know, I think—hey, look at that. Hey buddy, I think yer the one we're looking for."

They stood in front of me. Their upside down faces sneered, showing tobacco stained teeth.

"Boss'll like this one," Bubba said as they shoved and pulled bodies away from the pile. The people cowered together as they hit the grass, too afraid or too weak to try and escape. "He looks real healthy."

They lead me to a line of tents.

There was a silver lining to everything. No more meat pile, no more disgusting smells. I inhaled as much of the cold winter air as I could, glad to be away from the stench.

My thoughts went into overdrive as I looked everywhere for an escape while we walked. We were on the side of a road by a truck rest stop. Five large tents were set up some distance away from the trucks these raiders stored us in. Dense forest flanked either side of the road. A green sign said Everett was five miles away.

I let my body sag, forcing the rednecks to take my arms and carry me. I needed to buy more time to think. They grunted but didn't say anything. Our pace slowed.

I wouldn't make it on foot down the road. It was unlikely I'd be able to steal a truck. Couldn't kill all of them since I didn't know how many there were and didn't have a weapon. My best option was to escape into the forest, get as far away as I could, and make my way back to the town. They'd be looking for me there if they were hell bent on catching me, but I had to get Pickle.

We stopped at the biggest tent. It was a pavilion tent, each of the plastic panels closed tight.

"Immortal Son," Bear said. "We found the redhead."

A man pulled a panel aside. The moment I saw him I knew he was bad news. The name was a big clue, sure. His appearance even more so.

He wasn't like any redneck crazy I'd ever seen. He was immaculately groomed. His tan robe touched the ground and was tied at the waist with a rope. Long blond hair was tied at the nape of his neck. Above all his eyes set him apart. Not dull and animalistic like the rednecks. They were calculated. Slow. But no less insane.

He flashed a pearly white smile. "Hello. Welcome. Please, carry this man inside."

I planted my feet and straightened, yanking my arms from Bear and Bubba. If I was going to get eaten, the least I could do was have some dignity going in. More importantly, if *Immortal Son* was the only guy in the tent, my chances of escape looked promising. Going in willingly would benefit me.

"I'll walk, thanks."

They closed in on me again, their grip on my arms tighter this time.

He laughed. "You are very humorous, friend. Please escort him inside and tie him to the chair."

He disappeared in the tent. The rednecks pushed me inside, towards an ornate wooden chair. Parts of it were stained red. The trampled grass it stood on was darkened with what looked like blood.

"Nourishment does not usually speak. It takes much prodding for them to even say their names. They cry in joy that they might serve such divine purpose, but they certainly do not joke," he said as they tied me.

I kept my hands flexed as they wrapped the ropes. Once I relaxed later I'd have an easier time wiggling out.

"Is that so? I guess I'm a spicy flavor. I've got kick."

He laughed again. It was practiced. I knew because I used to do it.

"Very good, very good."

"You need anythin' else, Immortal Son?"

"No, Bear. Thank you, my beloved Great One. You may leave."

The rednecks left without another word. I was alone with the new crazy. I shifted in the chair and looked around. The tent was sparsely furnished. A cot, and a folding desk with an assortment of books and notebooks. A shining tin container of lighter fluid. I spotted a trunk in my peripheral. Hanging from the middle of the tent was a lantern that cast a yellow glow.

Natural light drifted in around the perimeter of the tent. I followed it until I found a vertical line of light where the walls of the tent met. It was small, two inches at best, but through it I saw forest. If I could get through, I might be able to make it to the forest without anyone noticing me.

"What is your name, friend?"

"What's it to you?"

"I like to know the name of my nourishment so I might thank Him for sending it."

"Oh, that makes me feel better. My name is Cyrus. Cyrus V. Sinclair."

The V was going to stand for victim if I didn't get myself out of this clusterfuck.

"It is wonderful to meet you, Mr. Sinclair. My name is Kevin, though my followers call me Immortal Son." He smiled. "As I said before, nourishment does not usually speak."

"I've got a lot to say. I could tell you all about how I was just being crushed under a pile of people that you plan on *eating*. I guess you knew that already."

"You treat it very lightly. Aren't you disgusted by being in the nourishment pile, Mr. Sinclair? Most are at first."

"I'm *disgusted* by how no one tried to get out of it. The people on the top could've rolled off. Freed the rest of us. There were only two of your idiot crazies watching us."

"Fear. Deep rooted fear is what keeps them there," Kevin said. "When told they would be nourishment for the Son of God, they feared the repercussions of escaping."

"They feared getting fucking eaten."

"No. Should you learn the doctrine of the Immortal Son you would understand. Other nourishment is taught their purpose in this world. As they learn their faces show their enlightenment. They become very peaceful."

Or they were so terrified by how insane Kevin was they completely shut down. I was on the verge of shutting down myself.

"You see, most people are not chosen to serve a high purpose. Some are meant for consumption, their flesh nourishing those of greater stature. In return, as those who are great consume them, their souls are cleansed so they might be saved in their next life."

How could he be serious? He spoke with raw sincerity. He believed every word. The crème de la crème of crazies who happened to have a taste for redheads. Fantastic.

Kevin paused. Brushed his hand against the top of the cheap folded table. He looked up at me and smiled. "You are quite intelligent, Mr. Sinclair."

"Sure am."

"I don't think you know the most important thing, Mr. Sinclair."

"Yeah? What's that?"

"That I truly am the Immortal Son of God, bringer of the Light in these Dark and Dead days. I have received revelation and—"

The glob of saliva I spit didn't reach him, but as it splattered onto the dirt floor it shut him up. Then he lost it.

He flung the table, its items scattering on the ground. Kevin crossed the distance between us and grabbed my shoulders. He squeezed. His eyes shone with rage and tears. A turbulent mixture of emotions flashed across his face, but they all added up to one thing.

Crazy. So fucking crazy.

"—and that these messages I am offering you, and the rest of the people outside, is true. You are very lucky I am giving you this personal sermon so that you might have a better chance of understanding."

I grinned. "No. I think I'm in here because you like to eat redheads."

Kevin turned away from me, rubbing his hand on the back of his head. He stepped to the edge of the tent and peered through. When was this going to be over? I'd rather be eaten then listen to crazy talk any longer than I had to.

"When the group of people you call 'crazies' found me, not long after the dead rose, I had been inside a basement for three days surrounded by dead bodies. My brethren elected me as the vessel that would aid in their ascension from this mortal life. If we died any other way but by gunshot to the head, we would come back. Our souls would be trapped in rotting bodies, wandering this hell forever. Naturally suicide would be a grave sin, so I was given the opportunity to send them to their next life."

I twisted my wrist while he spoke, using the time his stupid monologue bought me to try and find a weakness in the knots. There was a bit of give. I felt a flare of hope.

"So you shot them?"

Kevin nodded. "I did what I was asked in order to do right by my brethren."

"Technically they used you to murder them. Don't you see? They didn't want to commit suicide since it goes against your 'faith.' By having you do it, their hands are clean. But you're a murderer."

He paused. His fingers tapped against his side rhythmically.

"You do not see the light now, friend, but you will, just as I did. You see, on the third day I received revelation." Kevin turned back to me. The smile on his face sent a chill down my spine. "I persevered. The trial of isolation was testing my devotion. I succeeded and an angel came to me and revealed my purpose: to save the children of earth, by force if need be. He told me my brothers died so that I might be provided with nourishment until I was found. After another three days of being in that basement, knowing what my mission was but held back by fear of entering the undead world, my disciples found me. I taught them my mission, gained their trust, and am now here before you offering you the same truth."

The apocalypse weeded out everything between saintly survivor and jacked up crazies. I was encountering everyone on the bad side of the spectrum. This guy topped the charts.

I shifted my hands. No luck with the knots. No luck getting this guy to shut up. I was low on energy and worried about Pickle. I did what I always did in a situation like this.

"Sounds to me that your friends didn't care about you, the newcomer, so they had you kill them. Sounds like you ate your dead buddies because you're *crazy* and you wanted to, then taught the rest of these rednecks to do it, too. And finally, sounds like you came up with a good story to justify the whole thing. Am I right, Kevin?"

His right eye twitched three times. Stopped. "Mr. Sinclair, I am not going to eat you."

"What a shame. I hear redheads taste super. I bet I taste like sugar, spice, and everything fucking nice."

"From the short time I've spent with you I can tell you are a very smart individual. You are also smothered in sin, and I now know that it is one of my duties to save you. It will be a challenge, but your position should be at the right side of the Immortal Son, and I will do all I can to make it so."

Great. Why can't he just eat me like a normal cannibal?

Kevin righted the table and cleaned up his mess. "Before I go, I will tell you one last thing. To help you understand why I'm doing this."

I heaved a sigh, squeezed my eyes shut, and wished it would stop.

"Six months ago I was drawn to a house, and trapped there was the future bearer of the Chosen One. From a city of wickedness, chaos, and death I found a pure light that was destined for me. We cleansed the house with fire, but within were wicked souls. Many of my followers were lost, but the bearer of my future child, my closest disciples, and myself were delivered from the battle unscathed. Later she spoke of a redheaded man who was quite saintly. Brutal, but saintly." Kevin smiled. "A miracle. You cannot deny it."

"I can actually," I said. "I do. If you only eat redheads you were *destined* to find someone who fit the description, weren't you?"

Someone rapped on the tent door before Kevin could continue. "Immortal Son, they're ready."

"I will be there in a moment." Kevin tightened the rope around his waist and donned a fur cloak over his robe. He stood behind me and placed his hands on my shoulders. His fingers were red and blistered. I tried to jerk away but he held firm.

"Mr. Sinclair, I do not yet know what your purpose is. Clearly you will not birth the Chosen One." He paused to laugh at his own joke. "But I know there is another plan in store for you. The new world I am creating will need men of strength, honor, and intelligence. I have not met anyone who possesses all those requirements until you. I can only pray when He tells me what to do with you, it will be to put you by my side. Until I find that out, you will be under my direct protection. I look forward to speaking with you more when I return."

He pulled the tent flap aside. Morning sun sliced through the shadowy interior, blinding me for an instant before my eyes adjusted.

"And if you ever betray the protection and trust that I am showing you now, fear not. I know it is merely another personal trial for me and not wickedness on your part. I will not blame you. But I will find you if you try to escape. I will hunt you. There will be punishment, because no misdeed can go unpunished. Now, in the mean time I will mark you with our seal of commitment so you should never forget your connection to me. Bear, please mark Mr. Sinclair."

Then he was gone.

Chapter 2

Bear had a sick grin on his face as he strode in. Three men trailed behind him. One of them wore heavy gloves and carried a charcoal chimney. A thin metal rod protruded from it. Ashes dusted the ground as they jostled each other while situating around me. The heavy scent of hot metal engulfed me. I could taste it.

How many people had they branded with that exact rod? How much burnt flesh was caked onto it? Nausea swept over me. Fear made it worse.

Bear pulled the rod free from the coals. An insignia of a sword with licks of fire around it glowed red hot. Its light reflected in each of the crazies' eyes. I turned my head away. I couldn't look at it or them.

"Where you want it, buddy? Forehead? So everyone can see it?" Bear glanced as the other men for validation. The goons chuckled.

"How about you shove it up your ass where *no one* can see it?" It wasn't my joke that made them laugh harder. It was the shake in my voice.

"Look at 'im, boys. Trying to sound tough!"

"What a pussy!" I said.

Beneath his beard, Bear flushed. "Shudda fuck up, bitch. Ain't nuthin' you can say to stop me."

Another one piped up. "Immortal Son said to put it over his heart, so that's where we put it, ya hear?"

The three converged on me. Two held me down while one unzipped my jacket and lifted my soggy layers of clothes up to reveal my chest. I struggled but I couldn't move.

"Looks like yer gonna be one of us soon," one said. "Won't be able ta eat ya."

Bear stood in front of me and let the branding rod hover over my chest. "Nah, brothers. We can still eat 'em. Just have to eat ever last bit, so you don't know who he is."

Ambient heat caressed my skin as the rod came closer. My gaze flashed down. The sight of it so close to my flesh made my heart race harder. My breath was labored, my chest tight. This was worse than being shot or stabbed. I could see it coming closer, closer…

He grinned and, without preamble, pressed the emblem into my chest. At first, nothing was real. It wasn't my chest the smoke wafted up from. It wasn't my skin and muscle that smelled burnt and bloody. It wasn't my body that sizzled under the heat of the brand. That loud, continuous scream? Not me.

But it was. And it all hit me at once. My blood pumped so hard I felt it in my chest, my ears, my head. The scent of cooked flesh—*my own fucking cooked flesh, oh fuck oh fuck*—made my stomach rumble. Ragged screams tore up my throat. When I ran out of air, I sucked in more and shrieked again. As pain engulfed me, I never thought I'd stop.

When he pulled the rod away, the pain stayed, as though the rod was still there.

They left, laughing while I gasped for air and tried not to pass out.

I was wriggling out of the ropes as soon as they left. The pain of the burn pulsed with my heartbeat. It took everything I had to steady myself. Every movement took double the effort, but not having any choice was good motivation.

There were three zip ties connecting the two pieces of tent I noticed earlier. I needed something to cut through them and fast.

I went to the trunk first. It was locked. I searched the junk on the floor that had fallen when Kevin flipped the table. Nothing of use.

What if no one is even watching the tent, Cyrus? Did you check?

I peeked through a crack in the front. There were four crazies strolling the camp site, all of which would be attracted to the sight of someone coming out of Kevin's tent.

Great. I stepped back and scrubbed my palm against the side of my head. All that stood between me and freedom was some plastic. If this was the end of me, my life hadn't been worth living.

I ground my teeth as I stared at the items on the ground. What would I do with a notebook, pen, map…

Notebook. Spiral notebook. I snatched it up and uncoiled the thin metal wire. It was sturdy enough. It could work.

The papers slipped to the ground as the last loop came free. I took my wire to the zip ties, pinched the connector in my hand, and slid the wire inside. There was a small tab in the tie that only needed to be pressed for the tie to release. The first try didn't work.

I folded the wires in half and twisted them, creating a stronger poking device. This time the tab pressed in and the thick plastic popped off and hit the ground. I had the second and third ties free in no time.

I pulled the edge of the flap open. In front of me and on all sides there was forest. Kevin set his tent far from the rest.

Arrogant jackass. Didn't think anyone could ever escape?

I took a deep breath of the crisp morning air and tried my best to sprint to the forest. It ended up a determined, awkward lop. I didn't look back. If they were chasing me, it wouldn't matter if I saw them coming or not.

They'd get me, just like they got me in the forest before.

***

My lungs ached. I ran until I couldn't run another second, then I walked. I couldn't stop. Walking was better than being stationary. Had Kevin or his crazies found out I was missing yet?

I went straight into the forest then started jogging in a wide arc to the left until I saw glimpses of road. I didn't hear any voices. No roar of truck engines, either. I had to keep up the pace.

Eventually I passed the gas station. I kept far away from it.

Fuck if I felt naked. I had the clothes on my back and not a damn thing to defend myself with. I tucked my chin down into my coat and thought about getting to Pickle and getting far away from Kevin. I made fun of the situation, but now that I was out of it the gravity of my near death experience hit me. If I hadn't been snarky Kevin would've eaten me.

The sun was almost entirely risen by the time I made it back to the house I'd left Pickle in. I climbed through the back window I left open. The house was small and set back from the highway in a wooded area. I chose it for its privacy. It hadn't let me down. There was no sign of entry. Not a single Z wandered the area.

When I cracked open the door to the bathroom where I'd left Pickle, I wanted to hear an angry scurry to the door. But I didn't hear anything. She'd burrowed into the blanket I set in the bathtub. She lifted her head as I approached, her beady red eyes dull.

"I'm sorry, girl," I said as I picked her up. "I hope you weren't worried."

I stroked her thinning white fur and kissed her head before putting her back in the blanket. There would be time for apologizing later. I needed to change my clothes, pack my gear, and keep on moving.

I wasn't sure who owned the house. There weren't any family photos on the walls. Clothing in the closet and dressers indicated a man and a woman. No kids. As I sorted through moth eaten sweaters, I wondered if the house was empty before the apocalypse.

The jacket, jeans, and sweatshirts I found were a size too big, but it felt good to shed my damp, urine scented clothes.

I rummaged through the pantry and found two cans of soup with pop-tops. It wouldn't last me more than a day and a half. I hoped I'd find more once I had the chance to stop.

I cleaned my brand wound with rubbing alcohol and cotton puffs. They didn't have bandages big enough to cover it. I made one out of duct tape and gauze.

I placed Pickle in the top of my pack and left the zipper open a few inches for better ventilation. Then I left.

Chapter 3

Even though it felt like acidic tapioca coming up my throat, I coughed up another ball of phlegm and spit it in its designated bucket. After a few seconds of relief, more throat snot worked its way up until I needed to repeat the process. By now the aroma must've been beyond vile, ranging into intolerable. If I could smell it, I would've been disgusted with myself.

A thick fog hovered outside. I couldn't see Monte Cristo or any of the buildings past it. I vaguely saw the Parks building that housed the student store straight across from me. Today would be a good day to scavenge if I wasn't on the verge of death. For all I knew I had some form of the bubonic plague.

Somewhere under the desk, Pickle moved around, making herself more comfortable in the tiny bed she'd created over the weeks we'd been there. I found it humorous she had a better setup than me. My bitter laugh was cut short as I involuntarily hacked out another yellow package.

Everett Community College was supposed to be a pit stop where I could rest and fend off what I thought was a head cold. After walking for a half a day and reaching the main city of Everett, I began feeling lightheaded. My throat itched and my nose dripped. I needed to stop.

Just like I'd thought the gas station would be a quick stop, this also ended up being a bigger ordeal than I bargained for.

I wasn't familiar with the town itself, but I was drawn to the campus because I'd taken some classes there years ago. I knew its layout.

Remembering the names of different buildings was comforting. Knowing the land didn't hurt either. Any advantage helped.

The campus was a ghost town, which was one of the reasons I thought it would make a good rest area. I was still running on the assumption I was *just* getting sick. Mildly sick.

I'd spend just a day there. That's all.

Then, after searching a few locked buildings, I walked across a sky bridge which led to the second floor of a three story building called Rainer. The heavy glass doors downstairs were shut and locked, so I didn't have to deal with securing more than one entrance. The only thing I worried about was the door I came through, which I locked with a crowbar, in addition to its normal upper and lower locks and their manual bolts.

On day one I searched the bottom story. Day two my cold turned into something nasty, and that was it. No more searching. I whimpered like a baby as my nose clogged and my throat got dry. I grew afraid there were undead roaming the areas I hadn't cleared. As time went by, a new sense of paranoia set in. Weakness and fear gnawed at me, and it only grew worse the longer I didn't search. Each time I thought I heard something I paced behind my closed office door, secretly hoping the soft padding of my feet on the carpet would lure any undead out, but dreading the moment when it did. It was a vicious cycle.

And Kevin? I imagined hearing the convoy outside the building. There to come take me back. I remembered his crazy, made-up verse and dreamt of it on bad nights.

Dreams of Blaze plagued me since the night I couldn't find her in Startup. They'd been growing darker and more frequent since I'd been searching for her. Now that I was sick and sleep deprived, the dreams were becoming more hallucinogenic. Sometimes I woke up smelling cigarette smoke or feeling like she was in the room. I chalked it up to a guilty conscience and gave up trying to make peace with the situation.

I huddled in my makeshift bed of padding ripped out of couches and chairs and I shivered. I carried one thermal blanket in my backpack, but winter was coming on and that wouldn't be enough. Hell, I even layered on tapestries and wall quilts from the offices. Not like it mattered.

I glanced outside once more. The scene hadn't changed, but my willingness had. My head swam as I removed myself from the blankets and I grabbed the filing cabinet for support. My nose dripped and my body convulsed in an onset of shivers.

There was one thing about my situation I particularly hated—my lack of weapons. I suppose my adventures in the summer were far too easy because ammunition was abundant. Even during desperate times I had something, whether it was a handgun or assault rifle. Now all I had was a 9mm with a few rounds, a flashlight, and a baseball bat. The bat had modifications, though. Just some nails here and there. And a lady's face I drew on it—her name was Barbara, in case you were interested.

Gathering my two weapons, I opened the office door and peeked out. To my left there were no windows and the hallways faded into blackness. Even if I waited for my eyes to adjust, I wouldn't see anything. Well, except part of a corpse. Half the body was obscured by a right turn in the hall. All I saw were the legs. That half of the building was creepy. It instigated my paranoia. So still and dark. When I went to search that floor, I could only take a few steps into the bleeding edge of blackness before I had to retreat. I'm not sure what it was about down there, but I didn't want to find out.

Look at me, Cyrus V. Sinclair, afraid of the dark and the boogeyman.

I stepped out of the office and closed the door securely behind me. Yesterday Pickle escaped, bent on having an adventure. I still hadn't seen her. Since then, I'd been keeping the door shut.

The hall was vacant and chilled. My boots made no noise on the carpet. At the right end of the hall were heavy wooden doors that led to an open space before the staircase. I heaved one open. Blinding light dazed me and I squeezed my eyes shut until the burning went away.

Once my vision returned, I took a few steps towards the window until I had a good view of the campus. Taking my time, since I had a lot of it, I scanned the area for any signs of life—or death—of which I found none. Not even a breeze moved the leafless branches of the bushes and trees.

I was as confident as I ever would be. I opened the stair access door and headed one floor down to the sky bridge landing. Each footstep echoed, bouncing around the cement stairwell.

Too loud. Stop being so noisy, I chided myself.

I was soon in a room similar to the one above me. Open and chilly. I assessed the area around me then stared at the door to Parks.

It was just across the sky bridge. Like most entrances in the college, it was glass with a metal frame bisecting it at waist level. As far as I could tell, my only option was to break the glass and squeeze through the lower half.

Swallowing an incoming slime ball back down my throat, I unlocked the double doors, yanked the crowbar out, and crouched to open one and slide through. If I walked across the bridge, I would be visible.

I was convinced death was around the corner, but I could make some effort to prevent it.

My legs were rubbery as I stayed low and moved across the bridge. The cool air felt like it was freezing my mucus. There was no hope of breathing through my nose. And was it just me, or was it cold enough to freeze my eyeballs, too?

Clutching my bat, I came up to the overhang of the Parks' roof. In front of me were the doors, to the left was a wall, and to the right was a slanted walkway to the parking lots. As the coast was still clear, I moved forward. I was right when I said the door was the same as Rainier. There was a primary key lock and peg locks on the top and bottom.

I took the bat, gathered as much strength as I could, and swung at the lower half of the door. The sound of it cracking was so startling I had to fight back a reactive shout. To the undead out there, this noise was a dinner bell. But I had to keep going. Bringing the bat back once again, I gave it another hit and it gave way. I chipped away as much of the remaining glass as I could with the heel of my boot.

You don't need to hear a moan to know one's coming. I was well aware when I broke that glass I'd be surrounded in no time. Even though I hadn't seen any Zs, it didn't mean they weren't there. Whether it was minutes or hours, I had to hurry.

I set Barbara in and squeezed through the tiny opening. My gloves made getting through the broken glass a hell of a lot easier.

Down the hall was a skylight, barely lighting up the linoleum floor. Posters and bulletin boards promoting nonexistent clubs and programs lined the walls. To the right were glass displays with mannequins sporting school apparel and backpacks. Behind the display paper would be the student store.

I started forward. Once at the end of the hall, I glanced to either side. Left was fine, but the right made my heart stop.

The store security gate was closed. The metal grid barred me from everything I wanted.

Why hadn't I thought of that? The school was clearly closed down when the apocalypse came, so why wouldn't the gate be closed? Being sick put me in a foul, spacey mood. But look at where I was? In a disappointing situation with Zs coming from at least a mile radius to eat me up.

I'm not giving up. Get your fucking act together, Cyrus. You're getting in there.

I walked past the gate and headed farther right. There was a book buyback window, like a drive through window, but nothing else.

At least I had an option. Gritting my teeth, I struck the pane of glass at the buyback window, which broke faster as it was thinner than the entrance doors. I threw the bat in and tried hauling myself through. The first attempt didn't work, and I fell back onto the ground while releasing a loud sneeze. My throat throbbed in pain and my vision blurred.

Wiping the dribbles of snot off my nose, I got back up and put everything I had into lifting myself over the counter. Glass clinked on the ground. A series of tearing sounds was enough to let me know jagged pieces were snagging on my clothes. Then I was through, both feet on the ground, inside the store.

Minimal light filtered through the front gate, casting most of the store in darkness. It smelled dusty and unused. Heart pounding, I remained in a crouch and listened, though my ears were ringing from the silence. If something was in the store, it wasn't voicing it.

I grabbed the flashlight from my jacket pocket and clicked it on. A subdued yellow beam hit the floor and I raised it up. Binders, notebooks, backpacks, and all manners of school supplies were pristine on shelves and walls. My spirits soared when I saw school sweaters and jackets. On the back wall, beside the backpacks, I saw two large drink refrigerators, in front of which were racks of snacks that might prove more substantial than the junk going stale in vending machines.

Finally, my luc—

Every time I gave myself a high five for finding something, or thought things were looking up, I jinxed it and things went bad. Cutting my thoughts off before the cosmos could work against me, I stood and began my search. Cautiously.

My heart and stomach wanted to rush for the food, but the store was small enough to clear in no time. I held Barbara in one hand and the flashlight in the other and searched each aisle. Each row yielded no corpses, moving or otherwise. Relieved, I went to the back wall, grabbing a backpack as I passed. My hand shook from the stress of feeling out of sorts and on a time crunch. I unzipped the bag and filled it with anything useful.

Repeating the process with three other backpacks, I forgot about the impending doom waiting outside until at least ten minutes had passed. Before I could forget, I moseyed over to the sweaters and grabbed a hoodie, pulling it over my head. I repeated the process until I had two sweaters on. There were definitely more clothing products that would help me out, but I'd have to come back later to shop more. Returning to the last backpack I'd been filling, I resumed my work.

Outside I heard glass crunching. Dropping into a crouch again, turning the flashlight off quickly, I relied on the cashier island in front of the gate to obscure me. I forced my breathing to normalize and stayed still, trying to formulate a plan of escape.

Should've thought of that sooner, you idiot.

As ideas raced through my mind, a nearby shelf caught my attention.

Nyquil. Dayquil? Mucinex!

An over the counter respiratory dream. Knowing I might forget them when things got hot, I took them all and crammed the medicine into my fourth backpack. Even if I made it out with just that one, I'd be pleased.

Pleasure evaporated quickly when I heard squeaking drawing closer. I didn't need to guess what was making it.

What was there to worry about? It wasn't as though a zombie had the dexterity to climb through the buyback window. And besides the gate, there wasn't any other entrance. If worst came to worst, I would just stay in the bookstore until they cleared out enough for me to escape.

Footsteps grew louder and I peered around the cashiers' area to see an ordinary man standing in front of the grate. I estimated he'd been dead about five months, since he was emaciated and on the verge of snapping. Dark splotches stained the front of his striped polo and down his khakis. A ragged chunk of his face was missing. He looked around blandly, but even though he found nothing he remained.

Minutes passed and another one, an Asian woman, walked passed him and began a slow ascent up a staircase across from the bookstore.

Still, Khakis remained. Occasionally he wheezed and shifted positions, but wasn't leaving. If I was in this situation four months ago, I would've pulled out an assault rifle and popped one in his head. No problem.

Now I was as desperate as any other survivor out there. My primary form of defense was a baseball bat. I asked myself repeatedly what to do, but the backwoods part of my brain didn't produce any suggestions.

If I waited longer, I risked more zombies coming. I wanted to wait until he cleared out, but the plan was flawed. If too many of them arrive, there was no way to know how long it would take them to leave. Feeling a little dejected, I turned my head and looked at the three resource-filled bags. I had one with me, mostly filled with drugs, but some food, too. I doubted I'd be able to make it with more than one backpack, but leaving them behind was out of the question. I *needed* those supplies. What if I never had the chance to come back?

To my left was a pegboard where the sweaters hung. I realized it was behind the display windows. I couldn't leave the same way I came in—too dangerous—but this gave me an idea. As slow and quiet as I could manage, I made it to the pegboard. It was made of multiple panels, allowing it to span ten feet across.

Each panel was on a hinge, which was how people must've gotten behind it to create the displays. A rectangular notch acted as a handle. If I was right, tugging on that would let the panel swing open.

Then, if I broke the glass, I could toss the other three backpacks out and make a run for it with just one. Once the commotion subsided in a day or two, I could just run out and grab the other three. This plan wasn't perfect by any means, but I was pleased with it.

I heard a groan from Khakis, an alert to the others, and knew my grace period had expired.

I sprinted from the pegboard to my packs, looping their straps around my forearms, and dashed back. Hinges squeaked and apparel fell off hooks as I pulled the panel open.

Lunging forward, I heaved the backpacks with me, stepping into the display. I dropped the backpacks and Barbara as I was blinded by the bright light from outside. Stumbling, I knocked over what must've been a mannequin.

The window took two hits from Barbara before it cracked. A series of deeper fractures spiraled out from my initial strikes before the glass cascaded to the floor. While hoping Khakis was too dumb to go around, I threw the packs into the empty hallway. Broken glass crunched under my boots. The hallway was empty, and outside appeared to be, too. But how could I really know? There was a blind spot to my left outside the door. I wouldn't discover if something was there until I stuck my head out.

I set Barbara just outside the door dropped to my knees, and crawled through the opening. I looked to the left and I saw her. Saw her real, *real* close.

The Zs chest cavity was gaping open, grayed organs still intact. Ragged, torn skin framed the gruesome corpse. The face was mostly intact, though one eye was missing. She was a foot away, leaning down. I was probably the first living bag of flesh she'd seen in months.

I propelled myself forward. In my attempt to avoid her yellowed mouth, I skittered on some broken glass. She fell onto my back, her arms locking around my waist.

This is why I saved ammo. Sometimes there were circumstances where a bullet was the only thing that could save you. I couldn't use Barbara. I wasn't at an angle that gave me the leverage to destroy her zombie brain.

Jerking the 9mm out from my vest holster, now under the sweater, wasn't easy. The seconds it took brought me closer to death. More so than I was comfortable with. When I finally got it out, I twisted around as much as I could. The stiff's head rose and her arms loosened, one swinging up for my neck. I dropped to the floor with her and rolled onto my back, bringing the gun up between us, under her chin, just as her mouth opened.

Pop.

The stiff had been dead for so long all her blood was congealed. Nothing came out of the hole through her chin or the top of her head. I quickly shoved off her lifeless body, sending it to the floor with a fleshy thump.

Barely able to breathe through my congestion and exertion, I scrambled up and rammed the gun into my front sweater pocket. I looked at the door behind me. Khakis was making his slow way toward me. There was no telling how long I'd have to stay cooped up in Rainier again. I took the risk of reaching through to get another backpack. My heart pounded. I thought of everything that could go wrong. It could get caught on the doorframe, another Z could come up behind me—but no risk meant more suffering later on.

I pulled another pack through without a hitch and ran across the sky bridge, straight into my haven. I wanted to stop and take a look around to see what was coming for me. But after months of the same results, I didn't *need* to stop. I knew.

Once in, I shoved the upper and lower locks into place. After the first try at shoving the crowbar into place, and it clattering onto the ground, I had to leave it. Instead I rushed back upstairs. Aside from the echo of the slamming door and my own wet breathing, no noise came from inside or outside the office. Beyond the doors downstairs, I heard a faint, confused moaning.

I made it. The first thing I did was crack open a bottle of blissfully sweet cough syrup.

***

Too cold. Freezing. Wake up.

My eyes opened, but my body seemed to be paralyzed. Between all the sweaters and blankets I was steaming myself to death. A cottony texture coated my mouth and teeth. Despite the numerous layers, I felt cold. Rigid.

The fever didn't wake me up. It was the dream. I was back in the crashed Mustang, just past Startup. All the darkness surrounding me was constricting. My body hung by the seatbelt, but this time it was cutting into my flesh. I could feel blood trickling down my chest and stomach, dripping into the cold river swirling around me.

I didn't want to turn my head, but I had to. To know what was next to me.

This time she was in the car with me. And this time, she was dead. Her face was rotting and her eyes were opaque, but I knew it was her. Instead of gnashing teeth and groans, the dead Blaze looked at me blankly.

"You left me," she wheezed. "Didn't see that coming."

I opened my mouth to apologize, but nothing came out.

"You thought I was dead. I wasn't." Black liquid and smoke seeped from between her cracked lips.

And I woke up. Like I always did when I had that dream.

Blaze wouldn't leave me alone. She plagued my mind when I was awake and lingered when I slept. In my adrenaline-induced mania after raiding the store, I took too much cough syrup. Later, I saw her standing over me before she walked out of the room. My logic was getting shaky. For a split second, I considered running after her.

I groped around in the darkness for a bottle and my fingertips brushed against a familiar plastic surface. Rolling over, I grabbed whatever it was and cracked it open.

The citrusy smell of Sprite assaulted me. I drained the flat substance before throwing the bottle across the room. It must've struck Pickle, because I heard an angry squeak and the sound of skittering feet.

Dizziness overcame me. The room tilted until I blacked out again.

Chapter 4

Spicy jalapeño chips became an hourly sinus-clearing routine. I'd eat a whole snack size bag in a minute and wait until the magic started. Adding in shots of Dayquil seemed to help out other symptoms, too. Afterwards, I felt pretty good. For a while.

One day had passed since I'd gotten ahold of the drugs and food. My brain was still melting inside my skull, and my body protested against the lack of nutrition, but I was still alive. I wasn't sure if that was a good thing anymore, but I kept on going anyway.

I chewed and swallowed, ignoring the pain as the jagged end of a chip battered my throat, and I tried to imagine what I'd do when I was better.

Can I say post-apocalypse? Or was it still occurring? As far as I was concerned, it was done. *Sick*!

I wanted to continue, to toughen up like they do in the movies and defy the stress my body was under, but as the days passed I realized how cockamamie the entire idea of finding Blaze was. How in the hell would I search? It's not like I could track her down through the internet or hire someone to track her. I couldn't call her on the phone. Couldn't send her a letter. In fact, probability of finding her was dishearteningly slim. In the midst of an undead world, expectations were a joke.

But what else was I going to do?

Licking my fingers, I crumpled the bag, threw it at the computer desk, and yawned. I cast aside my nest of blankets and stood up, stretching my arms high over my head and groaning. I felt Pickle crawling up my jeans and I picked her up, holding her close to my chest.

"I'm sure you're ready to go, huh?"

Her beady red eyes stared at me before she began struggling in my grasp. I placed her on the floor and walked to the window.

There was a woman in the parking lot. But not just any woman. It was Blaze. She was walking across the empty expanse of cement like she owned the place. Not a care in the world. She didn't have anything to indicate she was traveling—no backpack, no rifle. Nothing. But I recognized the confident walk, the crazy black hair.

I burst out of the office and ran till I reached the doors, armed only with the delusion that I'd finally found her. When I unlocked the doors, a strong wall of cold air hit me, stealing my breath away.

Khakis happened to be out there and seemed surprised as I ran past him. I gave him a good shove onto the bridge as I sprinted towards Blaze. She was still in plain view. Breathing hard, I made it across.

But as I turned the corner to the side walkway, she was gone. I should've just turned around, killed Khakis, and gone back into my junk food laden den of illness.

I kept going, though. My face stung in the icy morning air. My chest heaved against the strain of physical exertion. I ran until I was in the empty parking lot.

"Blaze!" I screamed. "Blaze!"

There was nothing. I walked in a loose circle, but saw emptiness. A single truck sat in the parking lot, but I knew the vehicle was locked. A bleak feeling coursed through me and I dropped to my knees. I pressed my face into my hands and breathed out.

I was certifiably crazy. Off my rocker. This kind of thing was bound to happen eventually, I guess. How could a man stay by himself for that long, with that amount of guilt and cough syrups, and not put himself into immediate danger? Somewhere in front of me I heard running. The clinking of gear. It didn't matter. It could be a runner or just my imagination, but I wasn't sure I could keep going.

"What in the hell are you doing? Get up!"

Fuck you, hallucination. Now voices? I wasn't falling for it.

The steps grew closer. I finally gave in and looked up when a shadow fell across my vision.

"I thought everyone was dead. I haven't seen a living person in weeks," he said in a rush. The jangling of his gear ceased as he stopped in front of me. "Where did you come from? We need to get somewhere safe."

He looked familiar, but it wasn't as though I'd met him before. For all I knew he was from the East Coast. He was younger than me, for sure, but I wouldn't say he was in his teens. Dark eyes peeked out from behind shaggy black hair, and his skin rivaled my own in terms of paleness. A brown scraggly beard completed his mountain-man look.

"What's wrong with you?" he asked, while scanning for threats. His expression grew hard. He must have spotted Khakis.

The man grabbed my arm and jerked me up. I went willingly and my words came back to me. "Past those slows across the bridge is where I've been staying. It's safe."

"Glad you found your voice," he said, but he wasn't scornful. Instead he seemed jovial, which was out of place. Who had optimism these days?

Once I had my feet beneath me, he produced a lead pipe from somewhere. It looked heavy, but he held it with confidence.

"You don't have a weapon. Just follow me," he said. "I'll knock them out of the way."

He burst toward Khaki and another slow I hadn't seen before, pipe raised. I took a step forward and stopped thinking.

Stopped thinking because I fainted.

***

I was tired of waking up like that. With a splitting headache, a stomach on revolt, and major difficulties breathing. The chills from my fever were gone. Now I was burning from being under so many layers. The only thing different this time was that someone was right beside me.

"Oh, you're awake."

He looked at me kindly and patted the blankets that covered my shoulder.

After a cough that sent a stream of snot spinning end over end from my nose, I sat up and shifted away from him. How embarrassing. Fainting for no reason. Almost as though he read my mind, he said, "You must've exhausted yourself running down here. Between that, being sick, and the food you're eating, I'm surprised you were willing to leave the building."

"I—" I coughed again and said, "I can take care of myself."

That sounded stupid.

"No doubt. But all this indicates differently." He gestured at the vending machine crap that littered the room.

It *was* bad. The mountain of discarded wrappers growing in the corners threatened to topple and spread across the floor. I was sure my phlegm bucket smelled...ripe. Memories of my minimalist, clean apartment brought more shame.

"Right," I agreed and dropped the subject. I hadn't spoken to another person in so long I forgot how to be mean. Wallowing in self-pity softened me up. Even *looking* at another living human was strange.

"My name is Buford."

"Cyrus," I replied, a sinking feeling coming over me. This situation was a little too familiar. Meeting another survivor. Going on an awful adventure. Never turned out well, in my experience.

"Nice to meet you. I have some soup heating up. If you stop eating these chips and Nyquil, you'll be better in no time."

Once he mentioned soup, I smelled it wafting through the open office door. "Heating it?"

"I started a small fire. The ceiling's huge, and the concrete platform it's on reduces the chance of a fire hazard. Nowhere closed off outside to do it."

"All right." Silence engulfed us while I shrugged some blankets off. "How long was I out?"

"At least an hour. I had some time on my hands so I looked around while you were asleep. Found these on the body down the hall."

He fished around in his coat pocket and pulled out a set of jingling keys. "I think they belong to the truck outside."

Maybe if I had any shred of masculinity left, I would've found those keys and left long ago. Just to be difficult, I asked, "What makes you think that?"

"The truck outside is a Toyota. There's a Toyota key on here. The body had a janitor's uniform on. It was probably his truck." Before I could come up with another remark, he stood up. "I'll go get that soup. We'll split it and talk about what we're going to do."

What we're going to do? I didn't need his guidance. I needed to establish that before the kid thought he was going to be my savior.

After the soup.

The soup was beef and barley, and it tasted better than anything I'd eaten since I first arrived in the Rainier building. Buford even had two sporks.

As we ate he told me he had been traveling with a couple up until a few days ago. The woman was very pregnant, and they decided to leave the convenience store they'd been living in to find somewhere safer to hole up.

"I met them while scavenging inside a supermarket. Most stores are barren, but I look anyway. Even one can of tuna means having enough energy to outrun them. It was awkward at first. That moment when you aren't sure if someone is a threat or a friend."

"They're all threats," I said. I didn't know where his story was going, but I knew it would end badly for someone.

Buford's dark eyes flashed. "That's harsh."

"I'm alive because I treat people like threats."

"I'm alive because I don't."

He stared me down, a callous defiance in the look that seemed familiar. "As I was saying, we ended up talking and decided to travel together. Their names were Claire and Don, and they seemed trustworthy enough. Maybe a bit weak, but how could I walk away from a woman that far along?"

"Easy. Just do it."

I was pushing his buttons. One more snarky comment and I might have a fight on my hands. "She must've gotten knocked up right when the apocalypse started. Who does that?"

"She was raped. It was shocking how easily she told me. It's a fact of life for some survivors. Claire was working a late shift at the local ER when an outbreak started two rooms down. The whole town went crazy. It was day fucking one of the apocalypse and they all lost it. She was trying to walk home when it happened."

That was harsh. The raw depravity I'd witnessed since I'd stepped out into the undead world knew no limits. I never thought the first day of chaos would be enough for the inherent evil within people to surface with that much fervor.

"They lived on the outskirts of town in a farm house surrounded by trees. Don told me about how great they thought it was that they didn't have to find somewhere to hide because their house was perfect. It was the place characters go to in the movies and books, he said."

"They ran out of food, didn't they?" Only a handful of reasons would cause someone to leave their safe haven.

Buford's forlorn chuckle confirmed I was right. "That's what happens, isn't it? Claire wouldn't leave the house. She was too afraid. That left all the resource foraging to Don. He wouldn't go too far towards town because he was afraid something would happen to him and Claire would be left alone."

"A vicious cycle. Especially once they figured out she was pregnant."

He nodded and fell into silence as he scraped the remaining soup from the bottom of its can. The spoon rattled in the empty container as he set it on the floor. "Yeah, but only for a few months. I guess Claire had some type of realization she needed to do everything she could to make sure the child was born. She said she'd never felt that willful in her life. Don couldn't do anything but support her."

"I know that feeling," I said. "It's powerful."

"So do I. When I was a kid, I was picked on and..." Buford rubbed his temples with the tips of his fingers. He ran his hands over his face and inhaled. "Who am I kidding? It was more than bullying. It was beyond that. It was violent. But I got it in my head I wouldn't let anyone hurt me. The kids doing it were bigger than me, grades ahead of me, but one day I beat the hell out of the biggest one. That feeling was what carried me through."

His story was familiar. It sounded too much like my own tale of vicious schoolyard fights. The difference was that mine ended in me drowning another boy. I surfaced from my own sinister memories and found Buford still lost in his own thoughts.

"What happened then? After she decided she wanted to survive?" I asked.

"Oh, right. They decided to try and get to Marysville. It's a town north of here. Don's brother was a doctor. She said she'd rather die trying to get to someone who could help them than sit around starving to death. From there they made slow progress moving north, taking refuge wherever seemed safe for up to a week to prevent exertion. She was already having problems when I met them. Pains."

Buford shuddered. He ran his hands through his coarse, dark hair, pushing it away from his face. His breath came out in a quivering exhale. "It's hard for me to see people in pain and not do anything about it. I know better than to get involved with people, especially now, but it's like I can't stop myself. Growing up, I wanted to be like my sister. No matter how much someone needed help, or who it was, my sister didn't give a rat's ass. If she'd been with me when I met Don and Claire, she wouldn't have stopped to help. That's how I know she's alive. She just doesn't care about people."

"I'm like her."

"You think you are," he said, "but being around you...well, it doesn't *feel* the same as it would with her. I can tell with her. See it in her eyes. All I see is doubt with you. Struggle."

Silence. I waited for more from him. He didn't elaborate and I wasn't sure what else to say. Either he was unusually perceptive or I was an open book.

I hope it was the former. Based on my recent track record, I knew it was the latter.

"Back to Claire and Don," I reminded. "This isn't about us."

A suspicious look. A knowing look. Fuck. I hated it when people did that. Frank did it the most, though lately every person I'd met saw through me.

"Right, right. They needed to find somewhere to rest. I took them back to the house I'd been staying in. I knew it was secure. I hadn't seen any undead around when I got there or left. We slept upstairs in rooms across from each other. That night I heard screaming. I ran into their room, expecting to see them getting eaten alive. But it was just her on the bed. Thrashing. Blood was everywhere, soaking *everything*. The baby must've died inside her while she was sleeping. Once it came back it began clawing its way out. Her stomach was...it looked..." He brought his hand to his mouth. Pale skin tinged green with an onset of nausea. "...wrong."

I pictured tiny undead hands whittling away at her uterus. Beef and barley threatened to come back up. I hadn't seen it and I still felt sick.

"I had a panic attack and ran. I don't know what happened to them, but I know they're dead. With that much gore and how Claire was screaming, she had to be."

"Why didn't you do anything about Don? Was he hurt?" I asked, curious. Most good Samaritans would've tried saving him. Buford didn't want to see people in pain. Don would've been in a hell of a lot of pain.

He shrugged. "If it traumatized me to see that, could you imagine being him? But he was a brick wall. I want to help people, don't get me wrong, but there comes a point when you know there's nothing you can do. I wasn't sticking around. When I ran out, there were undead coming from their hiding places, drawn out by the noise. The house wasn't fortified. They would've broken in while I was trying to get him to leave."

"That's... Smart of you."

"Thanks, I guess," he said. "At that point you have to do what you have to do, right? I try to help anyone I can until it puts my own life at risk. That's where other survivors go wrong. All they think about is helping other people or only helping themselves." The look in his eyes didn't match the conviction in his voice.

"Would you have done it differently, if you could go back?"

"I don't know," he said. "When I can't sleep, I think about what I could've said to him, if there was anything, to get him moving. If I could've hit sense into him. Leaving him was the right thing for *me*, but if I could relive the situation I might do it differently."

His sentiment and sense of honor made me sick. What was done was done. He was alive, so he did the right thing. Doing it different meant he wouldn't be.

"Right. Now, where were you planning on going?"

"Farther north." Excitement flickered in his eyes, and he seemed to grab at this chance to end the story of his previous companions. "To an island my family used to visit."

I stifled my laugh. Barely. "I didn't know islands are zombie proof."

Buford glared. "It's not even on a map. It's just a stretch of land with nothing on it but trees and rocky beach. A seaplane would be the best way to get there. Just park on the water right off the coast."

"You can fly, then?"

"I know enough to get there. But even if I can't find a plane, it's possible to take a boat. It's just dangerous because of the distance and currents."

"Why didn't you go there to begin with?"

"I was trying to find my sister," he told me. "Then I realized she'd have the same idea as me. She's probably already there for all I know."

"Finding a person during the apocalypse is impossible," I chided. "Trust me, I know."

He shook his head. "I know she's there. I can feel it."

Feelings. I had the same feeling about Blaze all the time—that she was alive somewhere and I could find her. Irrational feelings, but they usually are. Feelings, that is.

"What are *you* doing here? You don't live here, do you?"

As if on cue, I hacked up a wad of phlegm. I sought out an empty pop bottle to spit it in.

Buford grimaced.

"No. I'm looking for someone, too. I doubt I'm going to find her, but why not try?" I told him.

"You love her?"

Love her? Sociopaths don't love. They manipulate, throw away, and lie...but love? Not in their vocabulary. Well, not unless they are using the concept to deceive someone.

But there I was again, trapped in the albatross of the title 'sociopath.' Telling myself what I should or shouldn't think based on a self-proclaimed definition I gave myself before *this*.

This being the experience of seeing the only person who ever understood me die. *This* being the sensation of weakness in the face of an unrelenting force. *This*...

This being the zombie fucking apocalypse.

I can make the hard choices. I can be a monster who leaves people for dead. A bastard who doesn't bat an eyelash at the harsh new realities of this crapsack world. I can be a selfish prick.

But that doesn't make me a sociopath. It makes me something else. Someone without a definition. A product of a life gone bad. A product of the zombie fucking apocalypse.

"Do you love her?" he asked again.

What was that in his voice? I couldn't read people, so I wasn't going to start trying now, but I didn't like the way he was looking at me. It reminded me too much of Blaze. It said, *don't bother answering. I already know.*

I didn't like the itchy feeling that started creeping over me right then, either. Like my mind was trying something on for size. The idea was still too foreign for me to even contemplate.

"Is it any of your business?" I snapped. After an uncomfortable silence I said, "I'm here because I got sick after being kidnapped by some crazies for their food supply. Once I'm better I'm heading out again."

"Two questions: First, how were you kidnapped? And second, what's your plan?"

"The kidnapping thing was so fucking bizarre I'm still trying to get over it." I didn't want to get into recollecting the events too much.

I wanted to move on. "Group of genuine cannibals abducted me from a gas station. They have a leader, *Kevin*, who only eats redheads."

"You're kidding."

"Does it look like I am? Anyway, I escaped. Here I am."

"And I thought zombies were something to worry about."

"Same here. As for the second question? It's hard to *have* a plan in this case. I don't know where she would be. I don't know where I should look. This is worse than looking for a needle in a haystack, you know?" I sighed. "It's unbelievable. Before any of this I was pretty damned content being emotionless."

"Being emotionless is impossible," he said. "I guess it took an apocalypse to get the ball rolling, but its rolling nonetheless."

"I guess." I sighed. "But this is the worst time ever to find some-one to care about."

Buford looked at me skeptically. "She isn't the only one you've ever cared about, though, in your whole life."

I laughed, but it turned into a wet cough. "I cared about a man named Francis Bordeaux who died because of me."

Buford raised an eyebrow.

"No, you idiot. He was like a father to me."

"No one else?"

"Not really. My parents died when I was young and I haven't seen or heard from my sister in at least five years."

"That's sad." He stood up, stretching. "But everyone's got their own problems."

He stepped over me and went to the window. He looked out for a few moments then turned back. "There aren't that many out there. They're mostly scattered in the parking lot where we were."

I forced myself to stand, ignoring the blackness creeping in at the edges of my vision, and peered out the window. There were only five or six of them outside, slow and meandering. One of them was particularly withered, to the point that it didn't look capable of walking around. I couldn't tell a gender—too much was eaten or ripped away.

"We can leave when you're better."

"What?" I rasped, turning to stare at him. "We? And listen here, I can leave whenever I damn well please."

"Cyrus, you may not recall, but I saved your life. You fainted just outside this building."

I couldn't dispute that, but the 'we' part still bothered me. "What about 'we?' Who said we were going together?"

"The way I look at it, I found the keys to that truck, if they are the keys. Finders keepers. If you plan on going wherever you're going on foot, then we can part ways right now. I just figured you'd want a ride."

He was right. I was sick and he was right. The last thing I wanted was to get into a friendship situation that raped me in the end, but this time around I wouldn't cave into other's peoples' desires so easily.

"We'll see," was all I said.

* * *

'When I'm better' didn't come as fast as I wanted it to. The days passed by, stormy and dark, without much improvement. Buford took away my pills and syrups, claiming mixing them just made everything worse.

So I lay in my cramped office, burning or freezing, asleep or awake, waiting for my strength to come back.

I hadn't seen Pickle since Buford showed up. I told him about her, and to always keep the door shut, but he said he never saw her anywhere. I knew it was his fault when he brought me back into the office. He'd left the door open. I didn't mention it, though. I'd wake up and expect to feel her curled against me or see her in front of me. But she was never there.

Buford rarely entered my den of illness, which was for the best. He stayed across the hall in another office, having made a neat set-up for himself. The only time he ventured into mine was to give me rations of medication and food. When he wasn't sleeping or taking care of me, he was checking the building for things I'd missed.

My perception must've been on leave when I looked around, because Buford kept coming back with stuff I'd overlooked. More substantial foods, like canned soups and fruit. Bottles of water. He even brought back little items I never paid attention to, like matches and batteries. Off to the side of his office I'd watch him make neat piles, which I assumed we'd each carry.

I still saw Blaze. She came to me in the form of dreams or hallucinations. Sometimes when I saw Buford I thought he was her. I'd see his dark hair flash in a door way and think she found me somehow. They had the same physique, tall and slender. The same walk, confident and quiet. Whenever he raised a brow in skepticism I had to look away. The similarity was unbearable.

Then there were the visions of *undead* Blaze. Those were the worst. The dream was vicious, repetitive, and always hit me when I was feeling guilty and restless. She hung, limp and bloody, from her seatbelt in the Mustang, and always said the same words over and over.

You didn't look for me.

You left me.

My sleeping mind put her back in the car even though she'd been missing when I'd woken.

In reality, if I met up with Blaze again I doubted she would spend effort on words. She'd probably beat the hell out of me as soon as she saw me. After waking from a nightmare, I'd fantasize about meeting up with her, but even those daydreams were short and incomplete. I didn't have a clue how things would go down if we found each other. The main reason?

I fucked her over, plain and simple.

Not on purpose, but I did. I'd looked for her, but there was no sign of her or which direction she went.

Undoubtedly, Blaze would be as mad as a hornet. If she knew where Frank's cabin was, she would've found me and killed me with her bare hands for leaving her.

Or was I projecting? Creating feelings for her she wouldn't have?

I had one other fantasy. An awkward one. The one I didn't know how to complete. I stopped having daydreams about women when I was thirteen, so I didn't have much practice. Ideally, I would miraculously find her and…and then what? I was already stumped. Hug her? Kiss her?

Hell, I couldn't imagine doing any of that. The idea was so foreign. Not unappealing, but foreign.

I'd figure it out if I found her.

* * *

Outside was all blue skies and sunshine. Billowing white clouds drifted above a pristine, sparkling white cityscape.

When I was a kid, my favorite part of the winter months was waking up to find an untouched white wonderland outside. Everything looked different covered in snow, almost like a foreign world. That feeling returned now.

The office felt like a freezer. As I stared out the window, bundled up in everything I managed to get my hands on, my breath fogged the glass and obscured my reflection.

Ah, my reflection. I looked like I went to Hell for an all expenses paid torture. My nose was reindeer red (appropriate for the time of year) and my eyes were puffy and bloodshot. I hated having weeks of beard growth, but there it was—almost half an inch of golden red.

I breathed out and wondered what I looked like a few days ago when I was at my sickest.

Buford's footprints remained across the bridge, and leading into the Parks building. He left in the middle of the night for more supplies, but hadn't come back yet. Well, not exactly. There were footprints going back and forth, which meant during the night he made several trips. Since sunrise I'd been watching for him to come back out, but nothing happened.

I considered going in for him. I *was* feeling better. I vetoed the idea every time. There was no way in hell I was going to risk a relapse. My throat was blissfully devoid of slime and my nose was only trickling, but going outside on another adventure was sure to set me back.

So, if Buford was alive, he was taking his time. If he was dead, he was dead.

I remembered my situation with Khakis. I only waited a handful of minutes before I'd acted, but the situation forced me to remain stationary. Buford might be in a similar circumstance, waiting for an opportune moment to make his escape.

I returned to my nest of blankets and cushions. Shortly after, my ears picked up on a soft scratching noise. Slowly, as to not scare her away, I turned my head and looked out the office. The light from my window cast far enough into Buford's room that I could see Pickle moving around his bed area.

My heart swelled, "Come here, girl!"

She rose up, as ferrets do, and looked at me. It was then I understood her disappearance. Pickle was upset about Buford. My furry companion hadn't seen another living person in months and this probably freaked her out.

I shrugged off the blankets and crawled to the doorway, beckoning. She stood as I was about to enter Buford's office, then disappeared farther into its depths.

"Drama queen," I muttered as I entered his room. Pickle scurried behind a filing cabinet. I paused and decided to wait.

I hadn't been in Buford's office. It was clean and neat. An absolute dream compared to my revolting cavern. It was in my nature to be organized, but I'd let myself go since settling in the college.

His sleeping bag and blankets were made up in the center of the office, while his backpack was propped up in the corner. Next to the head of his sleeping bag was an assortment of nightstand items—bottled water, flashlight, and…

A photo? Curious, I reached over and gingerly picked it up, but not before committing to memory exactly how it sat before I moved it.

When I saw who was in the picture, I froze. My hand went limp. The photo slipped to the ground. It landed face down, and I starred at the scrawled letters on the back.

Bea and Beau Wright.

Blaze.

Blaze Wright.

Chapter 5

Suddenly, everything made sense. Both looked years younger, but I still recognized her. Blaze was wearing a plain t-shirt and jeans, and her hair was longer, but the same scar and chipped right canine told me it was her.

Now I knew why Buford, or Beau, looked so damn familiar. He looked like his older sister.

The odds were astronomical—they had to be—but somehow the kid who knew where Blaze was walked straight into my part of town. If that wasn't fate talking to me, I didn't know what it was. Not only did he *know* where she was, but we had a car to get there and he could fly a plane for fuck's sake!

As soon as Beau came back, I planned on telling him I would absolutely love to travel with him. I would be de-fucking-lighted to.

As I studied their similar features, I wondered why I hadn't assumed a possible relationship to begin with. Well, aside from the ridiculous odds against it. Their noses were identical—sharp and slightly crooked. Their pale skin and dark brown eyes were the same.

A question popped into my mind and my eyes unfocused. Should I tell Beau I knew his sister? He was taking me to her whether he knew it or not, so technically telling him wouldn't change anything. If he knew everything, stuff could get messy.

Hey, Blaze's brother, I was snooping around and found this photo. I know your sister. Yeah, we got in a wreck a while back and she disappeared. Couldn't find her so I gave up. Crazy, huh?

I laughed aloud. Telling him was a bad idea for now. If it came up, I'd deal with it then. In the meantime, I was sure he'd talk about

Blaze, giving me an opportunity to learn about her pre-apocalypse personality. It's something I found myself interested in—it was time to stop denying my feelings.

Suddenly, Pickle shot across the room and hallway, scurrying into my office. I grinned. Things were looking up.

Before leaving, I replaced the photo and scanned the room to ensure I didn't leave anything behind. It felt good to have the upper hand again. Manipulating people for my own benefit was something I knew and was comfortable with. It made me feel like my old self.

My name is Cyrus V. Sinclair.

The V stands for villain.

I was standing in the hallway, feeling pleased with myself, when I heard the downstairs door rattling. It was probably Beau. I walked down the hall to the stairs. I made it a few steps down before I heard something else. The all too recognizable snarling and gasping of a runner. Then it scrambled up the stairs, coming for me.

Just as I turned to run, I saw him out of the corner of my eye. His mouth was brimming with saliva, blood, and dark ooze all undead seemed to produce. He had no shirt, revealing a clean torso with minimal splatters of blood on it, most of which came from a large head wound. At the sight of me he howled and climbed the remaining stairs on all fours. Flecks of liquid splattered the cement walls and steps as he moved.

A burst of adrenaline shot through me. I rushed through the stair entry and towards the hallway. My pulse was through the roof, and I knew it would only be seconds before the runner got me. Even as I ran, I knew escape was impossible. I was still weak and he was too fast.

I barely made it to the double doors when the bastard grabbed me by the waist and dragged me to the hard floor. His mouth clamped down on my shoulder.

If I wasn't wearing two sweaters, his teeth would've gone straight through. It still hurt like a bitch though. His mouth worked furiously, trying to take a chunk out, grinding the cotton fabric and bruising the skin below. Searing hot pain shot through me. I screamed, using my pain and fear as momentum to turn us both over. He was wedged between the floor and my back.

Sick or not, I had to fight. I lifted us both up, put my shoulders to the huge window, and hurled myself backwards.

A startling crack sounded. His arms and mouth released me. I sprung forward and spun to face my opponent.

At least the fight looked to be a short one. I was unarmed, and I wasn't sure who was going to be on the winning side.

The glass behind my new friend fractured into a spider web that radiated out from a bloody dent where he'd hit his head. He rushed me again. My shoulder throbbed, but I charged, too, grabbing him.

He didn't weigh much. The guy must've been starving when he met his demise. Grateful for this advantage, I took the opportunity and pressed forward, pushing him toward the weakened glass.

The Zs motions caused globules of ooze to flick onto my face. This struck a chord of primal fear within me as the drips approached my mouth and tried working into my eyes. I had him against the window and pushed at his shoulders. His head flew back and hit the same spot as before. Two more shoves and the glass began falling away in chunks.

One last slam and the rest of the glass shattered. Shards cascaded everywhere, landing with muted thumps on the snow outside. I bent him backwards over the window sill. My juggernaut motivation began to flag. My muscles strained from the exertion of keeping the undead at bay.

"Cyrus!"

Beau's voice came from outside. The bridge. I looked past the zombie and saw him running toward me. I heard the glass doors downstairs slam shut, and the loud clank of locks sliding home carried over the howls of the stiff.

Why hadn't he asked me to lock the doors behind him? That would've been the smart thing to do. But what was done was done. All I could do was hold Mr. Stomach Wound back until the cavalry arrived.

And it did. Beau rounded the last bend and burst through the access door at a run. Instead of helping me throw the undead out the window, he raised a crowbar above his head and brought it down on the thing's skull. Each hit brought forth bursts of bright red blood. Three more hits later and the dead was truly dead, body twitching before going still entirely.

Then I noticed the mark on his chest. Bile covered half of it, but I recognized it. Right where my own was. A sword and flames.

I couldn't keep staring. Beau grabbed its legs and motioned for me to get his arms. Together we rolled him out the window. I leaned out and watched as he fell, listening as his body landed in a snowy bush below.

"Where did he come from?" I asked. I was still winded but tried not to show it. Still thinking about the emblem, but unsure if I should share that with Beau.

"In that building." He motioned towards Parks. "Didn't you say you checked that place?"

"Once," I said. Apparently some Zs had found their way in since my last visit. "Where exactly was he?"

"In a room by the utility closet, where I found this." He raised the crowbar as proof. "It was close to the bookstore you told me about."

Unbelievable. There had been people in there the whole time. When I caused a ruckus getting supplies, they must've realized someone was around. If they'd made any noise to get my attention when I escaping, I didn't hear it. My need to get out of dodge superseded anything else. To the average starving survivor, the idea of another average starving survivor to team up with was an appealing thought. Had he been trying to find us and was bit in the process? I voiced my idea to Beau, and he shook his head.

"He wasn't a zombie. I hit him," he said. "When I opened the door, he was very much alive and acted like a bat out of hell. What was I supposed to do? Let him keep yelling?"

My mouth dropped. Before I could comment, Beau continued. "I tried to reason with him, but when someone can't be reasoned with an alternative choice has to be made right away. You know what that choice ends up being. I grabbed the crowbar and hit him in the head. He stopped screaming, but he dodged into a doorway and down some stairs to a library."

"Why didn't you finish him off? You know what happens. The last thing anyone needs is a fresh runner attacking them."

He moved away from the window and back towards the stairs. "This happened hours ago. I've been looking for him ever since. I must've hit him too hard and he died and turned. Anyway, I'm still surprised he tried to attack me. I didn't make any move to hurt him and yelled 'I'm human!' while he tried to beat on me."

I guess now was as a good a time as any. "He had a mark on his chest. A brand. I have the same one, given to me by that guy I told you about. Kevin. Him being here could mean they're still hunting me, and somewhat successfully."

Beau paused and seemed to be thinking. "No. This guy was skin and bones when I found him. Is it possible he tried to escape Kevin and couldn't make it on his own? He attacked me because he was probably starving, afraid out of his mind, and didn't know what else to do."

"It's possible. I guess there's no way to know for sure why he was here."

"Guess it doesn't matter, anyway. You or a stranger, right?" he shrugged.

The memory hit me hard. I was in the car with Blaze, Gabe, and Frank. Gabe was trying to pick a fight with us after we fled the scene of a massacre. She wanted us to save a bunch of useless survivors. We didn't. Blaze put her in her place after asking her if she'd die for a stranger. *You don't seem to value your life…right now, and for the rest of our lives, it's always going to be you or them.* What Beau said dredged up Blaze's statement. I was surprised I remembered it word for word.

"Hey, are you alright?"

"Yeah. I...I've heard someone say that before," I said. "That's all."

Beau tilted his head, remembering something. "My sister used to say it. Started saying it when I was a kid. She lived by it. Now I guess I do, too."

It was one of those one-sided awkward moments. He was just talking about his sister. So was I. But he didn't know it. I looked anywhere but at him.

At the doors were numerous bags and buckets he must've been collecting during the night, before his mishap with that crazy guy.

"Did you bring the whole store in?"

I received a smirk in response and unexpectedly became nervous.

He was Blaze's sister. He knew where she was. Nervousness and excitement blended, but there wasn't much I could do. I already decided not to talk about what I found out about ten minutes ago.

"It's for the truck. I figured we might as well bring everything we can." He began rifling through the bags. "Anything could be useful at this point. Before I met you, and even Don, I kept seeing groups of…I don't know. Raiders, I guess." He paused. "Have you ever seen that Romero movie? Dawn of the Dead?"

I nodded. Who hadn't?

"Yeah, like those motorcycle guys in the end. Like that. They were crazy. They had people in the backs of trucks, tied up. I guess this kind of stuff is going to be common nowadays."

"End of the world as we knew it also means a new world," I agreed. "Which direction were they going?"

"West." Buford frowned. "Which isn't good news because that's the direction I'm headed. It's strange, because you wouldn't think I'd ever see them again, but if they kept popping up on my route before, they could now."

Seizing the moment, I said, "Speaking of which, I'll go with you."

Beau's frown disappeared and he grinned. "Great. I knew you'd come around."

"And I'm feeling a lot better, although I don't look it," I added, remembering my reflection upstairs. "In a few days we should consider leaving."

Having found whatever he was looking for, he lifted a bag and straightened up. "We should lay really low for a while. If we're quiet for a few days, I'm sure our onlookers will disperse."

I nodded, realizing the ruckus I made earlier was bound to bring the crowd back again. We went upstairs, and as I passed the broken window I noticed a few slows wandering the courtyard to the left of Parks.

"What's in the bag?" I asked before we separated into our offices.

"Oh. Shaving cream, scissors, stuff like that. I found them in the store and figured cleaning myself up might improve morale." Then he added, "Plus if we encounter other survivors, looking clean would make me seem more…"

"In control?" I said, in total agreement.

One aspect of the apocalypse that was oh-so-hard to deal with was filth. If you had time to strip down and have a bath, well, fuck you. You're doing better than everyone else.

In reality, the grime layers on you until your skin is a different color. The skin beneath your clothes is ripe from sweat. Downright putrid in all those creases and pits. Everywhere itches from the buildup, but there isn't much you can do.

I hadn't been able to let my guard down enough to bathe in weeks. Every time I considered it, I pictured a zombie shambling in out of nowhere and… Let your imagination take you from there.

"The buckets downstairs are for water. If I fill them up with snow and wait until they melt, there should be enough." He looked at me. "Did you want some water, also?"

I tried to keep belligerence out of my voice. "Yeah. It's not like I *enjoy* being a walking trash bag."

Apparently he didn't register my comment as a joke or some kind of affront to his intelligence. Instead he just nodded and set the bag in the hallway. "I'm going to get started on the buckets."

I rubbed my tongue against my teeth and looked around. The end of the hall no longer held my unmoving housemate. Beau must've moved the body early on while I was delirious. I wasn't as frightened by that side of the building now I had living company, so I grabbed a flashlight and headed down.

Mortification swelled within me. There were only four offices and a bathroom down that way. What the hell had I been so afraid of? All that was left was a radial stain on the carpet from the body. Pressing the embarrassment to the back of my mind, I began trying doors. The first three were locked. Naturally, the bathroom wasn't.

Then I came upon the last door. Unlike the others, a thin blade of white light shone under it. I reached out and turned the doorknob. It gave way without difficulty.

The room was covered in a light dusting of snow. The single window stood open. Cold, wintry sunlight blinded me for a second before I acclimated to it. A chilly breeze wafted through.

There was something pristine about the room that relaxed me, sending me into a neutral state of being. The former occupant of the office kept furnishings minimal. I took another step in and a book on the desk caught my eye.

Weather hadn't been kind to it. The humor in seeing a book called *The Zombie Survival Guide* was almost too much to bear. I wondered if the readers of the book lived, or survived longer than others in the apocalyptic world we existed in.

I picked up the book, dusting away the snow, and flipped through the pages. Most of the author's commentary seemed to be spot on. I stood there reading until I heard Beau's voice behind me.

"What are you doing?"

"Reading." I showed him the tome.

His face brightened. "Yeah, I read that before everything happened. Funny thing is, it actually helped me."

"I'm not surprised. It should be a textbook these days."

We stood in silence for a moment. Beau leaned in the doorway, looking into the room. After a second, he said, "You probably shouldn't be in here. It's cold. Don't want you to relapse, especially after what just happened."

I nodded and took the book with me into the hall. As I walked, muscles grew stiff from my fight. They hadn't been used like that in a while. I settled into my shell of blankets and tried to ignore the weariness. Beau walked by my office door and I called after him.

"Hmm?" He took a few steps backward so he could see me.

"Where are you headed?"

"Just to take another sweep of downstairs before I clean up. There was a loading dock door I want to try and open."

"Loading dock?" Buford Wright seemed to notice a hell of a lot more than I did. I hoped it was because I was sick and not old or inept.

"Outside there were big garage doors, like the loading docks trucks go up, you know? If we can get the truck into the building instead of running everything out to it, it would save us a lot of time."

"Of course," I muttered. "Get to it, Beau."

His brows knitted and he studied me. "Why did you call me that?"

"What?"

"Beau. I never told you my nickname. You just called me that."

I had? It stuck with me when I'd read it on the back of that photo. I'd been thinking of him as Beau since. The slipup was fatal. "I grew up in the south. Knew a few guys named Buford. They always went by Beau for short."

It was half a lie. I had known a Buford once, but no one ever called him Beau. The concerned look on his face faded and he chuckled. I heard his footsteps fade away until I was left in silence. I leaned over to my door and shut it, blocking out the elements.

I needed to be careful. The barrier between what I knew and what I said in front of him was weak. This time was easy to recover from. Next time? It could be awkward. Yet, why was it so hard?

'Sociopath' was what I used to love calling myself, yet the sociopathic traits I used to have were fast disappearing. The persona I presented to the few people I interacted with was a complex lie, but I maintained it with no conscious effort. Perhaps what changed was that I was forced to rely on other people in some capacity. Keeping an image up isn't hard when you never got personal with anyone.

I thought of the summer and the role Blaze, Frank, and Gabe played. Each had saved me at one point, some more than once. Now Beau was taking care of me in every sense—feeding me, protecting me. Doing all the work. *All* of it.

The apocalypse let what I thought was my true persona take me over. I'd been consumed with apathy. Cruelty. Then, it played a sick joke—I found out that wasn't who I was. I thought my past personality was complex. But a truly complicated web of personality problems I had now become.

Then the difference between Beau and the rest of my old companions grew clear. No matter how much of an emotional, unstable wreck I was, I let it show in front of them. Now that I knew who Beau was, I was stepping on eggshells, wearing a mask, in an effort to make sure he stayed with me.

In short, I'd forgotten how to keep up an ongoing lie. I'd grown accustomed to, as they say, being myself. I couldn't do that with Beau.

At least not for now. Maybe once we were on the road, and I knew where to go on my own, things would change.

But for now...let it ride out, I thought as I opened my book up again. *As long as I get what I want.*

Chapter 6

When I woke up, it was dark out. Not the kind of darkness one experienced at night, but the kind brought on by a storm. The view through the window showed blue clouds mixed with charcoal gray. Rain threatened to pour any second. I heard a loud rumble from far away. Thunder.

The short nap I had made all the difference. My chest felt fine and my throat and nose seemed clear.

Stretching, I examined the room for Pickle and saw her sleeping on the desk chair, a round ball of sleek white fur.

I was honestly surprised she was still alive. Keeping her in the top of my various packs seemed like it would've crushed or suffocated her. Yet the little rodent kept on going as though she had something to live for, too.

A soft knock on the door caught my attention. I stood up and opened it to find Beau standing there, illuminated by the electric lantern. He'd cleaned up—cut his hair shorter and shaved his beard off completely. The grime that coated his face and neck was gone, showing his pale skin.

"I managed to get into the loading dock," he said. "Wanna come look?"

The kid was proud of himself and upbeat. His new look probably contributed to that, and I couldn't say no. A pang of jealousy shot through me. I wanted to freshen up, too.

"Sure," I said, then added, "When will I get an appointment at the spa?"

Buford laughed. "After. You'll never believe what I found in there."

He picked up the lantern and I followed him down the hall plus two flights of stairs until we were in the bottom story. When I first arrived, I figured out the bottom level was a tutoring center. Empty chairs and desks were scattered throughout the first half of the large room, then doors led to what I assumed were more offices. They had been locked, and I hadn't bother trying to open them.

The windows didn't illuminate much, so we relied on the white light of Beau's lantern to get us through. It cast hard shadows onto the motivational posters and the effect made me nervous. Nothing could be in there, though, since Beau had been in the room. Any undead would've come out before now.

One door was open. A short flight of steps led upwards into a high-ceiling storeroom. Orange glow sticks were everywhere, giving me a good view of the place. There were stacks of metal shelves loaded with boxes. On the far wall were two loading docks, void of trucks. Everything looked normal.

"What's the surprise?" I asked.

"This." He walked over to an open box on the ground.

Inside were four tightly packed silver cans. Beau moved the light closer so I could read the labels. They all said vegetable soup, followed by nutritional information.

When on the move, finding food in the outskirts of cities wasn't too hard. Stopping in smaller gas stations or houses that looked safe always produced needed goods. It was the cities themselves that were raped. People scavenged from what was closest to them, but the supermarkets and stores soon emptied. Because of traffic jams left with no one to clean up, most didn't make it out of main thoroughfares. So if you were stuck in a city, eventually it grew harder to find what you needed. You had to travel farther every time you raided.

Being cooped up in a school with no access to anything but chips and candy sucked. Beau didn't have much food on him when he showed up, and we were running out of everything from the bookstore. We both knew there was no point in searching the immediate stores and houses for food. It made our situation all the worse.

"What else is there?" My words came out a bewildered whisper.

"I looked at the boxes on the shelves. There's canned fruit, vegetables, and more soup."

How could the day get any better? I had the apocalyptic version of a spa waiting for me, and now we had substantial food again.

"Are those loading doors locked? Or can we open them?" I asked, drawing my thoughts away from the pleasantries.

"They have padlocks on them, but I'm sure I can find something to pry them open. If not, I could try picking them. They look simple enough."

I nodded. "Let's bring up a few cans of food then figure out what we're going to take."

"We don't know if the truck will run. It's probably been almost a year since the engine turned over last. It probably isn't worth it to get stuff ready until we have a ride."

"I guess," I said. "We need to find a ride anyway. If we can't get the truck, it should only take a day to find another car somewhere."

That's optimistic, Cyrus. You couldn't find one to get you to Everett.

"It's lunch time then," Buford said.

I laughed. "How do you know what time it is?"

He raised his wrist, showing me a digital watch.

"Why bother? Time doesn't matter."

"Keeps me sane," he said. "It's the little things that count."

***

Despite the occasional frozen chunk in the vegetable soup, lunch was delectable. Even had dessert: pears. We'd retired to our respective offices to eat in solitude. The storm outside brewed into a disaster while we'd been exploring the loading bay. I heard it raging through the windows. Hail pelted and wind whistled through the broken glass down the hall.

It'd been pretty quiet since we came back upstairs. If I leaned back, I could see into his office. He sat at his desk. Instead of turning on a lantern, he remained quietly eating in the dark. There were no windows over there.

I took a few more bites of soup before realizing I'd eaten half a huge can. If I kept going I'd puke from food-overload. With a feeling of resignation I stopped, took a drink of the pear syrup, and carried my cans to the stair landing. It was cold enough there that the goods would keep.

My stomach felt heavy and sleepiness came over me. I basked in my layers of sweatshirts as I trekked towards the bathroom, where

Beau said he left all his hygiene products. Once I arrived, I couldn't help but get a *little* excited. There was a bucket of melted snow by one of the sinks and an array of items: shaving cream and razor, scissors, and some kind of bath tissue wipe.

I wasted no time in making myself look like a human being again.

My name is Cyrus V. Sinclair. You might already know the V stands for vain.

***

After a restful night's sleep, Beau and I decided it was time to check out the truck. I felt like myself once more, with only a lingering sense of illness.

Beau opted for his heavy lead pipe and I took Barbara. If we did end up having to take out an undead, the quieter the better.

The storm messed up the virginal snow, leaving muddy brown slush in its wake. Water dripped from eaves and trees. Trash and other debris gathered in areas the wind had pushed it to.

Yesterday Beau broke one of the locks in the loading bay. It couldn't be relocked, but since the barrier was pulled to the ground I didn't worry.

"You stand guard while I get the truck going," he said. "Once it's running, jump in and we'll head over to the loading bay and I'll lift the door."

"You can't lift the doors by yourself, not without using the crank. I'll get out, too. Just lift it enough for me to get under and I'll manually raise it."

Beau nodded. "Once you're under, I'll drive in. Let the door drop."

The plan was in place.

Easy.

***

Why didn't it shock me? Because I was used to disappointments.

Beau turned the engine, but the truck wouldn't start. I heard a series of clicks each time he tried. If that meant the battery was dead, I wasn't sure what we'd do.

It was cold and wet outside. I scanned the area for any threats. Didn't see any stiffs, but that didn't lessen my anxiety. They were there. Somewhere.

Feeling desperately exposed, I moved closer and hissed, "The longer we wait—"

"Just a second. I'm going to try something."

He slid out of the vehicle and ran to the hood. I didn't know a damn thing about mechanics so I kept on the lookout, waiting to hear the engine roar.

It felt like hours, but then Buford climbed in the front seat and the engine cranked.

"Hallelujah," I muttered, jogging around the truck to the passenger side. My footsteps sounded too loud for my liking. Until I was safe inside Rainer, everything was going to be too noisy or too risky. Gripping Barbara, I kept listening for nearby moans.

"Half a tank of gas," Beau said as he jerked the truck into drive and did a broad turn toward the loading dock. "We're in good shape."

"We'll be in good shape once we're on the road," I contradicted, just for the sake of it. Truth be told, we *were* in good shape. Truck was running, we were nearing the loading dock…

"Look." Buford gritted his teeth, tilting his head to his left. "Two of them."

I leaned forward and glanced out the window. Sure enough, two mobile rotbags were coming toward us. One was in a tattered uniform, possibly army, the other was a male wearing civilian clothes. They were coming from around Rainer and would reach our truck soon.

"Take them out?" I asked. "Or should we just rush?"

"No time," he said as we came to a halt in front of the loading bay door. "You take the uniform, I'll get the other one."

Once the truck stopped we jumped out, melee weapons in hand. I broke into a jog, intending to go for the uniformed Z, but catching the attention of the other one. I veered to the left, intending to draw him away.

Beau would have to deal with the switch in targets.

The face on the one coming after me was atrociously rotten. I didn't think slugs made it through cold weather, but this guy managed to find some. They were slinking out of his oozing mouth, and a few bigger ones sluiced up the sides of his face and neck. I couldn't tell where his blackened teeth began and the baby slugs ended. He stank of decay and mildew.

My opponent was in worse shape than his friend, but a skull is a skull. I raised my bat and ran toward him. This time I *knew* my footsteps were loud. I reached him just as his hands came up and swung. My weapon met the side of his head, but he didn't drop like usual.

From my right I heard a shout, but didn't pay attention. Beau could handle himself.

The slow staggered and started to come back at me. I swung the bat again. It hit his head, sending him to the ground. The nails protruding from Barbara lodged deep in his scalp. She was pulled from my hands when he fell. No blood, but I could see the grayish rot of his brain oozing from a crack.

I put my boot against his head, grabbed the bat, and yanked it free.

"Hurry!" Beau shouted. I looked up. His zombie was down and he was already at the loading dock, pushing the door upward.

I sprinted over to help him. I had to drop Barbara on the cement because I'd need two hands for the job. With our combined effort, the door went up easily. As soon as I had enough space, I darted underneath to get to the manual chain, grabbing my bat as I went.

The steel was cold. I ignored it and hauled the door up, the pulley system clinking and grinding.

When the door was high enough, Beau drove the truck in. I watched outside for more undead as I lowered it. There were none, but I could've sworn I heard groans in the distance. I let the barrier touch the ground as lightly as possible. There was no sense in making more ruckus. I was so used to our hushed voices inside that my ears throbbed from the clamor of the truck engine.

The rumbling engine sputtered off and Beau opened the truck door, looking at me pleasantly. "We're going to make a good team."

Forcing a grin, I nodded. "We'll find your sister in no time."

Beau shrugged. He slid from the car. "Maybe. It's all I have to hope for."

It's all I have to hope for, I thought, terrified by how true that was.

* * *

"Now my brother? You're going to leave him, just like you left me."

I shook my head. "No. I would never. We'll both find you."

Blaze's dead eyes peered at me and saw through the lies. "I don't believe you. You left me. You'll leave him."

She unbuckled her seatbelt and splashed into the cold water swirling in the wrecked Mustang. Then she shifted towards me. Her hands looked like claws and her lips curved in a viscous parody of a smile.

"Let's see what you look like on the inside, Cyrus."

Just as her hands came to my throat I woke, gasping and clutching the blankets around me. The panic didn't subside until my eyes adjusted to the midmorning light. After a moment my heart stopped racing. A familiar, chilly sweat clung to my skin.

Another nightmare, I thought. *That's all.*

I threw my blankets off and searched for a bottle of water as I forced my mind to more agreeable matters.

Between the emergency supplies Beau gathered and the food from the loading zone, we were set in the resource department. The only thing we *did* lack was guns and ammunition. Melee weapons were fine, but whenever firepower was involved adventures like the one we were headed for became a lot simpler. If a stiff came out of nowhere at close range, there might not be time to swing a bat or bring up a crowbar. More effort meant expending more energy and putting our lives at risk. Yeah, guns made things a whole lot easier.

What time was it, anyway? Beau and I agreed we'd leave today, but I foolishly agreed to the precise time of 9AM. How would I know if it was 9AM or not? The sun wasn't all the way up, so I estimated the time to be before nine.

By the time I drank some water and felt the sweat dissipate, there was a knock on the door.

"You ready to go?" came Beau's voice.

"Yeah," I said meekly, then after clearing my throat, "Yes, in a few minutes."

"I'm going down to the truck. Meet you down there in ten."

I fished around for a cleaner shirt and sweater and pulled them on. I rustled around the heaps of junk in the office. All the gear I'd abandoned since I arrived at the community college, like my tactical vest, boots, and thigh holster, were buried in there, and I wasn't leaving any of it behind. It felt good to start suiting up again. The sound of snaps and zippers was invigorating. The purple school sweater looked silly under the black pocket-laden vest, but it was too warm to forgo.

We'd packed the truck the night before. Everything of immediate use went in the cab. I mentioned to Beau that if we lost access to the truck bed for one reason or another we'd be SOL. There were a few cans of food up in the front and other necessities Beau decided upon. Everything else was in the back, secured and covered with a tarp he found in the loading zone.

I finished tying my shoelaces and straightened up to take a look out the window. A light snow had fallen overnight, but would probably melt as soon as the sun came up. The world was dusted in white where the sun touched, and shadowed in a cold gray where it didn't. I could see my breath fog up as I exhaled.

The adventure was about to start, but my excitement was clouded by thoughts of Blaze. How was she going to react to seeing me again? To seeing Beau? What if she didn't even care about me once she saw Beau?

That's a natural reaction, Cyrus. It's her fucking brother.

I snatched up Pickle and threw her inside the backpack.

"Here we go again, right, sweetie?" I said, kissing the top of her soft white head before zipping her up.

The building I'd been calling home for weeks was silent. It felt like it was bidding me a sorrowful farewell as I walked down the empty hall and stairs.

As I neared the loading zone I heard the crackling of fire and smelled smoke. I wasn't panicked this time. Beau enjoyed creating fires from cargo crates and cardboard to heat up the giant soup cans. Apparently he had breakfast fixed already.

"Hey," I said as I passed through the doorway. "What's cooking?"

He sat next to the fire. It made him glow like an orange beacon in the dark room. "Chicken noodle. There's some fruit medley in that one." He gestured towards a can a few feet away.

I sat down crisscross and felt my body protest. I was only 27—*my birthday is soon, isn't it?*—but the apocalypse was finally taking its toll on me. Before I could stop myself, I cast an envious glance at my companion. I put him at about 21. I never pegged myself as someone who would envy youth, but there I was doing exactly that.

The fruit medley wasn't anything spectacular. Too-soft fruit swimming in overly sweet syrup. I spotted the giant, open box of plastic forks Beau found somewhere and took one. After a few bites, I couldn't take it anymore. Sure, I had a lust for sugary items. But only processed candies, chocolate, and condensed milk. I'm picky, even in the zombie apocalypse.

"I found a map in the truck and highlighted the route we're going to take," he said. "I lived in that area for a long time, so I know where you have to take ferries and bridges. I routed us around all of that, but it's going to make the trip a lot longer."

He reached behind him, produced a map, and handed it to me. I took it and unfolded it at my side. The path he'd mapped out was hideous. There were zigzags and turns everywhere. We wouldn't be on any one road for more than five miles. But if Beau said that was the best route, then fine. I also noted the drive was about 70 miles.

My gaze finally arrived at our destination, Samish Island. It wasn't quite an island since it jutted out from the mainland, connected by a narrow strip of earth. Beau had mentioned the possibility of flying there, but there didn't appear to be any need.

As if he read my mind, Beau said, "Samish isn't the place I told you about. Where I'm talking about? I think it's too small to even put on the map. On nicer days you can see it from the coast. A seaplane would be ideal, but I'm not betting on finding one. We can row over there. It would take a few hours."

"All right," I said, then started laying down some rules I developed during my travels from Kellogg Lake Road. "We should only travel during daylight hours and only when visibility and weather conditions allow. Forcing ourselves to continue in bad circumstances will end up slowing us down. Whenever we find a safe, zombie-free area, I say we find shelter and rest. Once we're on the road, I want to get this done right."

"Look at you," Beau said. "Taking command."

"I've been in this situation before," I said, remembering events from Seattle to Startup months ago. "I'll end up playing leader sooner or later."

We stared at each other before he looked away, prodding the fire with the trip of a ruler. "Who's driving?"

Regretfully, I said, "You."

"That's surprising."

I shrugged. "I can't drive a stick."

Chapter 7

Since I was a passenger, I had no choice but to view the apocalypse's toll on the city as we drove down the barren streets of Everett: skeletal remains of burned houses, tangled carcasses of vehicles. There were few cars in the roads, which surprised me. If someone had asked me before if I thought the roads in a zombie-filled world would be congested, I'd have asked if their brain functioned properly. Of course there would be cars bumper to bumper on every street and highway. They would be packed. But clearly, in some places, things were different than I'd have thought.

We passed by a RiteAid. In the parking lot, a Jeep and a Honda had merged into each other, with five or six cars behind them. All the doors were open, and the vehicles had been evacuated long ago.

Yeah, everyone got stuck in Everett. Entrances were blocked, leaving the roads open for those who managed to get onto it. I guess that was a bonus for those who survived.

Beau never exceeded about 25mph. I certainly had time to ponder. So I ruminated on the indistinguishable heaps of bodies and body parts lying everywhere. Some were only skin and bones, immobile and wet from the elements. Others were in piles, almost as though the living had designated that area for the truly dead. Those piles were an endless picture of limbs, rotting clothes, and flesh. You couldn't really tell where a body ended and another began.

Where the hell were the mobile dead? I knew the Zs didn't travel far from their last kill. They stuck around the corpse until noise or movement caught their attention. There were over 300 million people in the United States when this thing went down. Most had to be undead, a smaller percentage truly dead, and the tiny remainder living. Either my estimates were grossly off, or the majority of them were crowded in the bigger cities, or wherever groups of people made their longest stand. In Olympia, Washington's state capitol, there could be millions of them.

That made me wonder about the huge expanses of desert between the mountains and the cities in the far east of Washington. If enough people escaped there, they could build themselves a nice colony. Unless someone drew undead to a location, societies could be rebuilt.

"What are you thinking?" Beau pulled me away from my thoughts.

"Where's all the zombies, you know? Doesn't make sense." I reached into my pocket to retrieve my final pack of cotton candy flavored Bubble Yum. The smell made me salivate. I popped one in my mouth and offered the last one to Beau. Soon the noisy sound of lips smacking and gum popping filled the car. The atmosphere felt lighthearted, jovial almost, but vanished almost as quickly as it appeared.

Beau's lips formed a grim line and his knuckles grew white from gripping the steering wheel.

"What's wrong?" I asked.

"I know where a lot of zombies are. Yeah. I lived way south, near Oregon, when this happened. By the time I passed through Tacoma, on my way to Samish, there were thousands of them." He shook his head. "There were military bases set up. The living kept pouring into them, thinking they could be protected. They were slaughtered before they made it, and slaughtered if they did.

"Once I saw what was happening, I took advantage of the confusion and took refuge in a gym. I knew no one would ever go in there for supplies, so I was safe from the living. It had a lot of windows, but I stayed in the stockroom eating protein powder mixed in bottled water for about a week, until I stopped hearing gunfire and screams. There were still a ton of zombies, but they were all slow at that point. I found a bicycle and rode like hell until I found an unpopulated back road."

Beau seemed to have ample stories about the horrors he saw, but he stopped talking and I didn't ask for more. Not everyone enjoyed sharing their morbid travels. Most survivors I'd come across called them 'those things' or 'monsters.' These people weren't in tune with reality.

I snapped my gum. He blew and popped a bubble.

"Makes me wonder what my sister's story is, you know?" Another bubble. "She's callous. Served in Iraq, had a bad childhood."

Callous? Yeah, that was true. I remembered her telling me a bit about her upbringing.

"I haven't even shown you what she looks like, huh?" He reached behind him and rummaged through the side pockets of his backpack. "I guess since you're coming with me to find her, you should know, right?"

Trust me, Beau, I know what she looks like.

He pulled the photo out. Handed it to me and returned his focus to the road. There she was. Blaze. I wanted to keep the photo so I could look at it when my memory wavered. Yet it was the only one he had, and he'd been toting it around for who knew how long. Beau would miss it if it vanished.

I'd just wait until the time was right. When he was distracted.

We passed a street sign and he made a left onto Hewitt. Hewitt was straight and empty, save for the cars blocking the underpass half a mile ahead. As we came closer, I saw a bullet riddled sign indicating that the highway would take us to Snohomish.

According to Beau's route, we weren't going to pass through Monroe, but Snohomish was awfully close to it. Just thinking of the junior high fence filled with zombie teenagers made me shiver. I doubted they were still in there. With enough of them pressing against the chain link, it must've tumbled a long time ago.

I handed the photo back to him.

"Damn," he said, as the truck came to a halt. He put it in park and took the photo. Then he glanced at it before spitting his gum out, placing it on the back, and squishing the picture onto the dashboard. He held it, waiting for it to attach, as we looked out the front window at the scene before us.

There was no avoiding the highway. We had to use it, he said, as it was the most efficient way on our route. Beyond the two-car wreck blocking us it was hard to see anything, so there was no telling if the road ahead was even clear. To the right of the wreck was an on-ramp, I-5, to Seattle. It was empty except for an abandoned sports car.

"I guess the roads decided for us." Beau moved his hand away from the photo, and he caught me looking at it. "She's my reason for trying. Figured I should see her every time we drove, you know?"

I shrugged. Sure, fine by me. I didn't mind it being there. I refocused on the wreck.

"We only need to move one of the cars," Beau said. "If we find a chain, or maybe some strong rope, we can attach it and use the truck to haul it out. I saw a garage door repair store back there. It's the only building on this street that probably has something we can use."

"Good idea." I remembered the loud purple building we'd passed earlier. "Can you handle it yourself? I'm going to go up on that ramp and check out the highway. I'll be able to see most of it from there. No sense in moving a car until we know if the rest of the highway is clogged."

"We'll need the chain regardless. And yeah." He laughed. At me. "I can handle myself."

Not bothering with a reply, I placed Pickle in my pack and took Barbara out of the truck cab then slowly walked to the overpass. I didn't want to jog for two reasons. One, it would wind me. Two, and more importantly, it would be loud. Beau seemed to have the same idea, since I didn't hear more than soft footsteps behind me.

I passed a hair salon and a pet shop on the way. Part of me wanted to stop in the pet store since I needed real food for Pickle, but I didn't want to deviate from the plan without telling Beau. Having a companion meant they needed to know where you were, for your safety and theirs.

I skirted around the sports car carefully, but the doors were shut. Undead can't open doors. I drew closer to see if there was anything of use inside, but there was nothing but old fast food bags and some books in the back.

Before trekking up the incline, I checked my surroundings. Down the street, where we turned onto Hewitt, there was movement. The noise from the truck inevitably drew some hungry Zs from their hiding spots. They weren't coming our way, so I wasn't worried.

A quarter of a mile ahead a huge semi was rolled onto its side, blocking almost all the lanes. Cars had tried to squeeze past the open sides but got stuck, effectively creating a wall of metal. Behind the wall were more cars—hundreds.

Cars with bodies.

None of them seemed to see me, but I certainly saw them. They were disturbingly still, almost in a trance-like state, staring out of the windows. Each hideous face was blank, waiting for the prey that would never come. Only a few cars were inhabited, but their situation made me shiver. Trapped forever.

The other side of I-5, the one that went north, was blocked off by two humvees and one hell of a pileup. Cars were piggybacking each other for a block.

Edging along the concrete barrier, I finally got a view of Highway 2, the road we needed to get on. There was still a little luck in the world. There was only a small wreck between us and the open road.

I beheld the scenes with morbid fascination, reveling in my luck for a moment longer before I heard Pickle shifting in the pack. Her muffled squeaks were urgent. As I tilted my head to listen to her, I saw something in my peripheral. For a split second I thought it was a real, living Marine standing before me. The stiff was motionless, holding a standard M-4 in his graying, mottled hand as though he were still using it. His uniform was intact, albeit weathered by the elements. Even his helmet rested securely on his head, despite the straps being unlatched.

And he'd seen me. Who knew how long he'd been making his quiet approach while I gawked at the endless line of cars. If it hadn't been for Pickle, how close would he have gotten?

I silently thanked her before I let lust overtake me. I wanted that assault rifle more than anything. The M-4 was my go-to gun.

Raising Barbara, I rushed him before a snarl escaped his non-existent lips. The first hit ripped off his helmet. The impact sent violent vibrations through my hands. It skidded across the cement, the Z stumbling from the blow. I dashed for the bat and picked it up in one lucky grab then circled behind the Z.

The second blow caved in his skull. The sound of brain squishing made me squirm. The sound of Barbara splitting in half made me cringe. I jerked the bat back and the nails on the remaining half were covered with blood. Shards of wood protruded from my leftover chunk and the Z's skull.

I liked the melee weapon, but it wasn't looking too good. In fact, it was unusable. Even the strongest bat couldn't hold up to constant head bashing. I plucked a small sliver of wood from Barbara as a token and slid it into the side pocket of my pack. I gently placed Barbara on the ground and said goodbye. I hoped she fared well.

Before I claimed my new prize, I checked my surroundings once more. Beau still wasn't back at the truck. I bent down and pried the gun from the creature's hands and raided his vest. I turned him over and tugged off his pack. The Marine ended up being useful in the afterlife, too.

The Z had three clips of ammunition for the M-4, one clip of 9MM rounds, and a gun kit. More than I could've asked for. I stowed them in my pack then dropped the clip in the rifle and counted ten rounds, plus one in the chamber.

After my encounter with the Marine, every step I took made me wonder if the monsters in the cars were trying to escape their seatbelts. I didn't want to see either way, so I walked back to the truck and waited for Beau.

Minutes passed, yet I didn't hear or see any sign of him. I took the time to assess the rifle, but that went by quick, too. It was jacked. It could be repaired, though time and patience would be needed. The gun kit would help, as would rags and oil.

The pet store caught my eye again. Beau wasn't back, so I decided to head in.

The front window was smashed and bird cages were tipped over, with skeletal remains stashed among the old newspaper and bird feed. Enough light shone in through the window to show nothing was in there. I stepped around broken glass to the front door. There was no movement from the hair salon to the right or the café to the left.

Pet stores were familiar to me. It was a nonissue to find the rodent section and the untouched store of Mazuri dry food. I grabbed the five pound bag and cradled it in my left arm while I let the carbine balance in my right. I avoided looking at the aquariums and rodent cages, knowing they'd be full of dried out carcasses.

I stepped out of the pet store and heard a faint clinking noise to my left. Moving back into the building for cover, I leaned out of the doorframe just enough to look down the street. A subdued breeze sent pieces of old, torn paper up in a swirl. I still heard the noise but didn't see anything.

Finally, Beau came into view with a chain slung over his shoulder, keeping close to the buildings. I didn't think staying close to the buildings was a good idea. If we couldn't see any undead outside, it probably meant they were inside. I went to the truck to drop off the pet food and met Beau halfway.

The clinking grew louder as I approached. Beau took care not to let the chain drag on the ground. I came up behind him and took up the slack to speed things along.

"Once we move those cars, it's clear as far as I can see," I said. "But the noise is going to attract anything in the vicinity. If they aren't already on their way."

"I'm aware," he said. "We'll go fast and hope for the best."

Just as we made it to the truck, I felt my neck prickle. I glanced behind me and saw two waiflike forms coming over the crest of the hill. They almost blended in with the gray cement.

"Company. They're slow."

Beau looked back, sighing. "Let's get one of the cars out of the way. We have time for that before they get close."

We had to move fast. Beau and I got into the truck, slamming the doors a little too hard. He started the engine and pulled a u-turn in the three lane street, backing up to the wreck.

I exited the car without a word, dragging the chain with me. If the wreck had been more reasonable, we could've put the car into neutral and pushed it out of the way. But the two cars were tangled, one of them seeming to morph into the other. I went to the back of the larger car, a Jeep, and started wrapping the chain around the hitch.

It didn't take long before I attached the other end to our truck. The undead I saw before were getting closer, close enough that I heard their agitated groans. Once satisfied with the chain, I withdrew my handgun and gave Beau the go-ahead. I jogged away from the truck and toward the slows. They were coming faster than I originally estimated. I knew bullets would have to be spent. I thanked the Marine again. That one clip he had could mean the difference between life and death for me.

To my right, the chain snapped. The scrape of metal on metal sounded as the cars slowly pulled apart. The screech was so deafening, I dubbed it a zombie dinner bell. The Z's in front of me stepped faster. Bringing up my sight, I tracked one of their heads, waiting till the perfect moment to pull the trigger. It crumbled to the ground, but its companion kept coming, unfazed. I repeated the process, and that one went down too.

The kills only bought us minutes of safety, but I hoped that's all we would need. More of them came from the cross streets and hill ahead. I glanced behind me at the wreck as the Jeep completely dislodged from the other car. Beau dragged it until there was plenty of room to maneuver out.

I rushed back to the truck then dropped the gun off in the front seat. Beau was already getting out, his mouth set in a grim line. He ran toward the Jeep while I unhooked the chain from our vehicle.

One zombie was manageable. Even two weren't an issue. But when the moans and snarls of a horde drifted downwind, my nerves went into overdrive. There were maybe fifty, but it could've been a thousand and we'd be just as fucked. Instead of shaking in my little boots, I stopped thinking about dying.

Beau came up behind me with his end of the chain as I finished. We heaved it into the back of the truck and went for the cab.

The undulating sea of undead moved closer together. I hadn't seen that many in weeks. I buckled my seatbelt and stared as more came from buildings to join the ranks. Beau pulled a u-turn again and drove to our new exit, leaving the angry mass behind us.

I wasn't a seasoned zombie-fighter anymore. Due to weeks of inadequate supplies and firepower, my confidence plummeted and fear struck me whenever I had to deal with one. All it took was a fair amount of guns and good health to make me think I was unstoppable.

I wondered if Blaze felt the same.

Beau wasn't speaking. That didn't bother me. As long as the road was clear, we didn't need to do anything but drive. Our truck wasn't the quietest of vehicles, but the sound was comforting in a way. The heater blew a steady stream of hot air into the cab. A convenience I'd almost forgotten existed.

Outside, dark gray rainclouds moved in. Enough drops already pelted the windshield for Beau to turn the wipers on the lowest setting.

"It's going to get dark soon," he said.

Driving took twice as long as it should have for two reasons. First, navigating around even the smallest wreck slowed us down considerably. Second, Beau continued to drive slow, for caution's sake. Even though there were relatively few wrecks, there was plenty of debris on the ground. Suitcases, coolers, and abandoned bikes all implied people tried to make it on foot. Hitting one of these could result in crashing the truck or doing irreparable damage to it.

It was going to get dark soon. At this time of year, the sun went down around four. Technically we could press on—why not, since we had headlights? But that was exactly why we couldn't. The noise from the engine was bad enough, but adding headlights would make us a moving beacon for the undead. Once they caught sight of us, they'd be able to follow our general direction for a while. At least in the daytime we blended in with most of the drab surroundings.

We took an exit leading to a town called Lake Stevens, stopping when we spotted an old farm house to the side of the road. The house was shrouded in the white mist of lazy rainfall. It was off the side of the highway in an overgrown field. Behind it was more forest. I'm not sure why the house was there of all places, but it seemed like the best spot to stay.

Beau turned onto a winding dirt road. When we came up to the home, I wasn't surprised to see most of the downstairs windows broken. Curtains fluttered. I couldn't see any movement inside.

"Maybe we should stay in the car?" His hesitation was illuminated by green light from the dashboard.

"We'll be seen," I said. "Let's go in and take a look. If it doesn't seem safe, we can risk it in the car."

He nodded and pulled around to the back of the house to provide the truck with more cover. The windows here were also shattered and the backdoor was shut.

Pickle looked weak and her breathing was shallow. I found her underneath the back seats curled up inside of a sweater. How could she make it any longer? When I picked her up, she didn't move or protest. She knew exactly what was happening, and just looked defeated when I zipped her into my pack. I whispered an apology and swung the rifle over my shoulder before getting out of the car. Beau manually locked the doors to avoid the usual loud beeping acknowledgment.

We navigated through the overgrown backyard as best we could, stumbling over unseen clumps of wheatgrass and mole holes.

"Hold off on using your flashlight until we're inside," I said.

A twig snapped, Beau tripped, and he cursed. Once he righted himself he asked, "Why?"

"Do you *want* to turn us into a fucking beacon for whatever is out there?"

"No. But you don't need to be snappy about it."

Chapter 8

When we reached the house, Beau stopped me. "I should go first. I'm in better shape than you. If there's something in there, we need to react fast."

"Right." *If there is something in there, I'd rather it get you first,* I thought as I motioned him in front of me.

We moved close together at the backdoor and Beau reached out. "Locked."

Strange. "Come on. Let's look through a window."

I brought out my flashlight, making sure not to turn it on until it was pointed only at the window. We flanked the pane next to the backdoor and I leaned in. The curtains were parted, so I shined the light through the small crack. No movement. I nodded to Beau, who pulled the drape aside.

The kitchen was wrecked. All the cupboards were open and ransacked. Broken dishes littered the counters and floor. The sign of a struggle was marked in old blood on the tiled floor. Beyond the kitchen was a single arched doorway.

"Climb through," I told him.

Beau took a breath before handing me his pipe. He placed his hands on the window ledge and lifted himself up, climbing through. I glanced around while he entered. There was nothing coming from the garden shed or forest beyond.

I turned back to give him his pipe, but he was gone. A moment later the door clicked and swung open.

"Smells old in there," he said. "But not like they do. Just…unused."

I knew what he meant. After I went inside and closed the door behind me, I inhaled deeply through my nose. The house smelled stale and abandoned, but lacked the oily rot of the undead. I wouldn't write off the chances of them being in there, but it was still reassuring.

"Stay on guard. We don't know anything for sure."

Neither of us wanted to risk separating, so we began searching the first story together. Each room revealed the same tale of struggle. Chairs were overturned and broken in the dining room. The living room sofas were slashed with long, knife-like cuts that burst with stuffing. Family pictures hung askew on the blood-smeared walls. Despite all the signs of violence we encountered no bodies, living or dead.

Before we went upstairs, we checked the front door. Also locked. I wasn't sure how the windows were broken, or how there could be so many signs of struggle, while the doors remained locked. Anything could get in through the window. Why bother locking the door? Something was up.

Beau and I stopped dead in our tracks when we heard a floorboard creak upstairs. I pointed the flashlight up the stairs and sharp shadows cast against the walls from the railing. We waited, but heard nothing else.

"What do you think?" I asked.

"It could be nothing."

"It's always something."

I gave him the light and brought up my handgun, aiming at the stairs. We kept walking, slower than before, until I reached the top. Beau came beside me and looked down the long hallway. There were open doors to the right, and at the end was a bathroom. The flashlight revealed dirty white tile. A misplaced wooden chair stood intact near the end of the hall, but nothing came from the doors to the right. To the left there was a single closed door.

"If they knew we were here, they'd be out by now," Beau said.

"Let's just wait and give them a chance."

Minutes passed and nothing came out. The sun had completely set and the house was pitch black, except for features illuminated by our flashlights. Outside, rain beat on the roof. It made hearing difficult. Wind invaded through the busted windows, howling as it passed over jagged glass and split wood.

I shivered despite my gloves and sweaters.

Beau clicked his flashlight off and put it in his pocket. "I can't do any damage with one free hand."

"I have the gun. You hold the light," I told him.

We walked down the hallway and I stayed by Beau's side. I wasn't about to let him go up front and be in the line of fire. None of the rooms revealed anything different from downstairs. Furniture was broken and gore dried on the wooden floors. All the rooms we cleared were bedrooms, two of which were clearly boys' rooms and the other a girl's. The doors were intact and unlocked.

After checking another room, we turned and stared at the last door at the far end of the hallway. Nothing creaked and we heard no moans from behind the wood.

"Look."

Beau focused the flashlight on the bottom of the door, where a blanket was rolled up and shoved against the crack. We approached it, waiting for another sound. It came from above us. A slight shift. There was an attic entrance.

"Do you think—"

The whisper triggered the undead in the attic. More urgent shuffling began when Beau spoke. Before we even moved away from under the opening, wood groaned and a form broke through the attic entrance.

The Zs hands were reaching out towards Beau, who was closer now that I'd stepped back. Beau raised the flashlight and brought it down on the undead's head. It was a smaller figure, a kid, and the force knocked it to the side. I came in with the butt of my rifle and hit again. The Z went down, twitching. One more hit and it was down for good.

We went towards the stairs, keeping away from the attic entrance in case others would follow. After a few moments, no one followed.

"Find something for me to stand on," I said. "That attic might be the safest place to stay in the house."

"No way for them to get up," Beau agreed.

We stuck close together and searched the rooms. A sturdy nightstand in the master bedroom did the trick. My head was peeping through the attic, flashlight sweeping the scene, in no time.

Before the kid turned, he'd been living up there. There was a heap of sleeping bags and empty food cans in the far corner of the area. No signs of a struggle. He must've died from starvation and came back.

"Looks good," I said as I set my rifle next to me. I hauled myself into the space then I helped bring Beau up.

Unless the undead got smarter and figured out how to climb, we'd be safe up there. I was tired through to my bones and ready to sleep. As I tried to get comfortable, holding Pickle under my shirt to keep her warm, Kevin's face popped up in my mind. His clueless smile. The deeply sincere insanity.

"You okay?"

Beau had been searching through a stack of dusty boxes, but he'd stopped to stare at me. I wasn't sure why my expression set off his inner alarm.

"Yeah."

He chuckled. "Listen, I can tell when someone has something on their mind. I'm perceptive. Plus if we're going to survive together, I need to know if you're a mental case on the verge of a breakdown. That might change a few things."

I'd mentioned Kevin earlier on, just briefly. Beau knew I'd been captured, but he didn't know I was actively being hunted. Or that Kevin wanted me to serve him. I was never the kind of person that enjoyed talked about their feelings or concerns, but this time I needed someone to affirm my thoughts on the subject.

"Remember how I told you I was captured by cannibals a while back?"

He nodded.

"It was more complicated than that. They had a leader, this religious guy who wore a robe and spoke his own verse. He's a cannibal too, but he only eats redheads."

"Sucks for you."

I glared.

"Sorry." He shrugged.

"Anyway, when I was waiting for him to kill me, I talked back. I wasn't going to go down without a fight, even if it was just a verbal one. He loved it. Decided I was meant to be a leader in his army." I paused to stroke Pickle, who was motionless on my chest. I pressed my thumb gently against her chest. A faint heartbeat promised she was alive. "He said he'd hunt me down forever until he got me to see his way. I escaped, and I've tried not to think about it, but it's been getting to me."

"Having a personal stalker in the zombie apocalypse isn't something I'd predict. You'd think people had better things to do." Beau rummaged through a box, shoved it aside and sat down. "He has no idea where you are. He'll never be able to find you."

I thought of Blaze. I didn't know where she was, but I thought I'd be able to find her.

"Right."

He handed a crumpled piece of newspaper to me. It was an ad for a sporting goods store, claiming they had the best sale prices on last season's winter gear. The store was located in Lake Steven's, a town we'd be passing near anyway.

"We'll check the map tomorrow for the exact location, but if it isn't too far away I say we check it out. We need better gear, and this might be our only chance before we start driving in the boonies."

I agreed. We turned off the flashlight to conserve batteries, casting us in complete darkness. I fell in and out of sleep, dreaming of Kevin filleting flesh off my arms and legs while I was still alive, while Blaze told me I deserved it.

Chapter 9

Frost coated the bare nails in the eaves. Golden light pierced the dimness of the attic, coming through the slats of an oval window positioned high on the wall. Particles of dust drifted in the path of brightness. I wasn't sure how long I'd been staring at it, but staring beat facing the world just yet.

Something about the way the light played on the walls reminded me of growing up in Alabama. Memories of life with my grandparents and sister were fragmented. Recollections involving my parents were nonexistent. Yet on occasion one came to me, so vivid it felt as though it happened yesterday. Some part of my mind associated what I was going through to a moment in the past.

As I lay on the hardwood floor trying to ignore reality, I found myself thinking of a conversation I had with my grandpa. My parents had just died, putting me around seven. I was surprised I could remember *anything* that far back. They came to Washington to sort everything out and move me and my sister to Alabama to live with them.

I'd woken up crying. Crying because my mom and dad were gone, crying because it was the last day I'd be in my bedroom. Crying because I didn't want to get up and go to their funeral. Didn't want to admit they were dead. It had been a week since it happened, but this was the first time I'd really reacted.

My grandpa must've heard me from down the hall. He came in and sat on the end of my bed. He was kind, in his gruff way. When I was a kid I thought he was mean, but as an adult I could look back on him and appreciate his methods.

"I'm not going to ask you what's wrong. I already know. I came in here because I want to tell you something. You're a smart kid and I know you'll understand." He ran his hand across his balding head and sighed. "All night long, while you were sleeping, your brain thought about the bad stuff. When you woke up, everything seemed worse than it is. But I promise, Cyrus, once you get out of bed and get going for the day, you'll start to feel better."

What he said made sense now. Sometimes when I woke up, I was at my weakest. It was like my mind had been processing negativity in overdrive, pumping it into every thought, shoving aside confidence or optimism. You had to battle yourself. Fend off dread.

Do what grandpa said, I told myself. *Get up and you'll start to feel better.*

My extremities were numb. My face was numb. I was freezing to death. It wasn't an unpleasant way to go. You didn't even realizing you were dying.

Beau was awake. I could see his eyes, open and glazed, in my peripheral vision. I wondered if he, too, was dying. Or already dead. If he was at his weak point in the morning.

We shuffled around, getting our stuff together. Pickle looked emotionless as I set her into the cold pack.

Beau got up and dropped down through the attic entrance onto the table below. The thud was loud, echoing through the entire house. I followed.

Wood broke downstairs. We rounded the upstairs hallway and saw the front door splintering in the middle. An old trail of bullet holes had weakened the wood, and the relentless banging of the undead made short work of it.

"Come on!"I took lead and went towards the back door.

Winter air nipped at my skin and made my eyes water. It took a second to adjust. I blinked until my vision cleared, then I spotted undead walking towards the truck and house from the forest. The closest one was a scant twenty feet away. It was an older man whose chest was obliterated from a shotgun wound. Rotting skin peeled away from his bones, like a wall shedding old paint. His arms were almost eaten away, but he still flexed his hands and came towards me, unhindered by his deterioration. If I didn't have to shoot him I wasn't going to. He was far enough from us that it shouldn't be a problem.

Beau clicked the button on the truck keys to unlock the doors. Behind him, two women, young and intact save for their graying, rotted flesh, approached quickly.

As I slid into the truck, a hand with white bone showing through rotted tendons, grabbed the edge of the door as I pulled it. Slimy meat slid off and came with the door. The slow stumbled and fell. His whole body slammed against the truck and disappeared from sight.

Beau had the engine running. A handful of stiffs circled the front of the vehicle, and he threw it in reverse then hit the gas. Their fingernails screeched against the hood. I stared at their hungry faces with morbid interest, my heart rate already slowing down.

We were flung to the side as Beau made a hard turn and accelerated back to the highway. I took off my backpack and set it on the floor so Pickle wouldn't be smashed.

Beau released a shaky laugh. "Close one."

We pulled onto the highway, still dampened from yesterday's rain, and were finally on the way again. My stomach grumbled, but the engine drowned it out. The heater kicked in after a few minutes, which we all appreciated.

It was cloudy outside and, if I had to guess, below freezing. It was going to snow, and soon. Our truck didn't have chains on the tires, and that might mean bad luck in the future.

The trees quickly gave way to the occasional house and grassy field. The area was residential, and there didn't appear to be any useful shops. I was hoping for a car shop we could get snow chains from. If we could find that sporting goods store Beau saw an ad for, that would be even better. When the apocalypse started it was spring, and there were probably still heavier jackets and boots in stock, just going on sale. We both needed jackets and pants suited for the weather. My bulky collection of sweaters reduced my mobility considerably."I'm going to check the map, see if I can figure out how close we are to the store you saw."

"Good, yeah." Beau took a hand off the wheel and pointed to the glove compartment. "Check the map and see if it's on the way. I don't want to go too far off course."

I took the map out and viewed our highlighted route. We'd be on State Route 204 for about three miles until we had to get onto Highway 9. Market Place, where the store was, was long before we had to turn. Ammunition, guns, and food were the first things to be looted from stores, and I doubted we'd find any. What we needed the most were winter clothes, which the sporting goods store would have.

Raiding anywhere was a hit or miss affair, just as traffic seemed to be. State Route 204 wasn't clear of cars. Sometimes we had to drive off into side ditches to maneuver around wrecks or abandoned vehicles, but we made it to the turn.

We parked the truck in the center of the intersection and studied our route. The rest of 204 was blocked with battered military Hummers—powerful behemoths rendered useless without a driver. Walls of sandbags stacked waist-high stretched unbroken across all lanes.

Propped up against the middle of the sandbag wall was a large ply-board sign spray painted with the words 'By foot only' in red.

"This doesn't look good."

Excellent work, Captain Obvious, I thought but didn't say to Beau."It's fine. Let's just go to the stores and figure it out after," I told Beau, who followed the order and turned onto Market Place.

The back of a huge, red brick building greeted us. To the right was undeveloped land, with trees and overgrown bushes pushing at its edges. At our left was a grassy hill blocking off whatever was behind it.

'Haggen' in bold green letters revealed what the building was. It was a pharmacy and grocery store. At one point it was probably very well maintained, but the lawn was brown and muddy, grown out to at least a foot. A red SUV was rammed into the back wall.

We drove to the front. The area held a shopping complex with multiple real estate agencies and a movie store. Cars sat bumper to bumper in front of each establishment, blocking off any vehicle access.

Beau shifted gears and went faster, bypassing the parking lot. Only a few stiffs milled about. They were far from us, but shambled our way when they heard the truck.

We got to an intersection and Beau slowed down at the stop sign. I had to laugh. His shoulders loosened and he laughed, too. Still following traffic laws when no one was there to enforce? Priceless.

"It's habit," he said and continued past the stop sign into the next lot.

An *Albertsons* and *Payless* were the first businesses I noticed. We didn't need to go into the supermarket. There was food in the back of the truck. The more stops we could eliminate from our route, the more likely we were to survive. The *Payless* had shoes, but I doubted they had a better selection than the sporting store. Nothing useful yet.

We passed a *Rite Aid*. All its tall front windows were shattered. Black scorch marks rose up from the inside of the building, licking up to the roof. Despite the natural light making it through the windows, the *Rite Aid's* interior was black from fire damage. I saw movement somewhere in the back, but I couldn't distinguish what it was.

Not like it could be anything but a zombie, I thought.

The parking lot over in that area wasn't as congested as the ones by the grocery store. Evidently a hardware store wasn't as popular as a supermarket. Its front was beat up, though not at the level as the other stores. I guess no one thought to steal wood from here to fortify their homes.

Light, fuzzy flakes made it hard to see much and obscured buildings in a white haze. It was already piling up on the windshield. A slight breeze swooped flakes up, creating flurries that danced over the ground.

That primordial connection humans had with the earth spoke to me, telling me the sense of dread I felt was for a reason. My body knew a worse storm was coming. I could feel it. The charge in the air when a lightning storm was coming—I could feel it with the snow.

Although slows could only shamble, they'd made their way from distant parking lots and inside buildings to draw near. The closest one was only a hundred feet away. The cold made their movement more sluggish than usual, probably due to the stiffness the temperature induced.

I rifled through the assortment of junk on the car floor and retrieved the Mazuri ferret food. I needed to feed Pickle in case things got hectic when we found the sporting goods store.

The *womp womp* of the windshield wipers started. The snow came down harder. Beau leaned forward and looked intently through the clouding glass. I clicked the heater onto defog.

"I saw it across the street," he said

I cradled Pickle with one arm while she ate. Snow stuck to cement outside. At the rate it was falling, we'd have at least an inch in a matter of hours.

"We hit the sporting goods store and get gear for this weather then get back on track," I told Beau.

"Yes, sir." Beau reminded me of Blaze when he said it. The authority problem, the sarcasm.

Frost crept inwards on the side view mirror. It obscured the proximity warning on the bottom, but didn't block the view of distant figures following us. Some bodies slipped and disappeared, while others kept up their relentless pursuit.

According to our clock—which I doubted was accurate—we'd been driving two hours since we left the farm house. That meant we burned two hours of daylight and maybe, if we were lucky, had another six to go before we had to find somewhere to stay for the night.

We got onto Market Place again and came to an intersection. It seemed like a long way across to the shopping centers, but Beau had a plan and I wasn't going to stop him. I'm no backseat driver. We turned left onto Highway 9 and started the inexorable job of navigating around abandoned cars.

Highway 9? That's what we were supposed to be on. I got the maps out and verified. 204 came to a T with Highway 9. Taking Market Place ended up being an alternate route to highway 9. Happy mistake. Farther north the highway would reconnect with 204, the original T we'd been headed for.

An undeveloped lot filled with dense forest loomed to our right. An assortment of evergreen trees were dusted white with snow. I could only imagine what lurked in its depths. We passed cars with broken windows, where truly dead corpses littered the ground. They were so decayed and rotten it took a seasoned eye to recognize what the heaps were.

After a while we came to a strange intersection. It was a one way street we couldn't merge off of. Under different circumstances, we could've broken the law and gone down it anyway, but another three cars had tried and had become a tangled mess. A deep drainage ditch prevented us from trekking over grass, so we were forced to keep moving down the highway to find another entrance.

As we drove, I saw a huge building with red letters saying *Sports Authority*. The whole parking lot was filled up to the front windows, which were, surprisingly, still intact. I knew the store and had been in it before. They sold guns and ammunition.

We came up to an intersection that granted access into the shopping center. Beau turned right. We passed a bank and fast food restaurant before finally turning right again into the major shopping complex. Cars were packed tight against one another, and we only made it past one store on the strip before Beau pulled to a stop.

All of the shadowy metal crypts were on my side, and on his were two vacant shop fronts. "For lease" signs were plastered to the front windows.

"Well it's on foot from here. I can't get past any of this."

I couldn't argue. Directly in front of us was an overturned minivan. And the lanes to the parking spots were all filled with cars.

Beau didn't have a gun, but he needed one for this. I took out my handgun and gave it to him. Even after what I took from the Marine, there were only a few rounds left. Better than nothing. I checked my rifle and made sure the safety was off.

When I stepped out I took my backpack, with Pickle inside. Beau turned off the truck a second later. The quietness only an apocalypse can provide was unsettling. Snow made it even worse, and I felt more isolated than ever.

Sports Authority was three vacant shops and an eyeglass store away. We started walking. So far no undead were in sight, but they'd be there soon.

Glass crunched under foot as we walked around the minivan. No snow covered the front windshield, since it laid on an angle. Interior and exterior were darkened with dried sprays of blood. I heard shifting inside, then a rotting hand slapped against blood and dragged down glass. A zombie appeared after, pressing against the window. Half of the little girl's face was eaten. Her vocal cords were gone, and her mouth opened and closed futilely.

Beau was ten feet ahead of me. Ten feet was too much, since we needed to stick together. I stopped looking at the girl and started towards him. He was walking around a black Honda Civic when he fell out of sight behind the car.

Chapter 10

"Help!"

The whole scene went down in the time it took to run to Beau. My rush left me vulnerable to open car doors and spaces Z's could be hiding, but I had to get to him. I veered around the corner of the Civic and found Beau lying on his back, pushing the naked top half of an undead away.

Blood and body fluids dried up after a while. Zombies didn't keep producing these, so eventually their exposed intestines and internal organs wither as they drag them along. This one's were covered in mud and dirt. Rubbery. Almost looked fake. Pieces of glass glistened in its exposed bits. A bare back showed multiple bite wounds, almost hidden under dark tire marks. Strips of skin were rubbed off, revealing pockets of white bone beneath. Once shoved off, the stiff flailed like a turtle, trying to flip onto its stomach.

Beau reached under the Civic and pulled out the 9mm, sweeping the gun toward me. I backed up, unsure of what his problem was, and he pulled the trigger. My ear rang and I hunched over, clenching my rifle as though it would take the burden of my pain, but the pain never came. I turned to glance behind me as the zombie fell to its knees, then to the side with a loud *thump*.

Straightening, I tried to ignore the pain in my left ear so I could get a better look.

It was a woman once. She wore a dark blue tracksuit, the fabric ratty and torn. She had been a soccer mom, no doubt. Her hair was no-nonsense short, and she still wore a wedding ring. One sleeve was ripped at the elbow, showing the tiniest of bites—those from a child's mouth. I thought of the little girl in the minivan.

The stiff he shoved off was still on its back, wiggling. The thing grunted with each sway of its body. Beau leaned against the Civic, evidently deciding legless man wasn't a threat anymore, and rubbed the back of his head with his free hand. He breathed hard.

Any Z that wasn't truly dead was a problem. If you didn't put them down completely, even the most decrepit undead could be your end. Pressing the heel of my boot into its chest, I slammed the butt of my rifle into its head until it stopped moving. I released a shaky breath I didn't realize I'd been holding, and scanned the parking lot.

A few Z's weaved through cars, bumping against them. They couldn't assess their surroundings well enough to navigate tight spaces. One tripped and disappeared behind a truck. They hadn't made much progress since I first saw them when we turned into *Sports Authority*. None came from behind us, near the sports store, or from the highway.

"I hit my head pretty hard." Beau swayed as he walked forward. I pressed my rifle into my shoulder and held it downward with one hand, using the other to steady him. "That one was practically *waiting* for me. It was stronger than I expected."

"Can you do this?" I asked. "Or do you want to head back to the car?"

"I'll be fine," he said. "Just don't rely on me."

We reformed our line and kept moving. I wanted to thank Beau, but I couldn't bring myself to do it. After our power-struggle discussion earlier, saying 'Hey, thanks for saving me' seemed like a sign of weakness.

Yellow cement poles were evenly spaced in front of the sliding glass doors to *Sports Authority*. They were a safety measure, and I knew they'd been installed before the apocalypse, though I wasn't sure what the point of them was. If their goal was to stop cars from going into the store, they worked.

Two small cars of unidentifiable make and model had smashed into a pole. They'd been traveling in opposite directions. The wreck formed a V. The disaster spiraled outward, cars compacting so tightly after they crashed that some of their doors were crushed closed.

We couldn't walk in. We'd have to shimmy between cars, if we could. Our best route would be to climb over them or take the long route. If the circumstances were different—if I knew there were no

Z's approaching—these options wouldn't have been a problem. The apocalypse often forced you to pick the less desirable, and more dangerous, method.

"We need to climb over," I said. "I'll go first, then you."

I handed the rifle to Beau so I could climb over. I put one knee on the hood of an older tan sports car. It was slippery from the snow and my knee started sliding. Moving fast, I got my feet farther up on the car until I stood firmly on the hood. I leaned down and retrieved my gun.

The journey across the hoods and roofs of cars was tedious and frustrating. More than once the heel of my boot slipped against slick metal, sliding off the hood and wedging between cars. Each time I maneuvered my way out, my calves and ankles throbbed more.

I made it across the last car and jumped off the hood, landing in front of the broken sliding glass doors. Sunlight didn't make it all the way into the store, and the back was bathed in inky shadows.

I kept quiet and peered into the blackness.

While Beau made his way across the hoods, I reached around and pulled my flashlight from the side pocket of my pack.

Beau soon followed and fished his light out. We scanned the front of the store. Debris littered muddy, checkered linoleum. Old blood streaked paths in and out of the store. The registers were close to the front, and metal shopping carts were packed tightly against one another there, blocking the checkout lanes completely.

The store must've been a hoppin' joint for the undead months ago, but now it was as quiet as a mausoleum. Z's abandoned it for greener pastures. At least I hoped so. If they hadn't…Well, I didn't want to be in a confined space with no easy exit.

I went in first. We didn't walk more than ten feet into the store before I saw racks of untouched winter gear to our right—shelves of boots, jackets, and gloves. Some items were scattered on the floor, but I had a feeling other sections, like the ammunition and guns area, were trashed and empty.

Hard shadows created by our cylindrical light spooked me. They moved as the illumination moved. There were too many places where a zombie could hide.

"Planning a ski vacation in Aspen, Cyrus?"

Beau's voice was barely above a whisper. He looked like he was still in pain, and the joke seemed forced, but I grinned anyway.

"Should we put stuff on now or check the rest of the store?"

The store was big. Clearing it now had advantages. If we did, we'd be more at ease while gathering supplies, and we could possibly find more supplies. Checking the whole store would take time, though, and the longer we stood around the more likely Z's would gather. I doubted they could make it over the wreckage blocking the front of the store, but stiffs had a way of getting into places.

"Let's do it fast. Just a loop around the aisles," I said.

We began moving through the store, only walking where we were safe from potential zombie hiding spots. After going through the men's and women's sportswear, the videogame section, and tall aisles of boots, we came upon the guns.

The shelves were barren, as though they'd never been stocked. I was a bit disheartened, but we'd expected a lack of weapons. Partially eaten bodies crowded the floor, indicating a feeding frenzy broke out and everyone was on the menu. The smell grew almost unbearable as we approached. One corpse here or there wasn't that bad, but five or more was downright nauseating. Plus they were still juicy. Our shoes squelched in unavoidable remains.

It was surreal not finding any undead in a store like this, though. We completed our circuit and came back to the snow gear without seeing a single Z. The whole process took fifteen minutes. If there *had* been any Z's lurking about, they would've started making noise or following us by now.

I could only see past a few cars outside, but nothing appeared to be looming out there, either. While I kept watch, Beau tossed his old meager clothes and donned the new winter gear.

"We're making good progress." Beau looked snazzy in the new threads he picked out. When faced with hard times, people started looking older, but the snowboarder look he was sporting made him look more his age. It reminded me of the photo of him and his sister.

"Don't jinx it," I said, before wandering off to find new duds.

My first priority was to set the backpack down so it remained vertical. Then Pickle could be as comfortable as possible. I waited a moment before I heard rustling, indicating she was still alive, then got to work.

Before I stripped down to my skivvies, I gathered the clothes I wanted and laid them out. I found thermal long johns and a pair of Burton Baker gloves. They were warm and durable, but flexible enough to allow for good mobility when using a gun. I considered ski pants, but they were too noisy, so I opted for some heavier pants that didn't make a *swick swick* noise when I walked. I layered on a fleece vest before donning a parka with a stylish fur lined hood. After I pulled on a pair of sweat-proof, ultra warm socks, I decided it was time to select new footwear.

"Hey," I said, "I'm going to go get some new boots."

Beau snapped out of his thoughts and nodded. We walked to the back of the store where the shoes were.

A spattering of automatic gunfire sounded off nearby, followed by the rumbling of an explosion. We stopped dead in our tracks and looked back towards the front entrance.

Hearing gunfire and explosions at this point in the apocalypse was rare. Whoever caused them could be hostile. Kevin's face haunted my memory. If it was anyone, it was him. I knew it.

Beau rubbed his forehead. "Raiders?"

"Probably." I sighed. "Let's just finish this and get moving. We need to get back on Highway 9 and get some distance between us and whoever it is."

It didn't take long to find a pair of sturdy, waterproof boots among five aisles of hiking, hunting, and all purpose shoes. I selected Rocky Mountains, with a steel toe and zipper up the side, as well as laces. The box promised they were ergonomically designed and lightweight. They felt good when I put them on, but I knew they'd hurt after a while until they were broken in.

After we finished up in the boot section, I spotted racks of miscellaneous quick-buys. One of these held compact blades that folded into themselves. I paused to tear the packaging off and pocketed two. They were useless against the undead, but the world we lived in now made survival gear a requirement. Another cursory glance caught a space blanket packaged neatly in plastic. It was small enough I could shove it into my biggest pocket.

I heard the choir of moans coming from our left before we cleared the doorway. A horde of undead shuffled out of the driveway of an apartment complex across the way. They must've been drawn out by the explosion. They were heading in the direction it came from, all of them, until one spotted us.

I couldn't tell if it was male or female, but it raised its head and moved our way. Others turned and followed once they saw closer prey.

Across town, towards the *Haggan* supermarket, dark smoke billowed high into the sky. It stood out against the heavy white snowfall.

We wasted no time climbing over the snow-covered cars, our speed motivated by the fear of being eaten alive.

Chapter 11

Adrenaline coursed through my body. My heart thumped loudly in my ears, mixing with the crunching my boots made as I ran through the snow. Each breath came out white and cloudy. My lungs ached, threatening to tighten up and never release.

Across the lot, Z's continued to wander out of buildings. There were more in the vicinity than I originally thought. We might end up hitting a few on the way out, but I figured the truck could handle it.

But when we cleared the last of the cars and rounded the minivan, Beau and I stopped dead in our tracks. Walking past our truck were four men, one of them the man I hoped I'd never see again.

Crazy Kevin.

I dodged behind the van and jerked Beau with me.

"Mr. Sinclair, do not hide. I see you, just as He sees you, and I will still welcome you with open arms."

Too late. He saw me.

"Plan. We need a plan," Beau hissed. "We need to get into that truck. We can't make it on foot. There's a horde of undead coming our way."

"Fuck, fuck!"

"Please, let your heart be warmed and come back to me," Kevin went on. "These men will not hurt you or your heathen companion if you come on peaceful terms."

I peeked around the van. They were twenty feet from us. Kevin's men bristled and checked their guns. They were itching to shoot. Peaceful terms? I doubted it. But at least they weren't hovering at the truck.

"I don't think they know that's our truck," I said. "They passed it. If we can get to it we might make it out of here."

"They have guns, Cyrus. We'll be shot up before we make it anywhere."

"There's only four of them," I said. "We're doing this."

Before he could stop me I leaned around the van, aimed at Kevin, and fired. The bullet didn't hit its mark. Nerves got me. Instead it burrowed into the chest of the man next to him. He fell as the remaining two separated. Kevin came straight for me.

Then the rifle jammed. I hadn't cleaned it well enough, but right then I blamed the universe instead.

"Run! Run for the fucking truck, Beau!"

I flipped the rifle around and clutched it as a bat. Beau was already moving past the van. A crazy was on him. He raised his handgun and fired. I didn't see what happened after that.

Once I was around the van, I came face to face with Kevin. No more than two steps away from me, he stopped and withdrew a sword from within his robes.

"Mr. Sinclair, I will not give up on you," he shouted. "My goodness overcomes the darkness that consumes you!"

He waved the sword in an arc over his head. Flecks of liquid flung off and splattered against me. It had a strong chemical smell. I couldn't place it.

As he brought the sword full circle, it burst into flames. The orange glow cut through the grayness of the world around us.

I stumbled back. A flaming sword wasn't something I expected. I heard shouts and glanced left. A bigger group of men, more than I could count, navigated through the parking lot towards us.

"You will be marked again, but not out of love. You will be burned for your insolence!"

I heard another shot. Behind Kevin, Beau was fist fighting a burly crazy.

Now or never. I gripped the rifle and rushed Kevin, swinging with everything I had. My rifle clanged against his sword. Drips of flaming liquid splattered onto my arm. I let his momentum push me back then angled my body so he slid right off me.

Kevin spun around, but his foot caught in the gore of the soccer mom's corpse. He slipped. His sword clattered to the ground. I took one step towards him to deliver a final blow to his head, but had to duck as a bullet whizzed by my ear.

"Cyrus, come on!"

Beau was in the truck. The crazies were on me. When I turned back to Kevin, he was almost on his feet.

"Hey, Immortal One?"

Kevin stumbled towards me, his burned hands grasping. "This will not go without punishment, I will—"

"Fuck you."

He stopped talking the second my rifle connected with his jaw.

* * *

The engine turned over without a hitch and Beau reversed out of the parking lot. Kevin's men were taken down by their three friends, who came back as runners a moment after Beau and I got in the truck. I didn't see Kevin get up. I hoped he was dead.

We backtracked, leaving the same way we entered. Stiffs coming from the fast food restaurants closest to us brushed against the truck, some even getting a few grabs in before we cleared them and pulled onto Highway 9. They forgot about us the moment we were gone, opting to shamble after the crazies instead.

As we drove, I watched the darkening smoke, twisting my body around to look through the back window. It still crept into the sky, deep and oily, but the plume was diminishing. Had that been an attempt to draw me out from hiding? How did Kevin know where I was?

Those unanswered questions couldn't tarnish my smug satisfaction. I'd replay the sound of crushing Kevin's jaw over and over again when I was feeling down. I set my hand against my coat, where the burn rested underneath. It wasn't retribution for what he did to me, but it would have to do.

Beau slowed down to skirt around an abandoned red Corvette then sped up. The tires lost traction for a moment as the truck slid. He didn't hit the brakes—a good snow driving tactic—and soon gained traction again.

"I'd like to think I was hallucinating, but I'm pretty sure that guy had a sword. And it was on fire." Beau was still panting. His nose was bleeding. Other than that he was in good repair.

"You weren't." I stopped and thought, then I smelled my arm where the burning liquid hit. I remembered the lighter fluid on the table. "He used lighter fluid. Must've made some kind of contraption to disperse it onto the sword."

"Damn."

"I love saying this." I grinned. "I told you so."

Beau snorted, then changed the subject. "The snow doesn't look like it's going to let up and, after what just happened, I need a breather. We need to drive as long as it's safe then stop somewhere. There isn't much in the way of cities for most of the drive now. We can find an isolated house without a problem."

We came to the intersection of 204 and Highway 9, which was blocked by sandbags. I thought about the right turn we'd originally made onto Market Place and the barricade there. The smoke seemed to be coming from that direction. The convoy must've tried blowing through the barrier.

Great. Crazies with explosives.

The windshield wipers fought the snow furiously. Beau decreased his speed as a flurry obscured the view ahead. We hadn't been driving very long, but the trees were growing denser on either side of the highway. Pine branches sagged under heavy white mounds. I would've enjoyed the classic Northwest scenery had I not felt such dread.

Or maybe that feeling was just hunger. My stomach growled. We had plenty of food, but I hadn't eaten since the morning. Our abrupt exit from the farm house didn't leave much time for breakfast, and our determination to get snow supplies distracted us. But now I felt it—weak and in desperate need of protein.

There were a few protein bars in my backpack. I took the opportunity to check on Pickle, who was as tired and motionless as ever. Definitely not dead, though. I gnawed on the hard block of nourishment.

I was ready to forget about Kevin. There was no way he could've survived the battle we'd just left. Yet I kept looking in the rearview mirror, expecting to see his smiling face right behind me.

Chapter 12

Houses were set far away from the main road. They loomed behind trees and unruly sticker bushes, weeds growing over winding gravel driveways. Save for the occasional car coated in frost and snow, the road was abandoned. I felt the presence of anything—living or dead—begin to diminish.

The truck slid, drawing my attention away from the scenery. Each time it happened, I couldn't help but brace myself for impact. Though Beau was a good driver, eventually he would lose control completely. If we were lucky, we'd come to a halt on the road. It was more likely we'd ram into a ditch and have no way to get out.

We were both feeling woozy from the head wounds, but we were making good time. If we had to stop and find another mode of transportation, I'd be pissed.

He reoriented the vehicle and the slide smoothed out. I exhaled in relief and looked back out the window.

The fear of losing transportation pushed me to remember the Hummer. When it was stolen by that band of crazies last summer, I was devastated. We lost a fortress with guns, ammo, and supplies. That's what I expected to happen with the truck. At least, back then, we still had Blaze's Mustang, which almost got us to our final destination.

It had been early enough in the apocalypse that practically any car we found was usable. Even the sportiest of sports cars worked fine, since the weather was hot and the roads were clear. But now, since the weather was *terrible* and all the cars had been sitting around, it was going to be harder to find one that worked.

My head swam suddenly, and dark spots faded in and out of my vision. I felt light headed and unbearably tired. The day passed by fast and already it grew darker. If I felt this bad, I could only imagine how Beau was doing. Was it even safe for him to drive?

"Are you feeling okay?"

He glanced at me. "Yeah. I think we should stop soon. We're almost out of gas anyway."

Great. The truck is probably going to run off the side of the road and *we're almost out of gas.*

"We're making good time, though," I said. "How long can we go?"

"I won't drive this thing on fumes, and we're almost running on nothing." He brought a hand up to his head to touch his wound. His face contorted from pain. "This thing is eating up fuel from the load in the back and so much slow city driving."

We zoomed past a blue sign that said Lake Stevens High. Underneath it, another sign welded to the pole read *Evacuation Safe Zone.* I wondered how well that worked out before they were slaughtered. The thought passed quickly before my attention returned to Beau.

"What are the chances we'll find anywhere with gas?"

"If we can't find a station that isn't electric, we might be able to siphon some from a car. Just take whatever is on the top. As long as it doesn't have contaminants, it should be fine."

I took Pickle out of the pack and fed her some Mazuri. She ate without her usual vigor and looked at me with sad red eyes. I could tell she liked the warmth coming from the heater, and I made sure it was directed at her.

"I'm surprised that thing is still alive after all this," Beau said. "How long have you been carrying her around?"

"Since the moment I left my apartment, except when she was ferret-napped," I answered. "She isn't looking too good, though. I'm not sure how much longer she'll make it."

Just the thought of losing Pickle upset me. I knew she was suffering. After living in a backpack for so long and going through hell, I couldn't expect her to last much longer. She'd soon be in ferret-heaven, or wherever they went when they died. At least I liked to think so.

She wasn't a burden on me, but I couldn't take care of her as well as I wanted to. Keeping a pet during the zombie apocalypse was selfish. I could never take care of her adequately.

Up ahead, yellow and red indicated a Shell gas station.

It was obscured by an old white building that housed the mini-mart part of the station. Once we were closer and Beau pulled off the road, we saw only one car at a pump. Its doors were closed. The cover over the service station blocked snow, the gray cement underneath was visible. We pulled up to a pump.

"I'll keep watch and you take a look at the pump," Beau said and started to open the door.

"Hold on." I fished the space blanket out of my pocket and tore it open. It billowed into a large sheet, which I wrapped Pickle in, setting her underneath the backseat.

Normally I wouldn't leave her alone, but I wasn't going far. I couldn't stand the idea of shoving her back into the pack if I didn't have to. I felt like she understood my intentions. The space blanket would keep her warmer, too.

I took the carbine and opened the door, shutting it as softly as I could. Then I walked around the truck to Beau's side where the pump was. It seemed like it got a hell of a lot colder while we were in the vehicle, but my new gear made a difference. I didn't feel like I was freezing to death.

It wasn't surprising in the least that the pump didn't work. I'd been in the same situation before back at the station after Sultan. We needed some kind of hose or tube to siphon gas out of another car.

Beau proposed an idea. "I've been on back roads before, and some of the gas stations and smaller grocery stores have emergency backup generators. Especially when they're far away from the cities. It wouldn't take long to search around and inside this building."

The plan sounded reasonable, and we didn't have anything else to go on. Beau locked the truck and we walked off the bare cement into the snow. The cold seeped through my boots, but my feet didn't get wet.

The shop inside was dark. When we passed the front doors, I gave them a tug. They didn't budge. If we didn't find a generator on the other side, would it be worth it to break in just to look for one?

It had stopped snowing. Beyond the gas station was a cheap looking two-story motel. Its bright green trim and railing stood out against the peeling gray paint and pristine whiteness of the snow. No cars in the parking lot.

We skirted around the building, taking the corners wide so we didn't come upon any nasty surprises. I tried not to be excited when I saw what was at the back.

There was a fenced off area with some kind of structure inside. It was covered in snow, and the fence was chain link with dark green plastic woven in to grant security and privacy at the same time. The gate was shut, but I hoped it wasn't locked. Even if it was, one of us could climb over.

"I'll be damned," Beau said, as though he didn't believe his plan would come to fruition. When we got close enough to look through the small holes in the fence, he added, "That's a generator, all right."

Once we were closer, I noticed the back door. A cinderblock stopped it from closing. Snow was pushed up against this and the block. It was pitch black inside. Who put the block there? Someone who intended to go back inside? Maybe whoever had left it was still in there.

Flashes of what happened at the gas station in Monroe came to mind. The building had seemed so inconspicuous, but my complacency had almost cost me my life.

The past is the past. Focus on the present, Cyrus.

It took some strength to pull open the fence, since at least half a foot of snow surrounded both sides, but the gate gave and we both slid through.

"There's no telling how long it will run even if it does start," Beau said. "Our best bet is for one of us to be right at the pump when it turns on. That way we'll at least get something."

I agreed as we studied the generator. It was diesel powered. All it took was a few jerks of a chain to start up. Anyone could do it.

"Wait. It doesn't matter if we get the electricity on. We don't have a way to pay for the gas," I said.

Beau nodded towards the back door. "Get the electricity on, go in and hit the paid button at the register. I'll be waiting at the pump."

My head hurt and my stomach growled. I wanted to get this done fast so we could move and maybe eat on the road.

Beau disappeared around the corner. I gave him a couple minutes to trek through the snow, then I yanked the generator pulley.

It took three tries, and I almost ripped my shoulder out from the strain, but eventually I got the thing running. It sputtered to life and sounded angry to be woken up.

I pulled my flashlight out and peeked through the back door. The storeroom was in good repair. Products were stacked neatly on shelves, along with a cart of cleaning supplies in the middle of the room. There wasn't anything out of place. Nothing that indicated a rotbag ready to jump me.

A doorway with long plastic slats sat directly across from me. I readied myself. Run in and out. Simple.

The odds were in my favor. I crossed the storeroom and pushed the plastic aside to reveal an untouched convenience store. The lights were on. I went to the front of the store to the register. Outside, Beau saw me and gave me a cheesy thumbs-up.

I hit the paid button.

And since everything was peachy keen, I took a detour through the candy aisle on the way out. A bag of Jolly Ranchers, a bag of Sour Patch kids, and whatever else I could grab and shove in my pockets.

Before I left, I stowed my flashlight and brought the carbine up. I took three or four steps before my foot hit something soft under the snow. I fell face-first, gun flying out of my hands. Then I pushed myself up and stood.

Only half of a body stuck up out of the snow. The rest of it was either torn or eaten away. I wasn't sure which. But it lay dormant, unmotivated to move, until it was provoked to grab someone. It was nothing more than skin and bones, so I couldn't tell if it was a she or he. Its eyes were completely frozen and didn't move. I wondered if it could see. It's face wore a frosty, perpetual grimace.

The Z couldn't move fast. It could barely lift its hand to try and get me. I took a few steps back to compose myself, then moved in, bludgeoning its head with the butt of my rifle.

I collected myself and brushed the snow off my front before trying to jog around the building. The snow made it difficult. I found myself watching the ground closely for more undead.

When the front of the station came into view, I almost laughed at how normal the scene was. Beau standing at the pump, looking like any guy just filling his tank.

"Everything go okay in there?"

"Better than okay," I said. "Things are finally on track again."

"I'd have to agree."

A minute passed before the electric pump began to flicker and the gas station and mini-mart shut off. Six gallons made it into the truck before electricity failed. When the loud generator quit, along with the sloshing of gas, we were silent.

"We'll find somewhere to stop now, right?"

We were making great time. I still felt haughty from beating Kevin. Why stop when things were in my favor?

I was about to voice my objection, but he said, "I'm in bad shape, Cyrus. Can't you see that?"

Bad shape. He was my driver and I had to acknowledge his needs. Beau took a couple blows to the head, was hungry like I was, and wasn't handling the scuff with Kevin as well as me. If he suffered a nervous breakdown, or had a brain aneurysm, I'd be screwed and have to go on foot.

A moment of logic felt good. It reminded me that I was indeed using him. In a way, he was like livestock. I had to take good care of him or he would be of little benefit.

"Yeah, I see that." I managed a halfhearted, sheepish grin. I put the remaining candies back in my backpack. "The next place we see that looks good we'll stop."

We'd park the truck somewhere discreet, search the house to make sure it's safe, then wake up right when the sun rose. The roads might be rough, but if he drove slow and carefully we'd be at Samish Island in no time. There were more obstacles to come, like entering the Puget Sound and trying to find a small island, but it seemed doable now that we had gas and got rid of some extra baggage.

But I let myself get hopeful too soon. We were driving in silence when the truck suddenly drifted from the middle of the road off to the right. It was happening in slow motion.

"Turn into the skid!"

"I am, I am!" Despite his efforts, the vehicle did its own thing.

There was a drainage ditch to our right. It was filled with shadows and snow. We watched, helpless, as the truck glided across the road and straight into it.

Chapter 13

Our descent into the ditch was slow and gradual, bumping to and fro as we went over rocks and dips in the hill. Once we stopped, we shoved open the doors and began to squeeze out. Beau fell through snow as he climbed up to assess the situation.

Before I followed I took the chance I'd been waiting for since he stuck that damn picture there. I swiped the photo from the dash, folded it and tucked it into my pocket. I came up behind him, confident he hadn't seen.

The truck wasn't smoking or burning. No signs of damage, but the front end was covered with snow. There was no way to push it back onto the road without another vehicle to tow it. And if we had another vehicle, we wouldn't need to tow the truck out to begin with.

We were good ol' fashioned screwed.

I wanted to scream and curse the universe. This was the third vehicle I'd lost to stupid luck. It was less dramatic than the Mustang flying off a broken bridge, or the Hummer getting stolen by a group of crazy raiders. This was more of a joke. At barely 10 MPH, the truck decided to go headfirst into a ditch.

Beau put his hands behind his head and looked up into the sky. He exhaled a huge plume of foggy breath. "Fuck."

"Yep," I agreed.

"I don't think we can haul this thing out." He kicked the snow. "I just want to eat, sleep, and figure this out in the morning."

Beau's new plan sounded just fine, all things considered. We were far away from Lake Stevens, the explosion, and gunfire. If I'd learned anything, it's to take incidents like this in stride. Didn't mean I wasn't pissed off, though.

"Let's get our stuff. We take a can of food and hole up in the next house we see," I said. "Sound good?"

"I wish we had something lighter. Hauling those cans isn't the safest or most practical thing we could do."

"I know. What else do we have?"

"Nothing." Beau sighed. He ground the heel of his boot into the snow. "Maybe we'll find a car along the way? Get it running. Anything is better than going on foot."

"When's the last time you saw a car? I haven't since the gas station, and that was miles ago. It took us an hour to get where we are. Going back on foot will take even longer, especially since you're *jacked* up."

I guess that settled it. Beau nodded, saying nothing. He half-slid down the ditch to get his pack. I did the same, but instead of putting Pickle into my backpack I nestled her into my biggest inner coat pocket. Her space blanket went into my pack. I took my rifle and slammed the car door shut.

Up on the road, Beau stood cradling a large can in one arm and his melee weapon in the other. It was dark now, but despite it and the clouds there was enough moonlight to navigate without flashlights. When we got to a house, we'd need to break one out.

I glanced over and noticed a pensive expression on Beau's face. "What's wrong?"

"Nothing, I—" He shook his head. "I think I lost the photo of me and my sister. How could I have done that?"

I shifted from foot to foot. Coughed. "It's the apocalypse. Things get lost?" He looked like he wanted to say more, but I moved past him. "Let's get going, okay? No sense in wasting time."

We hadn't been walking long when we spotted a one-story house ahead. It was set back from the road. It looked like a quaint place someone left behind. Nothing more.

As we came closer, I noted there were no cars in the driveway or movement anywhere. The snow remained pristine and untouched, which meant there hadn't been undead wandering around recently. We treaded carefully down a slope to the front of the house.

"Let's walk around the perimeter," I suggested. "Look through the windows. Maybe we can see if there's something in there."

We tried opening the front door, but it was locked. Beau and I stuck close together, shuffling around the entire perimeter of the house, but only the kitchen window was free of heavy drapes. I let my rifle hang by its straps while I shined the light inside.

It was like any kitchen in America. Middle-grade appliances, linoleum floor, fake granite countertops. It opened up into a small, sparsely furnished living space. There were no signs of struggle or the dead.

The back had a sliding glass door that opened onto a patio. Since we couldn't see any immediate danger, we backtracked and tried to open it. With a crunch of icy buildup giving way, it slid open.

There was a distinct smell that defined these locations. This one was no exception. Old, dusty, and unmaintained. There were family photos on the walls. I couldn't help but look as we moved farther into the living room.

Only one person remained constant in the photos. It was an older woman, maybe in her late forties, with brown hair and a grin. Other happy people accompanied her, with their arms slung around each other. In each photo she was posed in front of rundown buildings or with equally rundown people. She seemed to be the kind of lady I'd see volunteering in soup kitchens in downtown Seattle.

Other than the kitchen and living space, the main floor contained a hall with three doors. One was open and showed a room with a neatly made bed and a dresser. Beau went ahead first and I lit his path. He opened the door closest to us. It revealed a garage.

Inside was a silver sports car. It looked like the kind James Bond drove, but I couldn't remember the name. We walked around it, finding keys were in the ignition, but in this weather the sports car was useless. Even if we got it running, we were better off walking. The car was too light and would have cumbersome weight distribution. We'd be fishtailing everywhere.

There was still one door left, however I doubted there was anyone left in the house. The undead couldn't open doors, but it was still better to check. We closed the garage behind us, and Beau went to the last door.

The bathroom was small, almost cramped, but immaculate save for the bathtub. When I shone the light inside the basin, it reflected off of red water and an old, rotted face.

Suicide, was the first thing I thought. Out of curiosity, I pushed past Beau and stopped when I neared the toilet. A note rested on the lid—a little dusty, but handwritten and obvious. I was surprised. It seemed common to leave a note, but most people didn't after the apocalypse. They were often too caught up in their own pain to care about how other people would react.

"Cyrus," Beau started to say, but I shook my head.

"Just interested. I've never read one of these before."

I blew the dust off the single sheet of lined paper and held the flashlight up high so I could read it.

Dear whoever-is-left...I don't see any point in living now that the dead *have risen. It doesn't make sense. I've spent my life trying to help people in need, but I don't feel like there is anything left I can do. Being a humanitarian was all I had. So I have nothing now.*

To be honest, I'm not sure why I'm writing this note. I guess for closure. I'm taking my husband's Colt and ending it after I'm done. We fought so much while he was alive about keeping a gun in the house, but now I'm glad I didn't get rid of it.

If you're reading this and the world we knew is still gone, I applaud you for being strong enough to press forward and live. If you're reading this and the world's returned to how it used to be...

Well, I guess I gave up too early.

The note was signed by *Kate* in sprawling, feminine handwriting. I felt an odd sense of intimacy reading this woman's last words. I set the paper back where I found it and looked at Kate. There was a dark hole coming from the top of her head. I recreated how the scene might have played out.

While Kate ran the water, she retrieved her husband's Colt from wherever it rested and brought it into the bathroom. She undressed and slid into the hot water, enjoying it one last time before chambering a round and putting the gun to her chin. She pulled the trigger and her brains exploded onto the tile behind her. Her death was instant, and ensured she wouldn't come back as a Z.

Her humanitarianism gave context to her note. She cared while she was living. A lot. Even in death her note would help people understand why she did it. What happened to her—it was almost too practical.

She looked like she died months and months ago. There were waterlines on the tub that showed the slow progression of liquid evaporating. The parts above water were papery and gray, almost mummified.

Kate could've pressed on but she didn't. She didn't have anything to live for. *I* didn't have anything to live for, not really, when the apocalypse started. Why didn't I off myself?

This woman probably had friends or family. She had to have someone to live for, to try and find or save. But she decided there wasn't anything worth fighting for.

I never thought of suicide when the world got loud, or after it got quiet when everyone was dead or truly dead. Besides my sister, I didn't have any remaining family, or friends. I wasn't a humanitarian and never contributed to society. If anyone had reason to kill themselves, it was me.

It wasn't worth any more thought. She was dead, I wasn't. Kate must've had a darkness in her that allowed her to pull the trigger. I simply didn't.

"Are you finished in here?"

I almost dropped the flashlight. During my contemplation, I forgot Beau even existed. He had been standing outside the doorframe and now leaned in, looking at me expectantly.

"Yeah, yeah," I said. "This place looks good. Let's eat and get some rest."

He found a can opener in the kitchen and we ate cold chicken noodle soup for dinner. It tasted gluey and slushy, but it did the trick. We found a bag of cat food under the sink and a case of unopened bottled water in the pantry. The water was so cold it hurt my throat, but it felt good to get some hydration down.

After the glimpse I had into Kate's personal life, I felt uncomfortable sleeping in her bed. I opted to take the couch when we finished eating. Beau shrugged and walked off to the room, shutting the door behind him. The lock clicked.

I took Pickle out of my coat and set her on the couch with her space blanket. She felt weak and limp in my hands, but she still breathed. I reached into the cat food bag and set a handful in front of her. She didn't move or even look at it. Was it my imagination or did I hear her sigh?

"What's up?" I asked her as I took a glove off and pet her back, each vertebrae painfully obvious, pushing against her skin. "What's wrong?"

Part of me wanted to scream, but the logical side reminded me this would happen sooner or later. How could I expect a ferret to live through an apocalypse?

Pickle raised her head, just a little, and looked at me. She was taking a long walk off a short pier. She was getting ready to push daisies. Check out. My ferret was looking at me in a way that said, "This isn't your fault, but the time has come."

At least that is what I wanted to think.

I haven't sobbed many times in my life. The times I have were short and for good reason. I didn't cry, but when I did it was induced by the most traumatic events in my life. This was the best time to sob, but I couldn't. I could barely move or think. Because right then is when Pickle closed her eyes and died.

The sense of loss and grief I felt was more profound than when Frank died, when Gabe ran away, or when Blaze disappeared, even put together. It penetrated me to my core and made my stomach tie into a thousand knots.

Her frame quivered, starting from the tip of her head, running down her tail, then released. She was nothing more than a limp ball of flesh. Whatever spark she had disappeared into the universe.

I wrapped her in her space blanket, squinting my eyes as hot tears trailed down my cold skin. I took her into the kitchen, where I placed her on the counter. I'd try to break the frozen ground tomorrow, or burn her body if I couldn't. But for now all I could do was turn, leaving my companion behind.

***

"You think it isn't your fault? It was your fault you left me."

Blackness surrounded me, but Blaze was illuminated by some unknown source of light. She held Pickle, limp and dead, in one hand. She looked dead, too, with washed out skin and milky white eyes.

"It's your fault your beloved pet is dead."

Gore oozed from her grinning mouth. Pickle was gone, and suddenly Blaze was right in my face. I smelled rot. I felt scared, more scared than I had been in a while.

"Everything is your fault. You're not going to find me. I'm dead."

Her clawed hands closed around my throat. I tried to scream but couldn't. My body was paralyzed.

Then white light surrounded me. I heard a rumbling sound from afar. Blaze shut her mouth and faded away into blackness.

* * *

There *was* white light in the living room. I wasn't sure how long I'd been asleep. It could've been a day or five minutes. I was still shaken from Pickle's death, and the dreams of Blaze always disoriented me.

The light was coming from the windows. It took a second, but I put two and two together and realized there were cars passing the house. The rumbling I heard in my dream was coming from outside.

To my right, the bedroom door clinked open and Beau came out. He didn't have to crouch or stay low as he approached. The curtains were heavy enough no one could see through, but the light from the cars still managed to filter in.

"It's a convoy," he said.

I stood up and slinked over to the window. Instead of pulling the curtains aside, I peeked through a small opening between the seams.

Some of the vehicles stopped on the road next to the house. They weren't too close, but it seemed evident they were looking at the place. People stood in front of the cars, and I saw only their silhouettes. Which had guns.

I'd only seen that many well armed, organized crazies in Kevin's company. My body tensed. I strained my eyes and tried to recognize any of the men. Specifically *him*. How could he survive the chaos we left him in?

"Let's slip out the back," Beau suggested as he glanced towards the sliding glass door.

"No, they aren't coming closer. I think they're just covering the other cars while they go by," I said. "I don't want to go into a pitch black forest buried under a foot of snow. We'll get lost. If we give them a head start maybe we won't run into them later. Let them get to wherever they're going."

Beau didn't say anything. I kept watching and, after another five minutes, all the cars were gone. I counted a total of 20 vehicles including trucks, humvees, ATVs, and a few other military grade vehicles. That didn't include the ones that passed before I kept track.

"Where do you think they're going? Do you think they're Kevin's guys?"

I didn't want to say it, but it slipped. "Yes. I fucking hope they aren't, but who else would they be? That many trucks, that many guys?"

Kevin was alive and looking for me. I knew it. I felt it.

"We don't know if they're looking for us. Maybe they're trying to find supplies. Slaves."

I wondered if they *were* hauling slaves. Or meat, rather. It was vain to think every crazy in the state was looking for me. Their primary objective was to gather food, wreak havoc, and gather followers for Kevin.

20 or more cars. If those cars each contained at least two people, that was 40 people. Minimum. There had to be more, of course, but I couldn't even imagine that many together at one time. Back in Startup was the last time I saw a congregation of more than ten. Even at Kevin's camp there weren't that many, nor at *Sports Authority*. This group was massive.

Time passed and we remained in the dark living room, waiting to make sure there were no more trucks. I thought of Pickle's lifeless body in the kitchen and felt cold and sick. Defeated. Alone.

What if I'd joined a group like that? Hell, what if I said yes to Kevin? Would things be easier? Would Pickle still be alive? I'd have been able to take better care of her, because people would've been looking out for me.

I clenched my fists, closed my eyes, and took a deep breath. In times of hardship, like when Frank died, it was easy to let negative emotions take control. They made you think things you wouldn't normally consider. What I thought, even for those brief moments, showed how much I was losing it.

It took a few tries, but I made my mind go blank. I kept breathing slow and steady, regaining control. We separated to go back to sleep.

Chapter 14

When I woke up, I found myself staring at a pot of dead flowers. The fallen petals were dark and crispy. The branches were nothing more than twigs. It rested in the center of the coffee table, as forgotten and useless as I felt. Pink and green bunnies were printed across the pot with word bubbles coming from their mouths. *'Happy Easter!'*

My eyes were crusty and swollen. Mouth was sticky, but my throat felt dry. It seemed like that was always how I woke up, feeling like I'd been through the ringer. Then again, I had been. This time the smell of food redeemed the otherwise unpleasant morning.

My head was throbbing and my legs were stiff from sleeping on a couch a tad too short for me.

Shuffling sounded from the kitchen. I pulled my boots onto sore feet and stretched as I stood.

Today we'll make progress. We won't get hung up by anything. Fuck, we might even get to the island.

I tried to be optimistic, hoping it would make a difference.

"Hey, I made...I don't know. Chicken and beans, I guess."

Beau stood in the garage entrance, holding a steaming plate of white meat with black beans scattered throughout. It didn't look appetizing, but when I saw the steam coming off of it my mouth watered.

"The end of times won't stop you from making hot food, huh?" I took the plate from him. The meat and beans held the metallic taste all expired canned foods had. But it was delicious, and I wolfed it down while I went to look through the front window.

"I was looking through the garage while you were sleeping. Found one of those camping stoves and felt like eating something other than half-frozen cafeteria food."

"That's fine with me," I said. "Thanks."

I didn't have a perfect view of the road, but I couldn't see any tracks from last night. It wasn't snowing anymore, though it must have fallen heavily overnight to cover the tire marks so well. The sky was perfectly blue, which explained why I was so cold. Clear days were always colder than cloudy ones.

The dead, white world outside sparkled in the sunlight. There were no sign of the undead or life of any kind. It was a nice day for a funeral.

"Pickle." I coughed to clear the phlegm from my throat. "Pickle died last night. I wanted to burn her body. Ground is probably too cold to dig."

Beau didn't look sympathetic, but nodded curtly. "I found a lot of wood in the garage. Lighter fluid near the grill."

We made two trips to carry logs outside. The ever resourceful Beau found a shovel in the garage and cleared away a circle of snow. Here, we doused the wood in lighter fluid. It took a little longer to find a lighter, but there was one in the kitchen, in the drawer right under the counter where Pickle lay.

I carried her body outside and set it on the top of the wood. She looked awkward and felt stiff. Just a lifeless, dead rodent. What made up her unique, resilient personality was gone. I wanted the whole thing to be over with, so I didn't stop to dwell. I lit the bunched up paper Beau had used as kindling and watched as the structure burst into flames. I didn't want to watch it happen, but I stood for five minutes until her body was consumed in fire. A part of me needed to know her remains were gone from the world.

Last night I experienced most of my grief, though this morning an emptiness in the pit of my stomach wouldn't leave me alone. As we shouldered our packs and walked up the little hill to the main road, I couldn't shake the loneliness away. I doubted I would for a very long time.

"She's better off now, Cyrus."

Beau's voice held sincerity, but not enough to make me feel better. I knew she was better off, obviously.

"Let's just focus on getting to the island, okay?"

We grew quiet as we trudged down a smooth expanse of white road. The emptiness inside me made room for another familiar feeling. The hair on the back of my neck stood on end. Something was up. I looked behind me, and my gut feeling was confirmed.

Multiple figures in pursuit. They were far off, a mile maybe, and no immediate threat. But they were coming. It didn't take a rocket scientist to figure out they followed the convoy. If I had to bet, I'd say they came from Lake Stevens. The horde from the apartment buildings.

Beau walked past me a ways before he turned to see what was up. I gestured behind us.

"Great," was all he said.

It was hard to trek through snow. The powdery ice caked onto our boots, but the exertion made me heat up, and my new gear kept me well insulated. The exercise took my mind off Pickle.

The zombies following us remained in sight. In fact, the line of them filling the horizon grew darker, as though more of them caught up.

Zombies could walk miles and miles in your general direction until they found you. A loud, meaty target like the convoy would keep a herd of stiffs in pursuit until their legs rotted or froze off.

There was nothing on either side of us but trees, power lines, and a house or two. Up ahead, the trees gave way to buildings. As we got closer to these structures, my gut tightened.

I heard the screams first. I knew they were women. The high, lilting tones reminded me of Monroe and that fucked up church in Startup. Our paced slowed, but we pressed on. There was no other way but forward.

We kept to the right side of the road. A large wood sign told me the shrieks came from a Baptist church. The yard and parking lot around it was filled with cars and trucks who passed by the house we'd holed up in. All vehicles appeared to be empty.

Alive inside. Help and be helped, another sign on the side of the church read. The banner looked old and faded. It was a sheet, I realized, with black painted letters. I'd never seen one like that before. Help and be helped? I saw plenty of signs seeking aid but none offering it.

Beau's expression remained neutral. We both knew something bad was going on.

"There must be guns in those trucks," Beau said.

Now *that* I didn't expect to be true, but I agreed. Would the raiders really leave their weapons behind? A quick look wouldn't hurt, though. However, someone would probably be guarding their vehicles, so we crouched and watched the scene. There wasn't an inkling of movement anywhere. Their mistake was our gain.

Mind you, there were a lot of places a guard could hide. In the backs of the covered military vehicles, or in the backseats of any of the cars. A handful of them could still be waiting, expecting someone like Beau and I to fall in their trap. Were crazies smart enough to think that far ahead? Idiots with power rarely had the foresight to imagine others would undermine them.

But having guns and ammo was such a tantalizing promise, I couldn't resist. Most of the snafus I'd been in recently wouldn't have gone the same way if I did. We had to act fast.

"Let's hit the humvees first," I said, jogging towards the closest camo covered vehicle.

Another onslaught of terrible screams reached a crescendo within the church. Shouts sounded, but I couldn't make out words. The double front doors remained shut, and I hoped they'd stay that way until we were done.

Since I had the carbine, Beau quietly opened the humvee door. I kept my back to him, hoping he'd do a thorough search without me. Seconds later, he grunted in triumph. I turned my head to see why, keeping my body towards the church.

He held a 9mm Luger, which he inspected before clicking the safety on then shoving it into his coat pocket. My cursory glance at the front seat revealed a brick of ammo.

"Looks unopened. 60 rounds," he informed me. "There's a shotgun back here. I think we should take it and run. The raiders won't stay in there forever."

"I agree. Hurry up."

In my world, good luck usually precedes a fuck load of bad luck. As Beau's feet touched snow, the church doors burst open.

The girl had been skinny before, I could tell, but the apocalypse had turned her skeletal. Blood stained ribs showed through a gaping tear in her shirt. Her bony limbs should've belonged to a Z. Red dribbled from slashes in her legs and arms. She sobbed as she stumbled, half naked, through the snow.

Battered men and women flooded from the church doors. But some of them were zombies. A handful of runners pounced on the weakest among the living, taking them down in a flurry of claws and teeth. A boy ambushed an older woman. I watched in fascination as arterial blood sprayed onto pristine snow.

A roar of automatic gunfire spewed from the church. Bullets connected with flesh, hammering living and undead with metal. People dropped to the snow, while the dead remained unfazed and continued to attack.

Most of the women, and some men, were naked or almost naked, confirming my rape theory. The convoy stopped to do what they did best, and one of them went too far, killing their victim. All it took was one runner to start a chain reaction.

The whole scene was tragic, sure, but no one had noticed us yet.

I turned to run towards the street, but Beau grabbed me by the shoulder.

"It's Don."

"Who? What the hell are you talking about?"

Amid the bloody chaos unfolding in front of the church, Beau pointed to one plain man rocking back and forth on the ground.

"Don! The guy I left behind!"

...but if I could relive the situation I might do it differently.

Impossible. Don. Don and Claire with the dead baby. It was *that* Don.

"Leave him! Beau, you're going to fuck things up if yo—"

Logic left Beau. I almost followed him, before I realized running through that was suicide. I watched in amazement as he made a wide arc around the carnage, towards a man he had a second chance to save. Towards a big mistake.

A grizzled man, missing an arm and most of his intestines, stumbled from the group and focused his attention on Beau. Ever noble Buford Wright didn't see the Z coming. I had to do something. I still needed him. Though I thought about abandoning him before, I wanted it to be on my terms, when I was ready.

I hadn't fired the rifle in days. I raised it up, gathered the undead in my sight, exhaled, and squeezed the trigger.

It wasn't a headshot, but it did the job. My bullet hit the runner's shoulder and knocked him off balance. He tumbled to the ground, getting up a moment later. It caught Beau's attention. He turned and raised his shotgun, obliterating the zombie's head.

That's my good deed for the day.

"Please, help!"

Almost ten feet away from me stood the same young girl who ran out of the church first. Her blonde hair hung in a scraggly mess, partially covering blue eyes that shone despite the blood staining her face. I wondered how she got so close without me noticing.

A tiny boy, younger than the one I saw before, came out of nowhere and sank his teeth into her calf. She fell to her knees with a howl, slapping at the toddler. She looked up at me, and I greeted her with a bullet to the head, saving her in my own way.

Beau was out of sight and so was Don. The fight moved towards me. There was only one thing left to do: run.

I didn't risk looking behind me as I weaved around cars, making my way back to the main road. I glanced into vehicles as I passed, but there were no other weapons in plain view.

I kept moving, even though my lungs were on fire and my throat felt unbearably tight. I wasn't sure if the undead or living were winning. The mix of ragged zombie screams and booming gunshots seemed about even. An image of the girl I just shot flashed through my mind. It was a mercy killing, but it felt like murder. I wasn't sure why.

Up ahead was a four way stop. If I turned left, I could loop around, come to the area where I last spotted Beau, and try to save him. However, if I went straight, I'd be headed in the direction of the island.

Beau planned on using a plane or boat to get to Samish Island. How bad off would I be if I took my chances and went alone? I did know the route, after studying the map so many times. I didn't *need* Beau, but it would make things easier.

My body decided before my mind did. I veered to the left. A small hill blocked off my view of the battle, but gunshots seemed to drown out the shrill cries of the undead. The convoy might be winning, so I had to be fast.

I spotted a semi surrounded by three large trucks. The back of it was open, and raiders pushed frightened survivors inside. Twenty feet away, Don struggled against two men. Beau laid face down, unmoving in the snow.

Is he dead?

As I came for Beau, one of the men got Don into a sleeper hold and the other noticed me. I stood completely in the open, since there were barely any trees or cars for cover. I bent down, getting ready to grab Beau, when the crazy bolted towards me.

"We got a healthy one over here!"

A burly lumberjack heard his comrade and joined the pursuit. I raised my rifle then squeezed the trigger, but it gave a dry click. Dropping the weapon, I tried to take up a defensive position, but it was too late. Lumberjack barreled into me and knocked me onto my back. He must've weighed 300 pounds. The wind went from my lungs as I was crushed.

"Get him into the truck!"

I wiggled one arm free and punched him in the jaw. His beard was so big it seemed to absorb the damage. I did it again, but it didn't faze him. Lumberjack pushed off me, and his friend delivered a kick to my side. Then another.

They closed in on me, but I scurried backwards, grateful my clothes and gloves protected me from the freezing snow. As Lumberjack came closer again, I took advantage of my position and kicked him in the stomach before scrambling to my feet. He grunted and swayed, but didn't fall to the ground.

"We're gonna eat you up, ya little fucker," he growled.

I couldn't take the two of them. They looked well fed and on the crazy side. The only thing I could do was turn and run, so I did.

That's when a bullet grazed my leg. A spray of blood splashed across the snow. The pain brought me to my knees.

Hands grabbed me from behind, hauling me back to the truck. I struggled, but Lumberjack and his friend hit me in the head and kicked my midsection. My leg was on fire, pain coursing down to my foot and up into my hip.

"This one has red hair," one of them said. "Put him in the food truck and save 'im for Him!"

Black spots darkened my vision. I felt weak. I'd vomit from the pain if I didn't pass out first. Lumberjack and his friend lifted me up into the truck. My face hit the wood bed with a loud thud. The door slid shut.

Before I fell into unconscious bliss, I thought again of how fucking bad I needed to dye my hair.

Chapter 15

Women were crying. No, not quite. They were weeping. It reminded me of my grandmother sobbing when my sister did something bad. A regret filled, *I knew this would happen* sort of sound.

My cheek rested in a thin layer of liquid. The smell was bad—a combination of blood and urine. I stopped trying to analyze after that. After pushing myself up, I opened my eyes. Others were pressed tight against me, and I bumped into outstretched legs.

"Is he dead? Is he going to turn?"

My head swam and my leg throbbed. The bullet wound hurt like a bitch. I needed to cauterize it or stitch it or at least sanitize it. Bullet wounds couldn't go untreated.

A memory of Blaze putting iodine on my wounds flashed through my mind. Seeing her dog tags—her real name, *Beatrice*—and the smooth skin on her chest. Even the pungent scent of cigarettes was crisp.

"Someone check and see if he is dead!"

"I'm not dead," I groaned. "Can you all just shut up?"

I opened my eyes. The faces blurred together, but then I saw him.

"Don, come here."

"W-what? Are you talking to me?"

"I'm looking at you, aren't I?"

He squeezed between the bodies, moving closer to me.

"Save the questions because I'm not interested in answering them. I'm a friend of Beau's."

"Who?"

"*Buford.* Nice kid who tried to save you a while back. Remember him?"

Don nodded.

"Did you see him? Was he killed?"

His eyes watered. He nodded again. "I saw him. But he isn't dead. They took him in a different truck."

It took a second to grasp what he said. I felt rage and anxiety coming on, but pushed them away. It was what it was. Beau was gone. I sat in the back of a *meat* truck with too many other people, no supplies, a bleeding wound, and a meek motherfucker who didn't know he was on my bad list.

"Okay." I ran my tongue around my mouth, desperately needing to work up some saliva, but my prodding was futile. "Does anyone know where we're going?"

The crying continued. Wind rushed through the truck from a small opening in the camo covered back. Thirty or more people were packed in here and none of them said a word. Some of them held others for comfort. Two older women stripped off extra clothes to help cover a near naked girl.

"They're taking us to their camp. That's what I've heard them say, at least." The voice came from a middle aged woman with a heap of frizzy brown hair and cracked glasses. "They caught me in Snohomish, so I've been with them quite a while."

"Caught you?"

"Yeah, just like the rest of us. If they see signs of survivors, they'll get you. They broke into my house. Tore the boards off the windows and took me and my two sons. If they don't catch you that way, they'll lure you out by acting friendly. Sometimes they get their megaphone out and drive up and down streets, pretending they're everyone's savior. Trust me, these people know what they're doing. Dumb as bricks, but resourceful."

I suppose that sort of thing was inevitable. If enough crazies got together and decided they had a mission, no one was going to be able to stop them. In this case safety *was* in numbers. The town of Sultan was the opposite of the convoy. They were sane, rational, and wanted to help everyone. They put together a chain of command and established reason. I'd never know for sure, but I bet they were still alive and kicking.

"What happens once we get there?"

"Probably what's happening now!" The man who said it had a vicious glint in his eyes. He had delicate features underneath the dirt on his face. "They're going to rape and eat us! Torture us. Let those *things* eat the ones who aren't good enough for rape or food. They get off on seeing it happen."

"Shut up, Jim," Frizzy Hair said. "But he is right. Nothing good is going to happen."

"Have you tried to escape?" I asked.

She clenched her jaw and stared at me before answering. "Of course we have. But they have weapons, we don't. They're fed and we're starving. We're terrified, abused, and on the verge of dying. *They aren't.* The only thing we have against them is numbers, and that doesn't do any good, all things considered."

"He probably thinks he'll be our savior," Jim snapped.

Michael and Angie, those pitiful "leaders" who hoarded emaciated survivors in a house in Startup, popped up in my head. They thought they were doing the right thing. They thought they were helping those people. In the end, I bet *they* were all dead. People got snide when someone who could save them came around, but underneath the belittling they wanted to be saved.

"I'm no one's *savior*," I said, and laid emphasis on the last word. "Thanks for explaining the situation to me, but I don't want anything else to do with you people. If you haven't escaped or done anything effective by now, you aren't of any use to me."

I felt a wave of tiredness sweep over me. The adrenaline from the fight had completely worn off, and the pain in my leg went from almost tolerable to kill-me-now levels.

"I can't disagree," Frizzy Hair spoke. "We do have incidents of *ineptitude*. Yet you *have* to admit that it's hard to get a grip on yourself in our case. If the dead monsters don't get us, the living ones will."

She said it like it was some kind of morbid joke, but I didn't get it. When a grin tugged at the corner of her mouth, I couldn't help but return the look. Something about her made me think she could handle herself better than the others. She was still alive for a reason. I didn't have any interest in saving her, or even lending her a helping hand, but mentally I wished her the best.

All conversations faded and the truck filled with murmurs of pain. I wanted to sit or lay, but the only bed was the wood floor that smelled like a sewer. I maneuvered closer to the cab of the truck and leaned against a wall. I caught Don looking at me from time to time, but couldn't muster up the will to care.

When I lost my supplies, transportation, allies, and any control my plan spiraled. But only for a short time. I looked back at when this had happened before, reminding myself that I recovered each time. A few times it required a hard slap on the back, but I *knew* I could get my act together.

First, I had to look at the facts. Beau was in another truck. As far as I knew, he was going to the same location I was, but there was no guarantee. Since I couldn't trust anyone's word on the matter, I had to plan accordingly. Getting to the island would be a lot easier with Beau. He had the experience needed to get from Samish to the island he thought Blaze was on. But I didn't *need* him. I knew the route. I could get there myself. That meant I wouldn't go out of my way to look for him. If he happened to be at the compound and easily savable, I would save him. Otherwise…

The problem of Beau is now resolved. Find out where he is, and if it's too hard to get him out, forget it. With that thought, I moved on to my next setback.

I didn't have a gun. Before, I'd never been without a weapon for more than a couple minutes. This was worst case scenario for me. Those who had the guns outnumbered me, and I was in a weak physical state. I needed to work around these disadvantages. If I could catch a crazy alone after we stopped, I could take one out and snag a weapon that way

Then there was the matter of my leg. I suffered from many cuts, bruises, and aches, but the bullet wound could end up being fatal if I didn't treat it. Until I escaped from the convoy's clutches, I'd have to play it by ear.

Although I'd only resolved two things—what to do about Beau and how to get a gun—it felt good to piece things together.

"It's my fault Buford was taken," a timid voice broke through my thoughts. "I'm sorry."

The coating of grime on Don's face wasn't thick enough to hide his expression of fear and grief. He seemed genuine. I didn't care.

Instead of having a Hallmark moment with the man, I said, "Okay."

He was expecting more, and the look on his face showed it. The truck hit something then drove over it. Judging by the thud-thud, I guessed the driver hit a Z. Or, since they were lunatics, a living person wasn't out of the question.

"It's just...when my wife lost her baby and Buford was trying to get me out of there, I couldn't move. I heard him yelling, felt him pulling me. I mean, do you know what it is like to lose someone?"

I pictured the scar on Blaze's cheek, and the way she'd clench her jaw when she was mad. Then Frank's scraggly beard and Southern drawl drifted into my mind. Yes, I knew what it was like to lose someone.

"Been there, done that. You have to move on."

"She's my wife!"

"She's dead, Don. Beau will be too because of you."

A young woman next to us inhaled sharply and glared at me. I rolled my eyes. Whenever I told it how it was, people acted like *I* was the monster. Living, breathing, Cyrus V. Sinclair—only slightly better than the undead themselves.

Everyone jerked forward. Most of them fell onto each other, and their wails grew loud again. The truck skidded before coming to a complete stop. Brakes squealed and the roar of engines died.

"Get the children to the back!"

The truck's occupants moved in unison as they began pushing anyone young towards the cab. Hysterical sobs grew louder once the front doors were yanked open. Daylight burned my eyes. I stumbled back, looking down until my sight adjusted.

"You 'uckers 'ick out 'unone yet?"

Half his face was burned and scarred. Most of his upper lip curled into his melted nose. His scars created a labyrinth of skin. I couldn't tell where features ended and started. When he spoke, his mouth barely moved. I wanted to laugh, but I knew doing so would draw attention towards me. The brute's face and speech were amusing. The M16 in his hands was not. The burned insignia on the side of his head, that matched the one on my chest, was not.

"Darryl, you're as dumb as a doornail," another man said. He came from around the truck, a riot shotgun tossed over one shoulder. Acting smart, he clarified for us. "He said; *you fuckers pick out someone yet.* Well, did ya?"

What is this? I thought, *casual execution hour?*

Burned Face and Smarty didn't wait for a response. They grabbed the man next to me, the guy with fine features who I'd heard someone refer to as Jim, and pulled him from the truck. The man's screams were primal. As he thrashed around, it reminded me of animals trying to escape the jaws of their predators.

I didn't care much about where they were taking him, but they left the doors open. My way out was right in front of me! Forest surrounded the road as far as I could see. If I barreled through the pain, I could easily make a run for it.

I stopped because Lumberjack came around the corner. Pushing back into the horde of people, I made myself scarce. I'll admit, Lumberjack frightened me.

He scanned the people in the front before tilting his head up and bellowing, "Darryl, you see that ginger haired one we caught earlier?"

A faint shout came back. "No."

Snow crunched near the truck and Smarty appeared by his side. I guess they hadn't noticed me when they grabbed Jim. For once, my red hair hadn't given me away.

"Just grab one in front, it don't matter. Boss says we gotta get to camp, cause Jud took the other trucks up north"

"Fine." Lumberjack huffed. "But when we get back, that pretty red haired boy is mine."

Smarty laughed and clapped the bigger man on the shoulders. "You got a refined taste for gingers, brother! Just like Him. But you know you gonna get caught eatin' that redhead and then you gonna get in real trouble."

My exit plan failed when the doors slid shut. Two gunshots sounded, but those didn't seem to kill him, since they were followed by ample screams. Ten minutes later the smell of cooking meat drifted into the truck.

"Lunchtime," someone whispered. "Jim's on the menu."

Chapter 16

At least our body heat warmed the confined space. The only small silver lining I clung to. Hours passed and the dim sunlight faded, leaving us in complete darkness.

My legs ached from standing. I shifted my feet, or leaned against the truck cab for brief comfort.

The anonymity of night seemed to soothe my companions, and they started to speak. Most shared their stories. I tuned out the gloom and doom tales and listened to the interesting ones.

A seventeen year old girl named Carry was on a bus from Nevada when, somewhere near Kirkland, a toddler turned. Carry was coming up to visit her parents when hell broke loose, and the toddler began attacking anyone in sight. Since the kid was so lightweight, people threw her off, but she'd latch onto whoever she landed on. So after hovelling in multiple safe houses, Carry fell victim to crazies. They kept her as a slave before trading her to the convoy for two boxes of whiskey.

The man talking to her, Craig, was well in his 50s. He'd been in the military for his entire life and was living in Lake Stevens. When he caught wind of an unexplainable ailment bringing people back from the dead, Craig boarded over the windows of his home and loaded up on supplies before mass hysteria broke out. Like me, he was a survivalist. He'd probably still be there, had the convoy not caught him on one of his monthly food raids. Now Craig's perfect haven gathered dust.

"Bad luck for me, but I hope someone found the place and got use out of it," he said before their conversation ended.

Craig's buddy Jerry was on a weeklong sailing trip with his wife, unaware of what waited for him on the shores of Washington. They sailed up and down the coast for months after they heard the news, but they were forced to go ashore for supplies. The convoy caught them. Jerry's wife committed suicide just two days before I met them. Suicide was easy here. Just offer to be the next meal.

Another woman, a porn actress, told a grotesque story. The third member of a ménage a trois had been bitten, and they turned during the filming of their porno flick. "It became a snuff film after that. I hid in a sound equipment crate in storage," she said. "I'm not sure how many hours passed until the screams stopped and I left."

Hushed voices filled our small prison, until everyone had their fill of storytelling. The sound of engines and muddled speech were all I heard until the truck slowed.

A rectangular sliding door I hadn't noticed opened beside me. Yellow light illuminated Lumberjack's grinning face. I looked beyond him out the windshield, desperately gauging our location for any escape opportunities. A metal gate slid to the right, pushed by three men. Though riddled with bullets, I made out *Richardson's Private Airfield* in blocky red letters.

"There ya are!" He waggled his eyebrows while he peered at the group. He spotted me and his eyes widened in evil delight."Home sweet home, ya skinny fuckers!"

Beyond the fence, a mucky road ran straight through forest, leading into an expansive open space. Raging fires billowed from metal trashcans, illuminating at least five shacks built from wood and sheets of tin. Firelight glinted off two massive metal buildings. They were reminiscent of aircraft hangers left over from WWII, but were obviously slapped together recently by the crazies.

We drove towards an unfinished three story building. Its exterior wasn't sided yet, and half the uppermost level still showed skeletal bars of metal and plastic sheets waving in the wind. Fire and synthetic light lit the rooms inside, but ratty sheets blocked my view of anything more. Outside, two guards were posted at the front doors. Maybe this structure was intended to serve as offices or a base of operations, pre-apocalypse. Six snowmobiles were lined up ten yards away from the side of the building.

One dangerously huge bonfire burned between the office building and the tin and wood structures. Men milled about with guns, dressed heavily against the cold. There were less outside than I expected, but I hadn't seen inside the building yet.

Smaller trucks and military vehicles broke away, driving towards the metal storage buildings. We came to a gradual stop. I shook out my arms and legs, limbering up in case a chance for escape opened.

Lumberjack and Darryl, the driver, exited the truck. The survivors grew antsy when they pushed up the rolling door. Bodies pressed against me, away from the crazies. Didn't anyone realize that wouldn't do any good? Did they think if they tried hard enough, they'd fall backwards into nothingness and escape their fates? I choked on the pungent scent of weakness trailing off them.

Three more men came into view, pointing their guns and yelling the usual threats until the people climbed out. They jerked Craig out of the truck and pushed him flat onto his face in the snow. My fists tightened as I thought how Craig reminded me a lot of Frank.

But there wasn't anything I could do, unless I wanted to fist fight five men with guns. So far Craig had taken care of himself. When I escaped this place, I'd try to cause enough ruckus for him to get out, too.

I moved forward with everyone else, keeping my head tilted down. Lumberjack had it out for me, and now he knew I was in the truck. The less he noticed me, the longer I'd live.

He was preoccupied, talking to a guy about "last night's lay" when I slipped past him, following the line of captives towards the big building.

Don snuck up to my side. "Do you have a plan?"

Who the hell was this guy? Hadn't I made it clear I wasn't interested?

"No," I said, voice low. "If you haven't noticed, we're fucked right now. Do *you* have a plan?"

Crazies catcalled at the women, provoking new sobs. One crazy plucked a woman I didn't recognize out of the line and dragged her towards the shacks behind us. Anxiety escalated among the survivors. Some darted off the path in attempts to escape. They met the butt of guns. These guys were good at what they did, and soon the outburst was over. Dead and the dying were shot once in the head before the crazies piled them up near the bonfire.

The living were pushed through the doors to the building, as though nothing happened. We first came into a room that would've been a reception area. Two hallways split to the right and left. A gaping hole in the wall should've housed an elevator.

The stink of unwashed human hit me hard once we were all gathered in the space. My length of time in the truck made me grow accustomed to it, but my brief walk outside refreshed my senses. Now the scent was back, combined with the hard smell of cigarettes, marijuana, and a sweet odor that wafted down the halls. It came in many forms, but I recognized the pungency of home cooked meth anywhere. Living in bad parts of Arkansas made me familiar with it.

The doors slammed behind us. Firelight blinked away and darkness descended. Moments later one of our guards flicked on an electric lantern. There were three of them, Lumberjack, Darryl, and another man, each made more sinister by the play of shadows. Garish white light made the sallow people around me look like the walking dead. After the incident outside no one spoke, but tears flowed freely.

"Ladies and kiddies, make yer way to the right side of the room," Lumberjack said. "Gentlemen to the left!"

The apocalypse was my rebirth. My second chance. I'd been running on adrenaline, bullets, and survival since the day I left my apartment, but I *loved* it. As long as I had a goal, I had a reason to keep going.

After I found Blaze, I was going to make the world a better place, taking out one sadistic clusterfuck of crazies at a time. It wasn't the need to save people or be a good guy that instigated the thought. More so it was the sick feeling I got in my gut when I saw lunatics like Lumberjack and Darryl using people just because no one could stop them.

To use someone for your own advantage, like I did with Beau or Gabe did to me, was different in my book. No one got hurt, though feelings and egos might get bruised. Bartering humans for your own gain was wrong. Even I knew that, and my mental health was less than sound most of the time.

Plus, no more crazies meant I would never get in this situation again.

We gathered at our respective walls and waited for further instructions. My mind was set on escape mode. I assessed the building, what I saw outside, and everything else I'd seen or heard since we came into the compound. Even as we were lead down the hall by Darryl and the other guy, I forced myself to focus.

Covered windows lined the walls to my left. We passed two shut doors, then another hallway. Music came from down there, and open doors cast light into the hall. After one more office, we came to a door. The guy with the light went first, pulling a metal pipe that served as a lock from the handle. We descended a twisted flight of cement steps.

Chunks of flesh and hair nestled in the cracks of a ragged brick wall that flanked the steps, which were slippery with melted snow and blood. I almost lost my footing before we made it to the bottom. The hard white light of their lanterns illuminated men sitting on the floor of a maintenance room. Uncovered piping snaked through the walls and ceiling. A gray boiler sat noiselessly in the corner.

There were at least twenty of us. The space the crazies corralled us in was too small, not like they cared. Darryl and his companion waited until we maneuvered into the room before tossing out a few more threats, though we didn't need to hear them. I doubted a single one of us didn't know what their intentions were.

Our only light source faded, along with the sound of their footsteps, as they went upstairs. The door shut. I heard faint banging as the pipe was put back into place.

No one spoke or moved. Labored breathing and sniffling were the only sounds, until someone close to me said, "Juan, I don't think they're coming back. Light the candles."

The familiar clicking of a lighter preceded a flicker to my left, near the boiler. A Hispanic man came into view. He pulled three more candles from behind the boiler and passed them to the group. It was still hard to see, but some light was better than none.

"Is anyone bit?" Juan asked. "Please, just speak up if you are."

A unanimous chorus of no's and nuh-uhs. Don had made his way through the crowd, back to my side. He was an annoying stray dog that followed you everywhere because you acknowledged him once. I imagined he did the same with Beau.

"*Now* do you have a plan?"

"Has much changed since you asked ten minutes ago? Why do you think I'm going to help you?"

Don's face crumpled. "I'm sorry. You seem strong. I need help. Besides, we're in a different place now. Maybe you have a plan."

My plan, once I escaped the building, was to get a snowmobile and a gun. Or I'd have to hijack a truck. That was me being optimistic. Worst case scenario was going on foot, but I was willing to fight for keys to a vehicle. The chances of me getting out of here without coming across someone who had a weapon was next to zero, so I decided my chances of finding a firearm were 100%.

Yet none of that mattered until I found a way to get out of the boiler room. After my eyes adjusted to the candle light, I looked for any exit other than the stairs. There were no weaknesses in the walls. Upstairs some of the walls were barely plastered, but down here it was cement. No windows, no nothing.

"We're in a worse place than outside," I said. "Different, maybe, but does it look better?"

Don glanced around. "No, guess not."

Most of the new arrivals found places to sit on the floor. They squished together in some areas, but as minutes passed everyone found a spot. I sat down too, my knees drawn close to my chest so I could fit, and thought hard about what I was going to do. As my thoughts drifted in and out, I felt a painful stabbing in both my sides where my coat pockets were.

Things are getting better, I thought as I remembered the *Sports Authority* knives I'd stolen not so long before. *A lot better.*

My focus on obtaining a firearm, or how I didn't have one, made me forget about other viable weapons. I remembered what a friend of Frank's told me. The 21 foot rule. A knife wielder 21 feet away or closer is more likely to win a confrontation involving a gun. An individual can travel 21 feet with a knife before another person trained to use a gun can bring the weapon to bear and fire with any hope of hitting their target. Useful, motivating knowledge.

When I was locked in the back of a truck, I couldn't do anything with the knives. Certainly I couldn't attempt to kill any of them when the convoy stopped or we were unloaded. I couldn't fight more than a few crazies at best with a pocket knife. But one guy? I could take him. No problem.

The two knives weren't much, but they'd be the difference between life and death. I wanted to take them out for a secondary inspection, but decided not to. There was no telling how the crowd would react. One of them could try and jump me for it and get stabbed in the process. Then we'd have a runner in a tight space, unless we bashed his head in fast enough.

No, better to keep them hidden and safe.

I *could* overpower a crazy the next time they came downstairs. The wall beside the staircase offered cover, but my maneuverability would be terrible since there were so many people. Fighting someone on wet, slippery steps wasn't something I wanted to do, either.

When we were in the truck, it grew warm and humid. The same effect occurred in the boiler room. So many bodies shoved into such a small space made me feel nauseated. I breathed through my mouth, but instead of smelling it I could taste it.

That's when I heard it—the chorus of a country song popular pre-apocalypse. I hate country music (it's on my top ten list of things to dislike) and the unbearably catchy tune about a girl wearing short-shorts threatened to get stuck in my head immediately.

No one seemed to hear it, or they weren't showing that they did. It wasn't coming from up the stairs or from another prisoner. Each note and word was so faint I questioned whether it was really there. But why would I hallucinate something as obscure as that?

I rescanned the walls and floor; nothing. Then I looked closer at the ceiling and found the source. Above the boiler was a grate the same gray as the ceiling. It was a square ventilation shaft I estimated to be slightly over 2x2 feet. If I had a pack, gun, or any form of supplies it would be impossible to get through.

I couldn't get to the boiler without navigating from the middle of the room to the edge, so stealth wasn't an option. I'd have to ask people to move so I didn't step on them, and when they saw what I was doing mass hysteria would erupt. They'd see a way out and jump on it.

Or maybe they were so afraid they wouldn't do anything? I almost forgot most of the men down there had been captive and abused for quite some time. While they didn't have Stockholm Syndrome they might be abused into submission.

If one of them asked what I was doing, which they would, I'd tell them the truth. From there…well, I was good at lying. I'd come up with something.

I stood and began moving towards the boiler, politely asking anyone I couldn't maneuver around to slide aside. Don, of course, followed in my path. I'd deal with him later. No one questioned me until I got to Juan, who was stationed at the boiler itself. As I approached I smelled the lavender and vanilla wax of the candle closest to me.

"Did you need something, buddy?" he asked.

"I'm going to leave," I answered honestly. "Through that."

He stood and checked the area I pointed to. The look on his face indicated he wasn't impressed with the idea. "What happens after? You're going to take them all out? I've tried going up there. There's too many of them." He tilted his face more toward the candlelight, revealing a fresh, ragged gash. "Never a good time to escape."

"Where does it lead? You've tried?" His depressing comments didn't kill my buzz. Any information he had would only help my cause.

"It goes through each story, but the only opening is in a closet on the first story. You can't climb up to the other levels of the building. The vent walls are completely flat. Doesn't matter, though, since every floor has a million of them. There isn't a good point to get out anywhere."

"It's a risk *I'm* willing to take," I said, then paused to look him hard in the eyes. "Wouldn't you rather die fighting than get taken upstairs?"

Juan turned his gaze to the flame of the candle. "I'm afraid of dying either way."

"I'm not. That's why I'm willing to take the chance, go up there, and give it my fucking all to get out of here."

"Yeah," Don said, a hint of vigor in his voice as he tried to step up. "Me too."

The other survivors grew agitated from the conversation. They mistakenly thought I might come back to save them. Sure, I had a long term plan to help get them out, but it wouldn't happen today.

I wasted no more words on Juan and his pessimism. Juan moved aside, creating enough space so I could climb my way up the metal structure.

As I bent my knee to place my boot on a pipe, my wounded leg gave way and I slipped, knocking Don back. The pain spread out, morphing into sharper discomfort as my elbows and back connected with the concrete ground. My head bumped into something soft, fleshy.

"Get off me," someone said. I complied, rolling off, only to bump into other people. A murmur of laughter went through the crowd.

"He's pathetic, trying to escape," came another voice.

The mass of people in the room were all a dark blur. They breathed shallowly, waiting to die. But they were a group, stuck together for who knew how long, and picking on an outsider brought them together. That often happened in apocalyptic scenarios I'd encountered. Could they be blamed?

"What an ass."

No, but I still felt vulnerable. That made me feel pathetic. Falling down, weak and incapable, as I tried to make an escape into certain doom. It was junior high all over again, with that buzzing sensation at the back of my neck that warned me people were watching. Staring. The knot in the pit of my stomach induced by embarrassment.

And what does someone do when put in that position?

"You idiots aren't even trying to escape," I snapped. "You've given up. *That's* pathetic."

Under other circumstances I would've left after my snarky comment. I didn't have that option, not this time, but I was saved from further embarrassment by boisterous laughter and quick footsteps coming from the stairwell.

"I feel like spic tonight, Ray."

"Nah, that gives me 'ndgestion. I want chink. Feel like sumthin' oriental, y'know?"

It was the truck all over again. Upon hearing the voices everyone, cowered away from the stairs. Juan blew his candles out, shrouding us in thick darkness. Elbows nudged against ribs. Clumsy feet stomped on each other. My back brushed against someone before I pressed beyond him. Our bodies slid together as I pushed him in front of me. My back hit the wall. Since Lumberjack had it in for me, I had to be as inconspicuous as possible.

Hoarse screams rose as one of the crazies used a hooked, metal prod to draw a man from the crowd. Frantic energy filled the cramped space, as the prisoners fled from the bloody mess.

I rubbed the back of my head, closed my eyes, and imagined myself out of this nightmare.

* * *

Just get through this, I thought, while I steadied myself with one hand against the boiler. *Then you'll find somewhere to rest. Push through.*

It was take two on the escape. If the prospect of being eaten alive wasn't motivating enough, the stench of truly dead rotted corpses was. The crazies tossed two partially eaten bodies down the stairs. They were ripe, many days old, and though I didn't see them, I could certainly smell them. Whether it was a joke intended to scare the survivors, or a macabre food offering, I wasn't sure.

As I studied the boiler, lit by Juan's meager candles, Don began to speak, but I cut him off with a curt shake of my head. "You're coming with me. I get it. Get this straight, though; you're *following* me. Not going *with* me."

I needed to ditch the baggage sooner rather than later, before things got out of control again. Beau might've been willing to put up with him, but I wasn't. Don was a tagalong. If he wanted to follow the path I cleared, good for him. I wouldn't make the same mistake Beau did trying to save him.

With considerable mental effort, I pushed the pain aside and climbed the boiler. The grate to the ventilation shaft wasn't bolted or screwed shut. With one shove, it moved up and locked into place against the side of the vent.

Another country song drifted through the opening. I heard the notes clearer now, along with boisterous laughing. Above me loomed a black abyss. Candlelight reached less than a foot into the vent, but I decided it was safe to stand. I did so slowly.

When I stretched my arms up, I didn't hit anything. I felt against the smooth metal sides. On one, I found a dusty ledge. The grip was substantial enough for someone in great shape, minus a bullet wound, to pull themselves up and shimmy inside. Without a boost, I wouldn't make it.

I crouched down and looked at Don. Finally he'd be good for something.

Chapter 17

After traveling through cold ventilation shafts for too long, exhaustion accurately described my state of being.

The sharp, aluminum smell permeated my clothing and stuck in my nostrils. My throat and mouth were raw from dust. On top of that, my bruised knees and elbows prickled from banging against walls while we made our way.

Yeah. *We.* After he gave me a boost, Don managed to press his body against the wall and scoot up until he grabbed the ledge in the vent.

Navigating the vents was easy. I followed the music and, after one more boost and some shimmying, came to the sole exit. Artificial light pierced the darkness of the maintenance closet.

If the music hadn't been so loud, I'd have felt nervous about pushing the grate open. There's no graceful way to fall face first from a small opening. I landed in a soft pile of clothes. Before Don fell out, I got out of the way. He grunted as he hit the floor.

I waited, expecting a crazy to open the door and recapture me any moment. Minutes passed before I felt confident enough to move forward. That heavy pit of anxiety in my stomach untangled.

The mouthwatering scent of cooked meat hit my nose. I pictured steak cooked to a perfect medium rare. Then I thought of eating human stew, courtesy of Judy-Beth long ago, and my stomach tightened. I knew that familiar beefy scent. It came from a *different* kind of cattle.

Eating other humans was unreasonable. The apocalypse had been in effect for less than a year. Though they were sparse, canned goods would be in many houses and, in some cases, supermarkets. These guys got off on the crazed-control aspect of cannibalism. I filed the thought away for later analysis and took a breath.

The door didn't squeak as I inched it open, revealing an empty hallway. It was the same hallway I'd passed through before. Music, yelling, drifted from the rooms. Sometimes I heard a faint scream, but it sounded far away. Outside of the building, most likely.

In the middle of the hall, ten feet away, was a lone Coleman lantern. Its white halogen light hurt my eyes. That lantern hadn't been there before. It was set outside a shut door. A temporary placement, I decided. Someone might come out to retrieve it after finishing whatever they were doing.

"What's going on out there?"

"*Quiet!*" I hissed at Don. "No talking. Got it?"

I didn't get a reply, so I had to assume he did.

Farthest away, I spied the wall of windows. The ratty sheets covering them were thin, almost papery, and the bonfire outside shone through them. Orange spots of light flickered against the floor and walls. Silhouettes moved about, some clear and others distorted depending on how far away they were. Just another night at camp for the men outside.

It was probably pure paranoia, but I couldn't progress past the lantern until its owner reclaimed it. I pulled the door closed and sat back. While I waited, I retrieved my knife.

Twenty years ago—*am I really that old? Where did time go?*— I'd play hide and seek with my sister. Hiding in the closet reminded me of one very important fact: I wasn't a good hider. She'd always find me within the first couple minutes. Closets, cupboards, and behind curtains were the best I could manage.

Two decades later my hiding spots hadn't changed. Every time I won it was because she was distracted by something and stopped looking for me.

That was it! Distraction. I knew I wanted to get to the snowmobile, but I also knew I couldn't walk out the door and just grab it. However, I could do *exactly* that if the crazies' attention was diverted elsewhere. Say on an epidemic of flesh eating runners? Also, I could probably find out where Beau was through my captive. If I detained someone uninterrupted long enough to question, kill, then release him...well, I just hoped it would work.

Whether it was Lantern Guy or someone else, the next person to come close to the closet would find themselves quite unhappy. My opportunity came before I had the chance to fully finalize my plan.

The point of light moved up along the doorframe. Someone had picked up the lantern, so I cracked the door open. One lonely man stood in the hallway, a rifle slung over his shoulder as he smoked a cigarette.

I pulled the door shut with an audible *click*, hoping it was enough to get his attention.

"Hey? Riggy, is that you?"

I stood to the left of the door, knife ready. A rustling sounded as Don moved out of the way.

"Stop," I said. "He'll see you and be distracted. Stay in front of the door."

"Are you sure? I—"

"I'm sick of these games, Riggy. You ain't scaring me!"

Footsteps, then the door opened. I came from the side and pulled him in, praying that the door slamming shut wouldn't bring unwanted guests. Part of me knew the sound wouldn't be out of place, considering the crazies' slack security.

Lantern Guy inhaled sharply, ready to yell, but I clapped my hand over his mouth. The cigarette crushed against his lips and he dropped the lantern. Beneath my grasp, he squealed in pain. I was grateful for my gloves. They protected me from skin-to-skin contact, which was good, considering his whole body stank.

Maneuvering in the heaps of clothes under me was difficult. I stumbled forward, Lantern Guy in front of me, and toppled onto him. My side clipped Don's as he attempted to dive out of the way.

I ended up straddling the guy, but it kept him down.

"Turn off the light," I told Don. "Quick, before someone sees!"

One flick later and we were submerged in darkness. Lantern Guy thrashed underneath me, but stopped moving once he felt the edge of my knife press against his throat. Anymore fight from him and he would've escaped. I had bursts of energy, but I was getting weaker and weaker.

I counted to sixty slowly. No one came. The country music never stopped. I had to question him fast.

"I've got a few questions then you'll be on your way, okay? Nod if you understand." After he did, I continued. "There was another truck.

I heard you have another compound somewhere and the truck might've gone there. Do you know if that's true?"

Nod.

"Okay. I'm going to remove my hand. Any word above a whisper and you can say goodbye to your throat."

Lantern Guy spit out his cigarette and coughed. I couldn't blame him. "It went to Burlington."

"Why?"

"We traded with the another Brotherhood up there. They don't follow the Immortal One, but He said if we were friendly we could bring 'em into the flock. One truck of meat," he paused. "One truck of people for some weapons, and they had to listen to Him give a sermon. It ain't a fair deal, but He wants more guns."

"Thanks," I said. "That's all I needed to know."

. Lantern Guy's hot blood spurt from the slice my knife left in his neck. I backed off as splatters hit my face. His screams of protest gurgled away.

"What are you doing? Wait!" Don knocked me off the crazy.

"He…he…" Don sputtered, and I surmised he'd touched the crazy's hot blood.

I reached through the dark and pushed him off Lantern Guy. "Fuck, Don! He's going to turn soon. Get off him!"

I couldn't waste a second in getting him out of the closet. I opened the door, hoping that no one was in the hall. I needed it empty so I could get him out and close the door. Once he turned and started running, I didn't care how many people showed. Propping the door open with one foot, I grabbed his boots.

Our voices had risen, but the music outside had, too. Don didn't move to help me. I heaved Lantern Guy's body out myself, feeling exposed. I expected someone to come into the hall the whole time, but I didn't have a choice. No one emerged as I left him in front of one of the closed doors.

If everything went right, the runner would distract the crazies enough for me to flee undetected. Even if they *did* see me, they'd be too preoccupied with a zombie to care. Before I hurried back into the closet, I snatched the rifle off his twitching body. As I shut the door behind me, the potent scent of fresh, coppery blood washed over me.

"This is your amazing plan? You're going to get us killed!"

Words straight from Gabe's mouth flowed out of Don's lips. There were so many of her "type" in the world. The kind that survived because they acted like rats, hiding and feeding off the efforts of others. Yet they had the audacity to complain. I knew I'd see more Dons and Gabes in my future. Unavoidable.

"It's the only plan I've got," I replied.

The weight of the rifle in my hands felt fantastic.

I took deep breaths, clutching it against my chest, mentally prepping for the run out of the building. Playing it by ear was my only option. Another minute and the runner would be pounding on doors, too stupid to open them. I doubted any of the crazies would expect it. I'd never dealt with someone who'd been bitten, but I figured they'd zombify soon after. Hopefully Lantern Guy would get a bite out of a few people before they took him out.

My distraction relied on the crazies' stupidity and lack of coordination more than anything. Should one of them shoot Lantern Guy in the head right away, I wasn't sure what I'd do. But, if everything worked out…

Best case scenario, the chaos would escalate. There were too many of them for the compound to fall apart. There might be twenty of them inside, but at least double that amount outside. All I needed was a window of opportunity while they tried to regroup and I'd escape.

The next series of noises explained everything. Lantern Guy, now a freshly turned runner, was up. Loud thuds indicated him running. Fast, rapid slams sounded when he banged on doors. Music stopped. Jovial laughter ceased. Then the shrieks of the living began.

Just as I checked the situation, the door Lantern Guy banged on opened and he rushed in. It swooshed shut and alarmed shouts became desperate screams of pain.

There was my chance. I made a run for it, dashing down the empty hallway. Don's footsteps followed. I risked a glance and, sure enough, he was sticking to me like glue.

I passed a door and halted. A familiar symbol was carved into it. The same one burned into my chest. A blade of light shone from underneath the door. Before I could stop myself, I turned the knob and entered the room.

"Mr. Sinclair. I knew you'd come back."

No time for theatrics. Kevin needed to die. No epic dialogue. No verse.

He reached for his sword, but I already fired two rounds. Both hit his shoulder. The rifle clicked. I dropped it, withdrawing my knife.

His face was too swollen to show any emotion as I lunged towards him, grazing the side of his neck with my blade. I would've slashed his throat if he hadn't hit my arm out of the way.

Kevin crouched low and swung with his better arm. His fist connected with my right temple. I stumbled back, bringing my arms up to defend the incoming blows.

"Forgive me, Lord! I tried to save him!"

Each time he screamed the sentence, it became louder and more frantic. I came in low for a stab to his kidneys. He knocked the knife from my hand.

As I dodged again, his foot caught under my own. I fell. My side hit the table and flipped me onto my back. My hand bumped into something hot. I felt it even through my gloves. I jerked away and saw I'd knocked over a coal chimney. The branding rod fell from it. The insignia was red hot and smoked as it settled on the wood floor.

Kevin had his sword raised over his head. I rolled and snatched up the rod. The blade burrowed into the wood with a loud thud.

"Forgive me, forgive me, forgive me!"

I was on my feet. Kevin screamed in frustration as he tried to free his sword. I swung the rod. It hit his brow bone. Sword forgotten, he tumbled to the floor. His screams took on a new tone. I placed my boot on his chest and shoved him back down.

"Please, Mr. Sinclair. Please see it in your heart to—"

His teeth broke first as the branding rod clipped them. Then steam poured from his mouth as it met the damp insides of his tongue and throat. Kevin's body went into wild convulsions, limbs striking the floor at separate intervals. I pushed until it wouldn't go any farther.

I pried the sword from the floor and positioned it over his eye. I never wanted to see Kevin again. Alive or undead. It sunk into his skull. I put all my weight into it until the sword cracked through to the wood underneath.

Don yelped. I forgot he even existed. By the stunned, horrified look on his face I figured he thought I was a monster.

I retrieved my dropped knife and rifle and exited the room, taking comfort in knowing I'd never see Kevin again.

Chapter 18

Don kept his distance as he followed me from the room. I pulled the door shut as we left. The entire scene only took moments to unfold. The other doors in the hallway were just opening up. Men looked out, dazed and confused.

"Hey, what's going on out there?"

"Zombies!" another one replied.

"Where?"

"Who are they?"

"Who the fuck cares! Go help Riggy and Tom!"

My lungs swelled from the effort to run and ignore every ache in my body. The crazies' confusion gave me enough motivation to keep going. I reached the end of the hall. At the end of the wall to my right would be the boiler room. To the left was the entrance. No one was coming in yet. So far the incident was isolated to the hall behind me.

I went left. Gunshots sounded off behind me. I heard a commotion coming from in front of me, too, just outside the entrance.

It was now or never. I slung the rifle around my back, then grabbed Don and spun him around so I had him in a loose sleeper hold. "Play along or we die."

He struggled. "What's going on?"

A handful of crazies burst through the door. Thinking fast, I risked using the names I'd heard others in their gang using. "Runner got Tom! And Riggy! This kid is trying to escape, I—"

I didn't need to say anymore. There were five of them, all toting guns, and each shoved past me.

Don didn't have to play-struggle. I felt his fear. I wanted to let go of him so I could make better time, but if we came across anymore crazies I'd rather be in acting mode than an exposed victim. We made it into the empty reception area. The double doors were still open.

I'd never seen a human on a spit before. I'd seen it in a movie at some point, I thought, but that didn't compare to *seeing* it in real life. It had been a woman, I could tell, but any distinguishing features melted from the fire and heat. Beside the spit lay another body, but it was too far gone to tell what it had been before. Both legs were missing as well as most of an arm.

"What the hell is going on in there?"

That's the question of the hour, isn't it? I thought.

While I stared at the bodies, two men walked in front of me. Their suspicion showed, so I used more crazy-lingo I'd picked up. "Some of the meat escaped. Bit Riggy and Tom."

The two looked at each other. They couldn't dispute the sounds of battle coming from the building, but they weren't buying *my* story.

"Why you got this guy?"

"I..."

Someone slammed into my back, knocking both Don and I forward. He broke my fall as his body hit the cleared path underneath us. The two crazies sidestepped out of the way.

I rolled onto my side in time to see an undead sink its teeth into the face of one crazy. It was a new runner. My plan was working.

Twenty feet away, my ride out of there waited. After I got back onto my feet, I stumbled towards the snowmobiles. The screams behind me helped me trek faster. Even if the runner situation was resolved quickly, it didn't mean I was in the clear. I was as tired of facing crazies as I was zombies.

"Wait for me!"

I didn't care enough to acknowledge Don. Instead I inspected the snowmobiles for keys. After the first five turned up nothing, I thought all was lost. Heart heavy, I checked the last one just in case. A lone key rested in the ignition.

"Hey, wait!"

My entire body shook from overworked nerves. Don was almost to the first snowmobile. Beyond him, a battle raged between runners and the crazies. I recognized the bulky form of Lumberjack, who shot wildly at a runner tearing into another man. No one saw me. This was happening. I was getting out of there.

I pushed the heap of snow off the seat and threw my leg over. The engine started with one turn of the key. I'd never driven a snowmobile before, but the upfront operation seemed simple enough. I squeezed the handle and the vehicle jerked forward. Before I ran into the fence, I steered to the right, taking a wide arc towards the gates.

As I ripped through the snow, I heard a shout from behind me. Don's voice couldn't compete with that of runners, crazies, and gunfire. He waved his arms, standing beside motionless snowmobiles.

Ones with no keys. Useless.

He started running towards me, but before he made it five yards two figures sprinted from the main building and tackled him to the ground.

Then I saw her. Spraying rounds of bullets into runners and shouting commands. There stood a girl I thought I'd never see again.

Gabe.

I couldn't believe it. I released the throttle and glided to a stop as I squinted. It was too surreal. What I saw didn't match up with what I thought was possible. My brain couldn't cope.

Her scalp was no longer bare. The blonde stubble had grown out, but even with the longer hair I could tell it was her. The angles of her face were unmistakable. Pretty, but young. She wore a white robe tied at the waist with rope.

The rednecks circled her like a Roman phalanx, guns poking outward. They shot anything that came near. They were protecting her.

I needed answers. I needed to know how she ended up there, why she was dressed like that, and why the *fuck* she was telling the crazies what to do.

Gabe looked at me. *At me.* Her chest heaved as she drew in a breath. Even from my position on the snowy crest I heard the words. "Kill him!"

Every head turned in my direction. Guns raised.

Oh fuck.

I squeezed the throttle. Bullets whizzed by my head and burrowed into the snow as I sped away.

I didn't need answers *that* bad.

Chapter 19

Was a full tank of gas in a snowmobile enough to get me to Samish Island? When should I stop and rest? Where am I? Why was Gabe here? I'm so cold. I can't feel my feet. I'm hungry.

Questions assaulted my mind as I drove. My brain was in overdrive, hyped up on adrenaline and guilt. I couldn't reflect on one idea before another overtook it. The sensation reminded me of when I had insomnia. A constant stream of incoherent thoughts smudging into one another relentlessly. There was only one man watching the main gate. When I approached, he didn't shoot at me or ask who I was. He dragged the fence open enough for me to slip through. I wondered why they put someone like him on duty. Letting "meat" right out the door. Shame on him.

After I cleared the forest and reached the main road, I went left. The road showed more signs of use in that direction. I had no clue where I was, but if I backtracked long enough I might recognize something.

That was almost two hours ago. The blue lit console on the dashboard of the snowmobile made sure I knew how much time passed, how much gas I had left, and how other important features were doing. When the crazies went shopping for snowmobiles, they made sure they got the nicest one.

It didn't take long to get used to the controls. The headlights were going to draw attention, but I needed them. Low, thick clouds blocked any moonlight. The forest surrounding the road curved overhead, thick evergreen branches becoming a canopy. Visibility was zero.

My fingers are numb. What is Gabe doing? Why are they listening to her? My leg is going to fall off from that gunshot. I need to stop somewhere.

Every now and then I passed the occasional side road. None of them were marked and most looked decrepit. I ignored them all. At least until the pain became too much to deal with. And the hunger. I veered onto the next one I came to, climbing up a small hill. I reached its crest, but instead of going down the hill I tapered off onto flat land. Thirty yards away, a cabin loomed in the moonlight.

"Cabin" sounds quaint, but the owners of this home probably said, "We're summering in the cabin" when explaining their vacation plans.

It rested in a circular clearing. A deck wrapped around its second story, disappearing around the sides. Its front was floor to ceiling windows. As I approached my headlights shone through the glass. Once I was close enough, I turned off the engine.

That unique silence of a snow covered forest hit me all at once. I couldn't hear anything because there wasn't *anything* to hear. I peeled myself off the seat then took a deep breath, waiting as circulation returned to my legs. Then I slung the rifle across my shoulder.

I left the lights on as I approached the cabin. Snow crunched underfoot, and the wood of the steps creaked when I went up the first few. Inside were high ceilings, modern furniture, and no signs of life. Luck was on my side, since I could see the whole first story through the front windows. The living areas flowed into one another. If I took ten steps to the left, I'd see the kitchen. Backtrack to the right and I'd see a dining room and living room.

No blood on the floor, or overturned furniture. I took my time treading around the cabin, through two feet of snow, peeking through windows and listening for signs of life. There was a raised patio. Mounds of snow piled on unused tables, chairs, and a grill.

My breath came out in a ragged sigh, sending white fog up into the air as I dragged my feet up a flight of steps and walked to the glass double doors to try the knob. It was locked, but that didn't surprise me. I ran my hand along the top of the door. There wasn't any snow on the ledge since the eaves of the cabin covered it.

Clink.

The presence of the key weakened my knees. These days, any luck I found was hard to believe. I gripped it in my clumsy, numb fingers and jiggled it into the lock.

It didn't work.

Inhale. Exhale.

Breaking the window crossed my mind, but instead I backtracked along the way I'd come and returned to the front of the house. People who left keys above doors sometimes thought they'd be tricky by leaving the front door key above the back door. Sometimes the key opened both doors, other times it didn't. After raiding enough houses, I knew all the tricks.

This time the key went in smoothly. The deadbolt clunked and I pressed the door open, wincing at the sharp *crack* of ice falling away from the frame. No one had opened it in a while.

I didn't want to leave the snowmobile on where its lights could be seen, but if something happened I needed to be gone in a jiffy. Should I turn the lights off, I'd be blind. Move the snowmobile, and I'd have more distance to travel to get back to it. I stared at the blinding lights, imagining figures approaching without my knowing, before forcing the paranoia away.

Fuck, I really need some sleep.

My first steps into the entryway were intentionally loud. "Hello?" My voice cracked. My throat was dry.

If any undead were upstairs, or hiding downstairs where I couldn't see, they would react and give their position away. The quiet made my ears ring. I would hear even the slightest creak, wouldn't I? I thought of horror movies where the characters called out "Hello" or "Is anyone there?" only to have a serial killer butcher them one scene later. That was me. The dumb guy yelling in a potentially zombie-filled house.

Hearing no reply, I conducted an in depth search of the first story, giving any stiffs more time to get their act together if they lingered upstairs. Photos of a couple rested on every mantel, wall, and end table, along with obscure modern art. The man in the pictures towered over his partner. His hair was gray at the temples, but otherwise dark and thick. With the healthy tan and polo shirts, he was your average, upper class rich man. A younger blonde accompanied him in the photos, body pressed against his or arm draped around his shoulder. She was young enough to be his daughter, but their intimacy was evident.

Mistress, I thought. *That's what she looks like.*

I broke away from the photo of the two on a yacht, basking in sunlight. It was easy to get lost in peoples' past lives. This wasn't the first time I became sidetracked, and certainly wouldn't be the last.

My preliminary search of the first story yielded nothing unexpected. I saved checking cupboards and drawers in the kitchen for after the entire cabin was secured. The living room, dining room, and entertainment room hadn't been touched in ages. Dust coated every surface. Even my footsteps on the carpet sent little flurries up around my boots.

As I walked back through the kitchen, something caught my eye. I must have missed it on my first pass. Resting on the top of the fridge was a medium sized flashlight.

I pointed it at the ground and pushed the switch. A warm, orange glow lit the gray tile floor. The beam was weak, probably from dying batteries, but would suffice for my search upstairs. The light was comforting.

Even if you'd never been afraid of the dark before, the undead world ignited the fear with a vengeance.

No sounds came from upstairs, even as I walked up the steps. I couldn't hold the flashlight and aim the rifle at the same time, so I opted to use the light. I held the gun with one hand at my side.

The second story was as spacious as the first. The top of the stairs opened into a loft with a loveseat and two chairs. From these seats, you could look down into the front entryway and living room. There was a door on the three walls behind this sitting area. All three were open. I stood in the middle of the room and shone the light into each. One was a bathroom and the other two were bedrooms.

Since the bathroom was small, I peeked in there first. Nothing but dusty fixtures and appliances.

Next was the guest bedroom. It was square and easy to search. No nooks or crannies offered hiding spots for the undead. The guest bedroom closet was huge, but empty.

Last was the biggest bedroom. Identical to the guest area, only bigger. It had a master bathroom with a gigantic tub, marble counters, and separate shower. I noted everything, but didn't dwell on any one feature. I had higher priorities than admiring the cabin.

The upstairs was cleared, so I went outdoors and drove the snowmobile to the side of the house, this time turning the headlights off. While I was inside the wind had picked up. Powdery snow danced across the ground. When the evergreen trees swayed, I heard them creak. I hoped the wind would cover up the tracks the snowmobile made. If the crazies, or anyone for that matter, were trying to track me down, fresh snowfall would hinder their progress.

Back inside, I locked the door behind me and began collecting supplies to fix my leg. In the smaller bathroom there were only towels and hand soap, but the master bath had an assortment of products in its cabinets. Among the many lotions, perfumes, and polishes that probably belonged to the blonde, a brown bottle stood out. Good old fashioned rubbing alcohol. I plucked the bottle from its colorful, feminine companions.

A hard white plastic case was shoved in the corner of the cabinet. A first-aid kit. My heart lifted. I took that, too, and sat back against the wall. Inside were bandages, tape, and gauze. Everything I needed.

My bare skin erupted in painful goose bumps as I shimmied my pants down over the bloody wound. Similar to the bayonet disaster in Monroe, it went through the meat of my thigh. It hurt, but wasn't fatal. A deep scratch more than anything. I tried to fight it, but my whole body began shaking.

Get through this. You have to.

I lined up my items in the order I'd use them. First I unscrewed the alcohol and soaked a washcloth, then pressed it to the hole. It hurt, sure, but *every* part of me did, too. I clenched my jaw, closed my eyes, and kept on pushing. Alcohol seeped into the wound, stinging my insides. When I couldn't take it anymore, I tossed the rag aside and took a fresh one, cleaning the general area around the injury, also.

I arranged gauze and bandages atop the gash and taped them down. Instead of redressing, I peeled the rest of my dirty clothes off. When I put them on at *Sports Authority* they were spotless, but now they were disgusting. The med kit had a package of sanitary wipes, which I scrubbed my entire body with, from my face to between my toes. My shaking intensified, but it felt wrong to tend to one wound and leave the rest of my body filthy.

The brand was scabbed over. Soon I wouldn't need to bandage it, but since the alternative meant seeing it I covered it up anyway.

I slipped a dusty bathrobe from its hook on the back of the bathroom door, shook it out, then put it on. My hand went to the doorknob, but I didn't turn it. One minute. I just wanted one minute to stop. I set my other hand against the door and leaned on it. My shoulders sank, my chest heaved. I screwed my eyes shut and let the waves of pent up fear and anxiety exit by body in long, bone-rattling shudders.

Right then I needed Pickle. I needed that look in her eyes, that callous indifference, that made my problems feel insignificant. *Get it together*, I imagined her saying. *Oh, and feed me.* My next breath caught in my throat. I couldn't think about her. Not now. If any thought could stop me from going on, it was of her.

The world was small, but never quite in my favor. I could run into Blaze's brother. No problem. I could stumble upon Gabe leading crazies. No surprise. But finding the one person I wanted? Why couldn't that be easier?

I choked back a whimper and gritted my teeth. A moment to breathe wasn't good. It allowed me too much time to dwell.

Find clothes, find food. Those are your top priorities. What are you waiting for, Cyrus?

I hit my fist against the door and exited the room.

The man in the pictures was of average build, so his clothes would probably fit. The carpet scratched my bare feet as I padded over to a large dresser. The first three drawers held women's summer wear. Definitely not what I was looking for. As I pulled out the bottom drawer, I was glad to see muted, darker colors. When I pulled some items out, they were durable instead of lacy. Cotton instead of satin.

My grandma called sweatpants and shirts "lazy clothes," and discouraged my sister and I from wearing them unless we were sick. I felt sicker than I'd ever been before. Lazy clothes sounded just right. I chose two pairs of worn gray sweatpants and layered on two purple school sweatshirts with the familiar *University of Washington* emblems on their fronts. My body protested with each movement, but I bit my tongue and fought through.

Any amount of adrenaline left in my system trickled away. With every passing minute, I grew more and more tired. I knew I needed to eat and create an exit plan. But when I turned away from the dresser and my flashlight illuminated the king size bed, everything I *knew* I needed to do didn't matter. Sleep became priority one.

I locked the bedroom door, though it wouldn't do much good if a crazy wanted in, and retrieved my gun, laying it on the right side of the bed. The inkling of anxiety telling me to stay up and do other things couldn't beat the natural force of my body wanting to sleep.

I pulled back a blanket, down comforter, and sheet then slid underneath them all. I barely had a chance to appreciate the softness of the pillow and mattress before I succumbed to sleep.

***

Warmth. My whole body was enveloped in warmth. Not the humid, feverish heat of sickness. This was genuine, good old fashioned *warm*. If I kept my eyes closed, ignored the dull throb in my leg, I could pretend I was in my apartment in Seattle, waking up from a particularly good sleep.

When the end of days happened, I didn't mourn the loss of modern conveniences. At first I was wrapped up in the excitement of it all, then the survival aspect, once I joined Gabe, Frank, and Blaze. The time of year had something to do with it, too. Spring, summer, and even early fall were forgiving seasons where one could forget the need for such items. When I was at Frank's cabin, I *had* conveniences. Safety, a place to sleep, food, and any supplies I needed.

But now? Winter came blundering in. On occasion, Washington suffered from hard winters. Lots of snow, ice storms, and wind. Last year was mild, but this year was making up for it. Since I began my insane mission to find Blaze, I found myself truly missing the basics. That's why I let my eyes stay shut while I visualized my routine pre-zombie era. My warm apartment with my scalding hot showers. The grapefruit juice in the fridge. Miscellaneous research on the internet followed by a five minute walk, zombie-free, to work.

"*That's* enough," I said aloud.

My eyelashes were crusty. It took a moment to open them, in which I cringed as the delicate hairs pulled apart. An off-white, vaulted ceiling greeted me. No smoke, no screaming. Nothing out of the ordinary. I was grateful.

The night passed by without incident. Either the crazies didn't want to track me down or they had bigger problems to deal with. Whatever the reason, I was happy and ready to start the day. It was amazing what a solid night's rest could do. I'd been learning to stave off morning blues, too.

But there was one thing. Gabe. Last night I wanted to go back. I wanted to talk to her and find out why she left me, or better yet why she was being protected by redneck cannibals.

I laughed. What the hell was I thinking? Did it matter why Gabe left me? She didn't fit into my grand plan then. She didn't now. If I backtracked to find her, I'd be no different than Beau risking his life to save Don. Twice. That wasn't me.

Whatever curiosity I felt didn't compare to my desire to find Blaze, stay alive, and *not* be subjected to any more cannibals. If Gabe had survived this long, I suspected I'd run into her again eventually.

Outside the blankets, bitter cold waited. I sat up, and that cold air attacked my back. As quick as I could, I tugged the sheet and comforter from under the mattress, twisting it around until it wrapped me like a shawl. I'd take this heat with me as I foraged for food.

I moved slowly, so my stiff muscles would warm up without getting too strained as I searched the chest of drawers again for socks. Last night was dark, and I hoped my efforts, with morning light, would yield better results.

All that I could find were the blonde's gym socks, a collection of small, ankle-less ultra stretchy slips. I layered three pairs on, but the fourth one kept slipping off. It was better than nothing. Compromising was a part of life and I couldn't complain, especially after the success of finding the house.

Each part of the cabin felt and looked different in the morning. I had a full view of the front yard through the giant windows. Golden light glistened off every fleck of snow. There were still no sounds of wildlife, undead, or other humans. Blissful silence reigned, other than my own breathing.

I tightened the blanket around me and went to the downstairs bathroom. Despite having drunk next to no liquids recently, my bladder was full. I relieved myself in the dried out, empty toilet. After I shut the bathroom door, I shuffled to the kitchen.

Opening a refrigerator was a no-no. Perhaps, after six or seven months, the food had rotted beyond the point of being smelly, but there wasn't any point in taking the risk. Nothing in there would be edible anyway. I returned to the cupboards I looked through last night and found dry goods. There were edible items that weren't high priority because they'd taste the worst, such as old cereal or crackers. What I looked forward to the most were canned goods. I found corn, French cut green beans, cream of chicken, and chunky beef stews. The hip, modern couple had some trendy flavored and normal bottled water.

After everything I'd been through, I wanted to reward myself with hot food. Last night I'd noticed a large fireplace in the living room. I went through the house looking for stuff to burn. I didn't want to go outside unless I had to. Fortunately there were two Presto logs stacked on the washing machine. I retrieved a butane lighter from the kitchen and started my fire. Since they self-maintained after being lit, I went back to the kitchen.

No, starting a fire wasn't the *best* idea, but I didn't give a damn. The smoke could draw unwanted attention, but I forced myself not to care. Right then, if I wanted to start a fire, I sure as fuck was going to. Lately I'd been putting myself second or third to other people's needs. That wasn't my usual approach, and I was beginning to remember why. When I started putting myself first, starting after my parents died, life got easier. Concerning yourself with the wellbeing of others only resulted in sacrificing what you needed. What you wanted.

Even before the apocalypse, I stood firm on my belief that what I wanted was priority one. That belief had faltered more than a handful of times recently, much to my chagrin.

I poured one can of beef stew into a heavy saucepan, grabbed a spoon, and returned to the fire, sitting cross legged in front of it. It crackled nicely and gave off a small wave of warmth, combating the coldness of the living room. I didn't want to wait for it to break down so I could set my pan on the embers. Instead, I held it patiently over the flames. Eventually the congealed mass thinned out and simmered.

Once I started eating I couldn't stop. Sometimes, after going hungry for a while, I'd get sick from eating anything. Now my body called for a gorging, and gorge I did. When I was finished with that can, I picked through the water, settling on lime flavor. Next I prepared a mixture of corn and cream of chicken soup. This time I crumbled a stale package of crackers into the heated mixture and ate it straight from the pan.

I'll leave tomorrow morning, I decided. *But for now, it's all about me.*

After my breakfast, I found a clean mop bucket. I used this to haul snow into the kitchen sink. I packed the snow tightly in, then heated up a smaller pot over the fire. I dropped this into the snow so it would melt quickly, and repeated the process until I had enough water. I then used the water to wash my clothes. The coat was bulky, but after much struggle it was sopping wet and relatively clean.

When I emptied my pockets, I found the photo—the one I'd worked so hard to steal from Beau—folded in half, damp, and ripped an inch down the middle. I finished the job, tearing brother and sister apart, and placed the side with Blaze in one of my vest pockets after it dried.

While I was outside, I found a mound leaning against the patio. It ended up being a stack of logs covered by a tarp. They were ice cold, but dry. I turned my measly Presto log fire into a house-warming, lively blaze. I laid my wet clothes over the backs of chairs to dry.

Hours passed. I did nothing but lay around in front of the fireplace, eat, doze, and think.

* * *

Happy birthday, Cyrus.

One year older. Ever closer to dying. I stared at the face of the atomic watch. It was December 26th. My birthday. I was twenty-eight years old.

I found the watch while looking through the man's personal items upstairs. The walk-in closet had a few cardboard boxes. All of its contents seemed to have a story.

The watch was in a small box with a note in it. *Patty, boy, you made the right choice divorcing that no good bitch. Now you have all the* time *in the world to spend with Jeanie!* An illegible signature was scrawled on the bottom and a smiley face. Patty, who had to be the older man in the pictures, didn't want to keep the watch with him, wherever he was. I wondered if it was because the blonde wasn't Jeanie, but yet another mistress.

Either way, it was still ticking away and the date and time seemed accurate.

And it was my birthday. Something about it made me feel sad, old, and lost. I'd been thinking about my age and accomplishments a lot, so I just let the feelings overtake me. It took an hour and sixteen minutes, 32 seconds to get over it. Once I did, I ate some crackers, re-cleaned my leg, put more wood on the fire, and went back to investigating Patty's stuff. But somehow everything I looked at reminded me of my past.

There was a recent copy of Hustler in the same box as the watch. That brought up a memory of some boys in junior high crowding around a playboy. When I went over to see what it was all about, they shunned me.

Oh, and the squeeze bottle of chocolate strawberry body topping? Sorry, *Erotic Body Treats*? I shuddered at the mere *memory* of my one and only ex-girlfriend, Nicky, and not in a good way. That was…well…her favorite.

The sunlight was almost gone. It wasn't until I picked up a worn journal with Spiderman on the front and tried to read it that I realized night was almost upon me. Where had the day gone?

My gaze fell upon the watch. Beau wore a watch. What was it he said? *"Keeps me sane. It's the little things that count."*

A wave of guilt hit me. Should he be too out of the way, I wouldn't go looking for him. And Burlington? I didn't even know where that was, but it sounded far away. But as things stood, I wouldn't bother. I'd been telling myself I needed to ditch him anyway. Yet the guilt still permeated my gut, reminding me I was a complete ass for abandoning him.

I didn't have anything against him. Despite his bleeding heart, he was a valuable companion to have around.

I secured the watch around my left wrist and clicked all the side buttons until one lit up. It was 5:30 at night. I stood slowly, making sure my legs didn't cramp, and wandered downstairs to the fire. I'd had it going for so long the house wasn't subzero any longer. Not well heated by any means, but enough that it was tolerable.

Tomorrow morning I needed to continue on. I didn't know where I was or what direction I should go, but I knew which lead me back to crazies, and that gave me a direction to avoid at least.

I had to start from scratch with my supplies. I used my flashlight because I found extra batteries for it in the kitchen.

Patty Boy's mistress was a hiker. There wasn't much in the master bedroom closet, but the guest closet was packed with hiking clothes and all types of gear. I wasn't sure if it was the sign of a spoiled girlfriend, or if she genuinely had that many interests.

There was a full sized, pink, day hiking pack, along with the compact accessories that went with it. Tent, cooking supplies, and a Camelbak. There was even one of those lightweight but extremely warm sleeping bags. Also in pink. The girl had a color theme, that's for sure. Why couldn't Patty have any of that gear? I looked around, hoping I might find something of his, but nothing came up.

Then again, it was the end of the world. Why should I care about someone seeing me with girly hiking gear? Actually, I'd need to ditch it before I saw Blaze. That was the kind of thing she'd never let me live down.

So I wouldn't waste my batteries, I gathered most of my supplies downstairs, using the fire to light my way. I took anything of use in the closet, kitchen, and bathrooms. When I was done, mounds of junk waited to be sorted.

I organized the contents of my pink pack as efficiently as I could, stopping once my fire had turned to embers. Then I returned upstairs for one last peaceful sleep before my journey resumed.

Chapter 20

Hours passed before I began to find other cabins and abandoned cars off the road. I searched them all, but you'd be surprised how few people carry any type of map. Then again, why would they? GPS, cell phone, Internet…I doubt pre-apocalypse anyone knew *how* to use a map. It took half a day just to find one. Once I passed a city limit sign and matched it up with the map, I knew where I was. More importantly, where I needed to go. Another half day got me back onto I-90, but by that time it was dark out and I needed to find a place to stay.

Not one, but multiple houses I tried were inhabited, both by the undead and living. The zombies I encountered were emaciated, with hollow cheeks and taut skin, and wore multiple layers of clothing. It made me think they died recently from starvation or cold.

Then there were the *living*. In the moderately sized towns I'd been in before, most houses were either abandoned, had suicide victims in them, or undead that were easily dispatched. But these Northern towns? A much different scenario. Their inhabitants must've heard my snowmobile from a mile away. I'd park the thing in a discreet location some distance from my hideout, walk towards the home, and circle the perimeter. More than a few times I heard voices inside.

"We're still in here. Go away."

"Find somewhere else."

"Get away, now."

I didn't want to pick a fight. Instead of begging for help or trying to reason, I turned around and left. Just knowing someone sentient was around made me paranoid. Instead of finding a house elsewhere in the vicinity, I opted to drive at least a mile. Every house I picked had someone in it. I wondered if there was some kind of community in the area. It would explain why they'd survived so long.

530 turned into Pioneer Highway, which eventually lead into a town called Conway. There the snowmobile puttered and slowed down. I searched each house and building and found one red can of gas. The snowmobile sounded awful when I started it up again, but it ran another blissful hour until it stopped for good and I went on foot.

But I didn't have far to go. According to my map, I only needed to walk a couple miles. I ate the remaining food from my pack and trekked across Bayview-Edison Road, which eventually turned into Samish Island Road. The snow thinned out, since I was closer to the water.

Reality hit me; I was almost there. With a spring in my step, I walked across the small strip of land connecting Samish to the mainland.

Gray, chaotic water moved on either side of me. A wind coming off Puget Sound whipped up small white caps, while snow swirled above the surface. Large, expensive houses flanked the single road that lead onto the island. The sky was almost black with an impending storm. I turned away and looked towards the houses.

One more night. Tomorrow I'd find Blaze.

PART TWO

Chapter 21

The residents of Samish Island walked out of their houses and disappeared.

That's what it looked like. Nothing else could explain what I found there. The first two houses were dusty, abandoned, and untouched. When I broke through the back door of a third, it seemed even more suspect. A note on the granite kitchen counter read: *Grant, I took the kids to Fort Christian. You know how He is. He told us you knew. Went on the Bank's boat, left the dingy. Love June.*

The note gave me the creeps for some reason. I set it down and roamed the house, but found nothing. I needed keys. There had to be a dock, and thus there had to be some spare keys laying around, yet the drawers and key hooks were empty. I walked out of the house with the note, and icy slush pelted against my face, making my nose even more numb, stinging my dry, cracked lips.

The storm had crept even farther over the town. It's never a good idea to roam around when visibility and sound were poor, but I wanted to cover as much ground as possible. Besides, if the rest of the island was as dismal and deserted as what I'd already seen…

Well, I'd be in good shape.

There weren't any car accidents or signs of destruction *anywhere*. Something about the gore-less, ghost town frightened me more than the horrors I'd seen in Startup or the streets of Seattle. At least I knew what to expect in those places; here I knew nothing.

My light bobbed up and down, shining through windows and onto porches. How could *any* town be exempt from even one rotting corpse?

Another looming house, more mysteries inside. There was no story of what happened, no clues that would help me. Outside the world sat in twilight. The only sounds were crashing waves and rain pitter-pattering. That note mentioned they—whoever they were—left. But that wasn't enough to put a story together.

The next house I went to had a wooden plaque over its double doors that read, "The Bank's Residence." I jiggled the door handle. Locked.

What would it take for me to catch a break?

Behind me came a series of crunches. I spun, dropping the flashlight, and pulled my rifle forward.

An old woman stood at the bottom of the porch steps, a plastic bag sunk in the snow beside her. She had a shotgun aimed right at me.

We looked at each other curiously, neither pulling the trigger. Finally, she laughed.

"Haven't seen anyone since, well..." She laughed again. "I guess since the grass was green and the birds still chirped."

She didn't lower her gun. This old lady was a survivor. Any genuine spark of liveliness was long gone. Her mannerisms seemed more out of habit than anything else. Motions that your body remembered so well you didn't need to think to perform them.

"You're lucky," I said. "I wish I hadn't seen anyone in that long."

"Well, are you going to shoot me or what? I don't want to stand here forever."

The storm finally arrived. Fat drops of rain fell against the snow, making a soft *whip* noise. A crack of thunder made me jump.

I wasn't going to stand here and fight an old lady. I slung the rifle back over my shoulder. She lowered her shotgun.

"I guess not. Too tired," I answered.

She bent down and retrieved the plastic bag, which I noticed bulged with cans. "One less thing to worry about, right?"

I stepped aside as she walked past. "What do you mean?"

"It seems like all I do anymore is try to evade or kill the dead. Not having to deal with a scrawny, redheaded punk is one less thing I have to do today."

After she set her shotgun against the front door, she pulled a set of keys from her heavy coat. There were only a few keys on the chain, and among them was a bright orange plastic bulb with a number on it. If I had to guess, it was the key to a boat. It had to be. People often attached floatation key chains to them.

"What does having red hair have to do with being a scrawny punk?" I shot back. I'd been defensive my whole life about my gold and red locks.

She laughed and shrugged, picked up her gun and walked into the house

I remained outside looking in.

"Doesn't have anything to do with it, I suppose. Just a stereotype, right? Anyway, you are scrawny and probably hungry. I haven't had good company in a while. Why don't you come in?"

No one was goodhearted anymore. I didn't believe anyone ever truly had been. In real life, people had an objective behind their kindness. It all came back to what they wanted out of you. This lady seemed nice, but for all I knew she kept her zombie grandkids upstairs, and her dead husband downstairs to cannibalize. That'd happened to me before. Why wouldn't it happen again?

But then there was the matter of that key. I was sure it was a boat key. The question was how I was going to get my hands on it.

That was me—always wanting something for myself. The difference was I couldn't often mask my true intentions with kindness.

But I wasn't going to kill her in cold blood for the key. I had a soft spot for elderly folks. Besides, I didn't usually kill someone for a reason *that* mundane.

She motioned me inside. "Come on. It's not as cold in here."

I'd never been one to revel in the size or beauty of a house, but I had to admit this one was in the top five houses I'd seen, along with Patty's house. Every type of excessive interior design seemed to be in effect: marble, real hard wood, wainscoting, crystal chandeliers, plush carpet. The house had it all. It never got dark as I followed her deeper into the house. Multiple skylights let what was left of the sun through.

"Was this your house from before?"

"Yes," she replied as our heels clicked on the marble floors of the kitchen. The bag of cans and her shotgun clanked on the counter as she set them down. "Doctors make a lot of money. What else would I spend it on? Two bratty trust fund kids or my spoiled rotten grandkids? I don't think so."

"You've got a lot of anger, Mrs. Banks," I said before I could stop myself.

"How did you know my name?"

"There's a sign outside."

She clenched her jaw and peered at the floor. "My husband made that."

Dead husband, definitely. Whether her husband died pre or post-apocalypse, it didn't matter. She still let it get to her. Her whole family was probably dead, or at least missing.

She exhaled deeply and slapped her hand against the black granite counter. as though dismissing her anger. "So, how about we get you something to eat and I'll take a look at your leg?"

"How did *you* know about my leg?"

My hand went to the aching wound. I'd picked up new clothes along my journey to Samish, so it wasn't a blood stain or rip that gave it away.

"Just because I'm retired doesn't mean I'm blind. You limp, and I can tell it's new."

Instead of fighting her, I nodded.

"Come with me downstairs. You can pick something out from my stockpile."

"Stockpile?"

"What do you think I do all day? Sit on my ass hoping for the sun to rise and everyone to hold hands?"

***

A stockpile was an apt term for the horde of goods in her basement. Neat rows of shelves flanked both sides of the rectangular space, looking much like a grocery store. Every type of nonperishable food I could imagine was there. One tower was devoted to soda. When I saw the Mountain Dew, the memory of guzzling so much of it back in Everett made me feel a bit sick.

There weren't any windows or lights downstairs, but Dr. Banks had a hanging lantern on the top of each set of shelves, illuminating every nook and cranny. As I inspected the goods, I noticed a circle sticker with a date written on each one.

"Expiration dates?" I asked.

She picked up a jar of spaghetti sauce. "Yes. It would be disappointing if I died from botulism instead of being eaten alive."

"Very funny. I love your sense of humor," I said, matching her sarcasm but meaning my words.

"Early on, I didn't go out much, but once everyone left to Fort Christian I started my raids. At first, every day, but then I had to fan out to houses on the outskirts." She set the jar down, looking at nothing specific for a moment. "Pick something out. I've got a miniature propane grill that'll heat it up. Tell me what happened to your leg, and I'll get the right fixins' for it."

I explained how I got my wound, but didn't touch on *why* I got it. Why dredge up things I decided to leave behind? Besides, it would behoove me to let her think I was a normal guy instead of a total jerk.

Dr. Banks did just as promised, though she didn't cook my two cans of chicken noodle soup for me. "I'm nobody's bitch. You make your own soup," she snapped when I handed her my choice. She led me upstairs and through a hallway, into a perfectly designed master bedroom. By then, only the sun set and the harsh light of one of her electric lanterns lit the area.

The room was immaculate except for one thing: part of the wall was open, creating a narrow entrance into a room I couldn't see into. Dr. Banks went straight for it, but I hesitated. No one in their right mind would follow *anyone* into a dark passageway.

"It's a safe room," she said. "It's where I stayed the first three weeks of the end of the world. The door slides right into the wall. Can't even tell it's there. Neat, eh?"

Eventually I gave in and crossed to the shadowy entrance. Once inside, the lantern lit up the rather big area. Unlike the panic rooms I'd seen in movies, this one appeared to be a normal, albeit plain, bedroom. Its walls were painted off white, and it had a two person table and two cots. Against one wall were shelves with—surprise, surprise—food, camping equipment, and an array of medical supplies. The floor was wood, but most of it was covered with a dark green rug. A kitchen area was set up on the small table, where I began my soup cooking.

I never got used to eating soup cold. Too goopy and tangy. Heat took the unpleasantness out of the experience. Dr. Banks watched me as I meticulously peeled the labels off the metal cans, popped their tops, and set them on the burners.

My pack and gun felt heavy. While my soup heated up, I shrugged the pack off and sat on the opposite cot from her. She rifled through a blue Tupperware container full of plastic packages.

She ran through some medical questions. Did I have a fever? Did I feel weak? Was the wound swollen? I knew she was trying to figure out if I had an infection or not. I figured I did. The wound hadn't been closing and smelled foul. I bandaged it whenever I could, but the damn thing kept splitting open if I exerted myself too much.

We made snappy comments and jokes about zombies while I ate my soup. Dr. Banks' sense of humor was on par with my own. Another slew of remarks flew between us when she told me to slide my pants down.

"Enough talk. Let's take a look," she said.

"That's forward. At least you took me to dinner first."

"I'm a doctor, you dimwit. Do you think I haven't seen it all?"

"Right. How could I forget?"

Dr. Banks gave me a stern look after peeling my old bandage off. "It's infected."

"What's with the accusatory tone? I don't have any medical experience. How would I know?"

"Look at this," she said, pressing against the edge of the wound. "It looks awful."

I winced, moved to bat her hand away and cease the pain, but then I pulled back. "Can you fix it?"

Her blank stare was answer enough.

Her meticulous cleaning and stitching of the wound was more painful than getting it. But I couldn't help but feel grateful.

"What's your name? I never asked," she said

"Cyrus V. Sinclair. The V stands for...Vexed."

She tied and clipped a stitch. "Is that so?"

"I'm not sure why you'd help someone you just met. Show them you have endless resources in your basement and offer to fix their leg. I feel like there is a catch and I just don't know it yet. I'm vexed because that's the last thing I want to deal with right now."

"I've been alone a long time. Haven't you?"

I'd been by myself my whole life. Until I joined forces with Gabe and Frank, then met Blaze, that is. I went to say my trademark 'I don't care if I'm alone,' but stopped myself when I remembered why I'd come to Samish Island in the first place.

"Being alone wasn't a problem until I met the right people," I said. "When I wasn't invited to parties in junior high, my grandma said, 'Cyrus, how can you be upset about something you've never even experienced?' When I rode my bike past one of those parties, it disgusted me. There wasn't anything to be jealous of, but I never would've known had I not seen it for myself. She was right, though. I didn't know I was alone until I experienced meeting someone like me. Better than me."

The old woman had finished another two stitches by the time I finished. "That doesn't sound bad. Would you rather you never met anyone that changed your world?"

By then I couldn't be stopped. I'd never told *anyone* as much as I had already told her. My only friend Frank died before I could discuss love, or who I was becoming, with him. I'd been stewing in my own confusion for too long.

"I don't *know*. I used to be so different. Nothing fazed me. I was indifferent. But all it took was *one person* to make my life a rollercoaster. It was easy to be a total hardass when I was alone. Now it seems like all I do is second-guess myself. If I hadn't let that stupid, manipulative girl into my apartment and saved her life, I'd be the same guy. Lately I've been thinking life would be a hell of a lot better if no one had changed me."

Dr. Banks' stitches were neat and professional. The wound leaked blood onto the big cotton pad she'd set under it. She began dressing the stitches without a word, and I kept going.

"So now I'm on this absurd mission to find a woman I knew for a week. And do I have a plan for after? That is if I manage to highjack a boat, cross the Puget Sound, find a tiny island, and find her? *Fuck no*! Because I'm acting without thinking. Letting my *feelings* get the best of me."

She taped a piece of gauze to my wound then gathered her supplies. After throwing the bloody clothes away, she sat down on her cot and leaned against the wall. I tugged my pants over my thermal underwear.

"Listen, kid. Some people grow up when they're young and know where they're going in life. Others, like me, we never find ourselves. Consider yourself normal. You're finding out who you are now. Maybe you'll go back to how you were, maybe not. I'm not an oracle, but I am a lady who still gives a damn and has a boat."

I opened my mouth, not even thinking of what words would come out.

Dr. Banks cut me off. "I get it! You don't need to keep bitching. I followed you from the moment you came into town. I saw everything. I'm not completely sure you're being genuine, but it makes sense. You've got a long lost love, you need a boat, and you want to get to Fort Christian. Do you think these bony arms could ever row again,?

Or these arthritic hands could even grip the ores if the motor went out?" Dr. Banks sighed. "We've got a lot in common, Cyrus. We're both hurt and confused by everything that's happened. By who we were and who we've become. Who we've lost along the way. We might not know the gritty details of each others' pasts, but it doesn't mean we can't help each other out. We're two people trying to set things right against all odds. It's like a movie, isn't it?"

Silence. Awkward, *awkward* silence. I regretted my outburst instantly. There I was, trying to be specific about my problems, while Dr. Banks instigated the logical train of thought I usually followed.

She knew I wanted something out of her, and while she related to me, she wasn't ready to hug me while I cried.

"I'm…sorry, I guess. For unloading all that on you."

She shrugged. "I'll admit, I was looking for a 'yes' or 'no' response, but if you needed to get it off your chest, so be it."

I stopped looking at her and shifted down so I lay flat on the cot. What was I supposed to do from there?

"I saw Fort Christian in a note a couple houses down. You mentioned it twice. What is it? Why do I need to go there?"

"You said you were going to cross the sound to a tiny island. There's a piece of land so small it's not even on the maps. Nothing's on it. Nothing *used* to be, that is. It was just a daytrip for the locals. Then everyone in town got riled up by the minister at the local church. I'm sure you know the drill. Judgment day, Hell filling up, damned souls walking the earth. At this point the dead weren't a problem yet. We're too far up and our population isn't dense. Minister Encler said he was taking a group of people to the island to hold out and start a new holy regime. Again, you know the drill.

"A few things happened after that. A handful of families left in the first wave. Anyone who stayed behind had their reasons. But one by one they succumbed to their inner fears of damnation. One of the last to go was my sister, Melinda." Dr. Banks paused. "When Encler left, he said they'd build the island into a safe haven for the worthy and call it Fort Christian. Fort *Cliché* if you ask me. No one has come back. They're either dead, prospering, or… History shows us what happens when a group of crazies confine themselves to one area."

The grouped crazy phenomenon wasn't new to me either, so the worst of what was happening at Fort Christian wouldn't surprise me. "Thanks for the warning. Was that all I needed to hear to get the boat key?"

It was too good to be true, of course. "Yes and no. I told you my sister is there, remember?"

Ah. Dr. Banks was about to broker a deal.

"And you want me to bring her back?"

"Absolutely not. Melinda left on her own accord, and if she comes back, I want it to be the same. I only want her to remember me. That I'm still alive and someone who loves her is waiting."

"Sounds involved," I said.

"It's not. You go there and, if she is alive, give her this locket. Our mother gave it to me when she died, but Melinda always wanted it." Dr. Banks leaned to the side of the cot, reaching underneath to withdraw a fist-sized wooden box. She passed it over the gap between us. "I know we're strangers. I know you might not do it. I'm not an idiot. After you leave this place, I doubt I'll ever see you again. I'm asking that you try. If you happen upon her, great, but I'm not asking you to go out of your way."

"Why even ask me to do it? Seems to me you already think I won't."

"Anyone who chose to cling to hope, honesty, and goodness in this world is dead or should be. Like I said, I *know* you might not. I'm asking you because it makes me feel like I at least attempted to reconnect with her. If anything, I'm seeking solace for myself."

I saw it then, for sure. That inkling of care and hope Dr. Banks was trying to mask with her deceiving façade of smartass meets realist. You feel the hard sting of her words, first. *I don't care, not really.* Then after, once you listened to the tone, you saw the pained look behind her gleaming eyes. *I do care. I really care.*

Even the hardest of survivors must do it. They have to. It's a defense mechanism. Show any weakness and you'll be thrown to the undead hordes, ripped limb from limb for being too nice. Maybe even the crazies do it, but it's harder to tell. It's in me, though I'd never admit it to anyone.

The realists in us spoke to one another. We both knew I wasn't going to do it. I wouldn't go out of my way because I wasn't going to try.

"I'll try, but I'm not promising anything." I tucked the box into a pocket on the side of my pants, zipped it closed. It wasn't too much to ask, no, but there were a million factors that could make the task impossible.

I'd keep an eye out. More effort than that was too much to ask.

Dr. Banks showed me a photo of her and Melinda—recent, judging by how Banks looked—but didn't let me keep it. I committed her face to memory, then she put the picture away. This time the silence wasn't unbearable. We lay on our cots, consumed in our own musings until we agreed it was time to go to sleep.

***

I rolled from side, to back, to side during my effort to fall asleep. My stitches itched. Flashes of blood pumping from Frank's old leg wound went through my mind. Was it chance, fate, or coincidence that I too got hit in the leg? Why couldn't I have died like he did?

Dr. Banks informed me she was "doubling down" on some sleeping pills so I wouldn't keep her up. She said the safe room door would stop an elephant, so she wasn't worried about any zombies getting in. I declined when she offered me some pills, though I regretted it once she was out cold and I could barely lay still.

Clicking the light button on my watch didn't help. As hours went by, I grew more nervous. Tomorrow, Dr. Banks was giving me the key to the last remaining boat on the docks.

When she told me about Fort Christian, I didn't consider how serious the situation there could be. Every time I imagined finding Blaze, she was on an abandoned island. Happy to see me, surprised I came after her. I didn't factor yet *another* group of crazies into it. They were probably like the lunatics in Startup or the prison leader in Monroe—using a distorted form of Christianity to fulfill their sick need to control people.

I closed my eyes and rubbed my eyelids with the tips of my fingers. A kaleidoscope of colors burst and receded. The stillness in the room was troublesome, memory inducing. With nothing to distract myself, I couldn't keep the flashbacks at bay.

As quiet as I could, I swung my legs over the cot and began clicking the light on the watch over and over, using it to find the green sleeping pill bottle I saw Dr. Banks using earlier. I doubled down and hoped for sleep to come.

***

Heat waves radiated off the summer baked asphalt. The smell of freshly cut grass and pool chlorine was all I could smell. There wasn't anyone or anything in front of me on the street. Houses, empty and still, lined the road. Robins sang their songs.

"It's really nice, isn't it?"

I turned and the world changed. The houses were skeletal, burnt remains of what they once were. Weeds burst from the cracks in the streets. Grass was overgrown. Icy rain misted the scene.

"Forgetting about my brother. My *only* living relative. It must be nice to forget someone so easily."

Blaze's teeth were blackened. Her gray skin was flaky and stretched taut over her skull. Milky whiteness washed over her once glinting brown eyes. She smiled.

"He's as good as dead," I tried to say, but only garbled noise came out.

"I'm as good as dead," she snapped. "I *am* dead!"

I tried to take a step forward and reach out towards her, but my body was stone. Behind her, far off, hazy forms drew closer through the rainy mist.

She laughed again. Thick, slimy chunks of flesh swimming in bile sluiced from her mouth, running down her chin. "You'll be dead soon, too, Cyrus."

Chapter 22

The room became a sauna overnight from our body heat. Add to that my sweating and thrashing from the nightmares, which made the humid space all the more stifling. When I woke to the grainy smell of oatmeal, I was tangled in sweat soaked blankets and sheets.

I only remembered bits and pieces, but the general theme of my dream was the same. Blaze was mad, blamed me for everything, and my guilt ridden conscious sure as hell let me know about it.

My mouth tasted like I'd been sucking on rusty nails. I ran my tongue over my teeth and tried to hock up some spit. All that came out was a strained cough.

"It's a side effect of the sleeping pills, that bad taste."

Dr. Banks clicked off her propane stove and ladled a heaping spoonful of gummy oatmeal into a clear plastic cup. The Coleman lantern was on a low setting, covered by a thin white sheet in the corner.

"There's a fire hazard if I ever saw one," I joked as I shifted out of the messed blankets.

"I don't like blinding myself *right* after I wake up." She handed me the cup and a spork. "Instant blueberry oatmeal. I'd offer you coffee, but I ran out a while ago."

"Never drank it anyway." With a grin, I blew on the steaming cup.

I had a total emotional hangover. The casual banter helped me think less about what I'd told her last night, and more about the day's plan.

"Sun should just be coming over the horizon," she said. "If you hurry, you can get out of here before you burn much daylight."

We didn't exchange many words after that. I finished her generous breakfast, geared up, and followed her out of the giant, empty house. My limp seemed worse, but I wondered if it was just psychosomatic, due to her drawing my attention to it yesterday. Or was I adjusting to the stitches? Pins and needles went up my thigh and down to my knee whenever my foot hit the ground.

Once downstairs, we made a stop in the basement, where she insisted upon giving me power bars, a few flavors of bottled water, and a half-full unmarked bottle of pills. "For your leg," she told me. "I insist. I'd say take two a day, but really? Do what you want. People always do."

Dr. Banks must've been a pill pusher when she was a practicing doctor.

"What are they?" I asked.

During my raids on houses, supermarkets, and pharmacies, I had unlimited access to any kind of drug imaginable; legal or illegal. Pre-apocalypse I never took any medications beyond cough syrups or cold remedies for anything, so why would I start? Despite suffering through physical pain and mental exhaustion, I never picked up a bottle of *any* kind while on my lonesome search for Blaze. In a world where no one cared, it was only a matter of pride and personal preference that was stopping me.

"Your standard Oxycodone," she said. "Trust me, you'll need it. If you make it back, stop by and I'll give you a refill on the house."

We both knew it was unlikely I'd be coming back, so our smiles didn't reach our eyes. Helpful people I met never survived, or I lost them along my way. Dr. Banks would be no different.

She ended the conversation before I could object to the pills, and we marched up the basement steps. Outside of the panic room, I heard the storm raging. The snow was gone, melted away by the fat drops of rain pounding down.

In the middle of the street lay a decimated torso, making painfully slow progress towards the house. It had an entire yard to cross and a flight of steps to climb. I didn't think it would make it. This guy was the first zombie I'd seen in some time. His throat was shredded. White-washed bone jutted from his face and chest, visible even from where I stood.

"I wondered where he went," Dr. Banks said, walking down the steps without hesitation. "Shut the door behind you."

"You know him?"

"Sort of," she yelled over the wind. "I keep track of everyone who stayed in the town. This is Benjamin, my neighbor from a few doors down."

She clicked the safety off her shotgun and aimed it at his head, but didn't pull the trigger.

"Don't waste your bullets," I said as I stepped next to her. I used the butt of my gun to break his head in. His skull shattered as easily as an eggshell.

"Thank you." She gave a look of regret and discomfort. Dr. Banks was a strong woman, but killing people she once knew seemed to hit her hard.

A pang of compassion within me stretched out for her. I knew what it was like to kill a zombie-turned friend. It took more strength to kill one you knew than a hundred you didn't.

"The dock is just around the street and down the hill." The old woman had to shout. The brewing storm was going to be rough. She said something else, but her words were whisked away by the wind. She waved off whatever it was when I indicated I hadn't heard. I hoped it wasn't important.

We kept our heads bent as we made our way down the street. The road was icy, and we each had our share of slips. Besides Benjamin, there wasn't another living or dead thing that moved on its own. The skeletal figures of maple trees and shaggy branches of evergreens danced wildly. Pinecones and twigs from bushes swirled across the road, caught up in the strong gusts of wind.

Great day for a boating trip. I'm sure the ocean air will do me some good, I thought, growing more pessimistic by the second.

Dr. Banks veered off the paved road and began a treacherous descent down a winding dirt path. Getting to the rocky shores of Samish meant traversing down the sides of cliffs. She led the way, her progress as slow as Benjamin's, as we stepped over fallen logs and debris. How was she going to make it back up these switchbacks on her own?

I stopped myself from thinking about it. If I let myself feel more sympathy than I already did, I'd lose any courage I had left and abandon my boat trip. Dr. Banks was strong. Old, yes, but if she'd made it this far, climbing up some hills wouldn't kill her yet. At least that's how I justified it.

We cleared the forest area and came onto a narrow, pebbly shore. Waves crashed relentlessly mere feet away from us. Ten yards off stood a chain link fence with a jagged tear down its middle. Beyond were rows of empty docks and boathouses.

Dr. Banks squeezed through the fence first and led me to the boathouse closest to us. *Boathouse* is an overstatement. The one she took me into was a claim shanty.

I thought the boat was going to be a nice yacht, since it was owned by the prestigious *Dr. Banks*. It wasn't. The craft tied to the bit was so small it looked like it might sink before I even got it outside. It rocked in the blustery wind that seeped through cracks in the boathouse, icy water splashing into the already growing puddle on its bottom.

"It's a dingy, Cyrus." The old woman laughed before handing over the key. "I never told you otherwise. You'll need to use the ores. I tried telling you outside the house that it has no gas."

My stomach tightened as a strong gust slammed against the flimsy, wooden shack. Blueberry oatmeal laid heavy in my stomach, threatening to come back up. My luck always ran out when I needed it the most.

Should I wait until tomorrow?

I'm going to drown.

Don't be a coward.

Too many thoughts boiled in my brain. Waiting a single day could prevent me from going entirely. How many times had my journey picked up only to come to a standstill? Tomorrow I could be kidnapped again and sold as meat.

I was getting into that boat.

"Why are you giving me the keys when I can't even use the motor?" I asked. Hanging on the wall was a plastic bucket. I used it to scoop water out of the bottom of the boat.

"These aren't for that piece of junk. This is for my sailboat on the island. Her name is 'Queen Banks,'" Dr. Banks said. "Once you get to the island, getting off it will be easier with her."

A few buckets later, the water level in the boat decreased by a few inches. Outside, the storm seemed to have calmed. The wind wasn't as loud. Dr. Banks gave me a lifejacket, which I would've declined since it was so unfashionable, but who was I to get trendy in a crisis? I still used the pink backpack from Patty's. Practicality came first.

"Take this and tie yourself down." Dr. Banks tossed me a yellow nylon rope after I settled onto the metal seat of the dingy.

She went to the front of the boathouse and cranked a pulley, which slid the wooden door sideways. The old woman untied the dingy and kicked it away from the dock surrounding it. She was surprisingly strong.

"Good luck!" Dr. Banks waved from inside the shadows of the boathouse as the current outside took me away.

***

My eyes stung from endless splashes of saltwater. My bones and muscles were frozen. I gave up on rowing after five minutes.

But there was an obvious break in the deep gray clouds above me. The storm quickly moved away. In the distance was the island. It was the last place I could search for Blaze. If she wasn't there… I stopped thinking. I wasn't in control anymore.

Chapter 23

When I was 13, my grandparents took my sister and me to Oregon to visit my great aunt. My grandfather warned me about the undertow the coastal waters were known for, but being young and defiant I did what I wanted. As soon as they weren't looking, I snuck off to give the water a try. It was a particularly hot summer, and no one was going to stop me from going in. I dove under and couldn't get back up. Wasn't strong enough. If it wasn't for my grandpa coming to save me, I would've died.

That was the first out of three times I almost drowned. The second was in Monroe in a slimy swimming pool. A rotting corpse held me under with the intent of having an underwater buffet. I almost got out on my own, but I would've been drowned if Blaze hadn't grabbed me.

The third time was when I decided to let a storm navigate my boat.

My throat felt as dry and scratchy as it did when I woke up. How much saltwater had I swallowed? I turned onto my stomach and vomited diluted oatmeal and water.

An icy cold shock of liquid crashed over me, pushing me farther onto a gravel shore. I opened my eyes, but shut them once the white, cloudy sky blinded me.

After one more cough I got to my feet, stumbled, then stood straight. I looked down and shielded my eyes with my hand then opened them again. The skeleton of a crab, now covered in vomit, greeted me. I focused on it while regaining my balance and thoughts.

Am I here? Did I make it?

I squinted as I faced the water, trying to figure out where I was. Sure enough, across the now relatively calm Puget Sound, sat a large body of land. It had to be Samish.

Sticking out amid the gray rocks and driftwood was my pink backpack, about fifteen yards away. My rifle was nowhere in sight. Gone, most likely, resting at the bottom of the sound.

I had to walk slow, picking each step carefully, in order to make it there without passing out. My hands shook as I unzipped the pack a few inches to pour the water out.

Dragon fruit flavored water quenched the dryness in my throat. I drank half in one long gulp, but set it down. My water supply was limited. Drinking it too fast and vomiting wasn't part of the agenda.

The shore was narrow, much like the one I'd just left in Samish, but this one didn't recede into a steep cliff. Instead it went straight into a dense forest of bushes and evergreen trees. A pathway I missed at first glance broke up the forest edge. It was too wide to have been created by animals.

I remembered the crazies Dr. Banks warned me about. Every part of me hoped she was wrong about them, because I was unarmed. I had a knife, but that didn't count. It wasn't going to do me any good if I was fighting a pack of them.

Then again, I *did* manage to get out of the cannibal situation. That was pretty damn grim, but the knife and my clever thinking made all the difference. I could do it again.

With a newfound determination, I searched the immediate area of the beach for the dingy or my gun, but found nothing. I didn't let it get to me as I headed toward the path.

My boots squelched as the ground turned from sand and rocks to viscous mud. There was barely any snow. That was Washington for you: inches one day, slush the next. The storm blew it away or the rain melted it. Other than the noise of my footsteps and wet gear, the quiet of the forest was unsettling. The pine trees were so numerous they could've been cutting off sounds of trouble elsewhere. But as I limped along the path, I swore I heard the soft echo of a gunshot.

Snap.

I stopped when a twig broke somewhere nearby. It could've been an animal, but I wasn't going to risk my cold, skinny ass on it. If I hadn't glorified the power of my knife and let my ego boost, I would've been scared out of my mind. Yet, this time, fear wasn't a factor.

Whatever it was, I'd find it and kill it.

That telltale groan gave him away. Directly to my right, but I wasn't sure how close. I crouched down on my good leg and waited for the attack, gripping my knife for all it was worth. The undead knew I was there, judging by the eager grunt that drew closer.

Tiny beads of water flew from the branches of the pine tree when my zombie friend emerged. His momentum sprayed me with water and sharp green needles. He was about my height and build, but I wasn't expecting him to come hurdling towards me.

I hadn't had to fight an undead for a few days. Between being rusty and recovering from my boating incident, I couldn't stop him from knocking me to the ground. Mud squished under the collar of my shirt and into my hair. The corpse snapped as I held him at bay, his decayed hands grasping at me.

With a burst of strength I pushed him back, placing my free hand flat against the middle of his chest. I rammed my knife into his head. I'd been aiming for his temple, in hopes of destroying his brain. No such luck. It went in at an angle, starting at the top of his cheekbone. It sliced through his mouth and emerged on the other side, through the bottom of his jaw.

The zombie's mouth parted. A trickle of bile splattered my face. I tried to block his swings, but he managed to get a fistful of my hair. He held on with an iron grip, intent on ripping my scalp off for easier access to brains.

I spewed profanities as I strained to push him off. His body hit the ground beside me with a loud thud. Unfazed, he wiggled in the mud for a moment before rolling onto his stomach and coming after me again.

My legs buckled and my head swam from getting to my feet too fast. I grabbed the tree next to me for support, just as the zombie's hand wrapped around my ankle. I kicked his hand away, turning in time to see him getting to his feet.

I wasn't playing around anymore. His mouth was stuck open from the knife. Now was my best opportunity to kill him, while he couldn't bite me. I lunged, knocking him onto his back near a large, moss covered rock. Skin sloughed off his neck each time I smashed his head into the stone.

I didn't stop until it caved in. Gooey matter clung to the boulder, while half-congealed blood pooled in the muddy water surrounding it. He lay motionless and truly dead, arms sprawled at his sides. There was a handgun resting in a holster under his arm. I hadn't noticed it when he attacked. His sweater was striped tan and blue, but thick mud blended colors together, effectively masking the dark leather of the shoulder rig. I leaned down and unhooked it. The bottom half of the gun wasn't as dirty as the top.

After wiping it clean, I recognized it as one of my favorites. I'd used a Glock .40 many times before. Its weight was familiar in my hands, and it had a full clip.

I yanked my knife from his mouth, making sure it was as clean of muck and blood as I could get it. I took the holster, too, since it would make storing and accessing the gun easier.

My lungs burned from exertion. My muscles protested each movement, but I forced myself to stand anyway. I ignored the pain as best as I could, but limped slowly down the path.

If there was one zombie, there were probably more. Still I hoped he was a fluke. One that had floated in from the sea and hadn't made it to the living yet.

All the hopeful thinking distracted me from the hodgepodge fence in front of me. I came inches from running into it, since the section blocking the path was created from thin wire. It was almost as tall as me, which put it at six feet. Traveling into the forest on either side were sheets of tin, wooden boards, or anything else that could be added to the barricade. Sections were lashed together with chains and ropes. I needed to get over it, but curls of barbed wire or boards with nails protected the fence.

I gave the section in front of me a hard tug, but it didn't budge. There was only one thing to do: follow it until I found a weak spot.

My breath came out in white puffs. My muddy, wet clothes chaffed as I maneuvered around the bushes and stumps pressing against the fence.

On the other side, there was nothing but more forest for at least fifty yards. Then I smelled it. The ripe scent of rotting flesh. My grip tightened on the Glock. No groans or shuffling, but that didn't mean there weren't any undead beyond the thicket of bushes now surrounding me. I tried to see through them, but they grew too wild.

I hate rhododendrons, I thought, as their plastic-like leaves and spiny twigs slapped against my face.

When I cleared the immediate area, I saw the source of the stench. A small figure was torn in half on the other side of the barrier. I couldn't be sure if it was a him or her. All of the skin was peeled off, the bones and flesh chewed. Yet the size of the skull and remains couldn't hide that it had been a child. Two bullet entry points rested side by side on the front of its skull, hairline cracks extending outward.

The body was fresh, which is what disturbed me the most. There were no signs of it freezing over or having the chance to melt into the ground. Thin ropes of intestines trailed out from the torso, congealed blood still coating them. Whatever—*whoever*—ate the kid did it within the past day or two. And since the body was on the other side of the fence, it meant there was an opening somewhere and there were undead beyond.

As for the bullet holes…Was it a mercy killing? Or was the kid killed post-consumption? I scolded myself for trying to put the pieces together when the facts were obvious. I had a challenge ahead of me.

I had no choice but to keep following the fence and searching for an opening. After another uneventful fifteen minutes of treading through muck and getting scratched up by sticker bushes, I found a weakened area. It was a chain link section tied to two adjacent wooden barriers constructed of miscellaneous wood. If I cut the ropes, it would be easy to push the fence down and get in.

It took forever to saw through each rope and undo their loops around the posts. I had to put every bit of my strength into pushing and pulling the fence until it dislodged from the mud and toppled inward. The metal wire clanged loudly and quivered when it hit the ground.

What was done was done. I paused to listen for any unwanted attention and heard nothing but a light breeze rustling the plant life. Above, the sun was at its zenith, burning bright white in a clear blue sky.

There wasn't a path to follow anymore, so I made do with trying to walk a straight line. I used a technique Frank taught me, using my knife to mark tree trunks with an X as I went. That way I wouldn't start backtracking. It sped my progress up and I made it deeper into the forest.

That's when I started finding more bodies. Men, women, kids. Whatever happened to the compound of people looked unintentional. An undead had to have gotten in somehow. This was too random. No one was being singled out.

They were all eaten beyond the point of returning. I'd already been feeling sick from my boat ride over. Seeing and smelling the ripped organs didn't help.

Somewhere ahead, a bush shook. I saw a small figure weave between trees. It darted behind a larger trunk. It had to be a living being. No runner or slow would go *away* from me. Judging by the size, it was a kid. I knew how to play kids.

"Hello? Is anyone there?"

I tucked the Glock into the side pocket of my backpack then splayed my hands in front of me. The universal sign of peace.

Look non-threatening. Gain their trust. Simple.

A pale face peeked out. Then half a body. A whole body. The girl stood twenty yards away from me. She'd been through hell and back, by the looks of her. I wasn't sure what color her long parka had been before, but now it was the trendy dirt-and-blood shade so many people sported. She wore an orange and white hat with two knitted cat ears poking from the sides.

"I'm lost and looking for someone. Can you help me?"

I cringed when I said it. *Could you sound anymore like a pedophile? I have some candy and lost my puppy…What an idiot.*

But kids were dumb. Every news article on a kidnapping made me feel awful, yet I was never surprised when I read a follow-up story on how witnesses saw the kid get into a van willingly.

This girl was no different. She began a hesitant walk towards me, glancing behind her every few steps. They were wild animals—kids, that is—so I stayed still, trying not to scare her away.

When she was within ten feet, she spoke. "Are you looking for Minister Encler? Cause they strung him up."

Her too-blue eyes were innocent, but sharp. A flash of memory hit me. Another child, just like her. What was her name? Jenna? Jenny? That's it, Jenny. The girl who saved me in Startup. Blew a hole through someone's head when I thought all was lost.

"They killed him?"

"Guess so. He was moving when I got away, but you know they turn into zombies. Who are you looking for? Pretty much everyone is dead."

Pine needles and small twigs clung to her knit hat. A splattering of blood covered her right shoulder, spreading out towards her right hip. It looked like castoff from a gunshot wound. Her eyes were sunken and red rimmed. Those of someone who hadn't slept in days.

This kid was too nonchalant. It was unsettling.

"I'm looking for my friend's sister, Melinda, and—"

The girl cut me off. "Dunno if she is dead."

"Okay." I took a deep breath. "Then I'm looking for someone with dark hair and eyes named Blaze. She's—"

"Oh, the witch? Yeah, she's in the cage."

I didn't like either part of that sentence. The casual, matter-of-face way she said it didn't help. When I looked at her expectantly, she stared back at me, clueless.

"A witch? What the hell does that even mean?"

Before she could answer, a symphony of ragged screams echoed through the forest. Runners. She turned to flee, but I grabbed her by the collar of her jacket and yanked her back.

"Let me go! They're coming!"

"Tell me which way Fort Christian is and where Blaze is, then I'll let you go."

She twisted out of my grasp and shot off like a rabbit towards the fence. Now closer, the sound of runners made my hair stand on end. I had to make a choice—follow the girl, face the runners, or try to outrun them. Following her was counterproductive. I wasn't willing to backtrack that much for a piece of information. If I made it to the camp, I'd find Blaze. Knowing more about the situation there would be convenient, sure, but not essential.

As for facing the runners, I wasn't sure I had a choice. They'd hear me just as they tracked the girl.

A flash of bright blue passed between two trees in front of me. They were getting closer. I didn't have time to consider what direction I'd go in, so I set off to my left. It was away from the runners, but maybe I'd run into the girl again.

Mud sucked at my boots and branches broke as I barreled my way through. The forest was old and overgrown, hindering me at every turn. My wet clothes made it hard to run. I felt rashes erupting all over my body from the fear.

Then I broke through onto another path. I went right, farther into the forest. Only a minute or two of running took its toll on me. I began to sweat and the cold air made my lungs burn.

I had to stop. I bent down, my hands against my knees, and coughed until the pain in my chest lessened.

Alone again. Could I really have outrun a handful of fast undead? I quieted my breathing, closed my eyes, and listened.

No, of course not. It only gets worse from here.

There was motion behind me—far enough away that it didn't concern me. Sounds of zombies seeking prey in the forest. But up ahead were different, faint screams. Living human screams with an intermittent gunshot. Apparently I planned a trip to Fort Christian during the worst of times.

Dr. Banks' locket and the torn photo of Blaze weighed heavily in my pocket. I wasn't going to let another obstacle get my optimism down.

Albeit at a slower pace, I made my way towards the sounds of chaos. This was it. The end of my journey. She might be dead, but she was there somewhere.

I'd found Blaze.

Chapter 24

Fort Christian reminded me of shanty towns I'd seen photos of in high school world culture classes. These places are, or rather were, some of the strongest examples of poverty, and it's very upsetting. The settlement looked like nothing more than a pile of junkyard scrap. Except for one relatively well constructed building, none exceeded one story. There were at least twenty of them. Their roofs peeked out from behind a stronger, more solid fence than the one I'd encountered before in the forest, which must've been a preliminary perimeter fence. The primary fence circling Fort Christian was mostly constructed from metal with intermittent sections of wood. There were few gaps between its slats.

The gunshots and shouts had almost stopped entirely by the time I made it to the area. I was glad. The reduced threat of conflict was fine by me.

I peeled my backpack off, retrieving a power bar and my unfinished flavored water while I came up with a plan. I was surprised the pink pack hadn't gotten me killed. It was a bright, shining beacon for crazies and potential living threats. However the undead didn't respond to it, but I wasn't sure they could see in color. Now I walked into a situation with potential alive threats, though, I decided it was time to drop it.

Shivers coursed from the top of my head throughout my body. I braced myself, biting down hard on the chewy power bar in my mouth and clutching the bottle. If I didn't get out of there within the next couple hours, I'd die from the cold. How embarrassing would that be?

The shaking passed after I stomped my feet and windmilled my arms to bring back some circulation. My gaze wandered to the two story building in the center of town.

Its façade was different than the other shanties. Instead of being thrown together from a hodgepodge of materials, it was made of consistent sheets of wood, 2x4s, and had a shingled roof. Was it Minister Encler's residence? Or a church? It was almost structured like a watchtower.

I wondered where a bunch of crazies would keep a cage. It could be on the outskirts of town, as some prisons were. Then I remembered the gallows and guillotines of medieval times, which were quite public.

Thus my plan developed. As soon as I got over the fence, I'd circle the outskirts of the town until I could get a good look at the front of the building. I couldn't assess how bad it was in there until I covered some ground.

I checked my Glock and knife and hid my pack underneath some sticker bushes. I crouched low, keeping an eye out for anyone outside the encampment.

An explosion erupted near the front of town. I saw a plume of black smoke rise. The scent of burnt oil carried on the light breeze. A series of faint shouts, then groans, followed.

The area between me and the fence had been cleared of bushes and trees. I dashed across the expanse, stopping at the fence and pressing myself up against it.

The fence was even more formidable than I thought. The metal sections were welded together, and it contained only a few sections of wood. It was a good foot over my head, too. There was another important difference; no barbed wire.

If I could get footing, I could boost myself up enough to slide over. My leg throbbed just from the thought.

Maybe you could squeeze through farther on, or find something to climb on for a boost?

I was better off taking a quick look before trying to jump a fence and hurting myself even more. I trudged down a ways, keeping my shoulder to the fence.

"Help! Hey, help!"

My gaze focused farther ahead. Through thick mud, a man wriggled out from under the fence. Only his head and neck showed. His features blurred under a thick layer of dirt. He was five big steps away from me. The head disappeared, and two hands began clawing handfuls of earth out.

He screamed his plea for help louder. A mistake. Soon I heard a zombie approach, then his hands jerked from sight. A ragged scream preceded a drawn out, gurgling death sigh.

I pressed forward. I didn't need to see what was going on behind the fence to know, but it didn't matter. I couldn't help even if I wanted to. Besides, I wasn't in the mood to backtrack.

Hot blood poured into the tiny ditch the guy had created, steam rising up from it.

I skirted it as quietly as I could, even though I knew the undead behind the fence would be too distracted to try and come after me.

Moaning and loud tearing made me cringe. I imagined three or four zombies pulling the guy in half.

I've seen that in a movie before, haven't I?

While I tried to remember what movie a torso-rip happened in, I drew closer to the encampment. Behind me, the sounds of the man being eaten slowly faded, but were replaced by a soft whimpering.

I rounded the sharp corner of the fence and found a wooden segment. Small gaps between each slat showed a figure standing behind it.

I would've kept walking, but it was the best place I'd found to try and climb over. Pieces of wood were nailed horizontally to the vertical posts. I could easily use these to boost myself up.

"Eddy, is that you?"

"Ah, no," I replied awkwardly. "But I'm not here to hurt you."

It was a woman about my age. She leaned close and peered at me through the slats. I stepped to the side, getting a quick glance of what was behind her. She was wedged between a shanty and the fence.

"He said he'd come to get me. That we'd leave," she whispered.

This shanty roof was only inches above the fence. Once I got up there, if the roof was stable, I'd climb onto it. Good plan. If I crawled to the other side, I'd be able to get a layout of the town, and—

"Will *you* save me?" Her voice escalated since I hadn't responded

"Shhh! Quiet. They'll hear you."

If it wasn't for her, it would've been perfect. She pushed her bloody fingers through the fence, reaching for me. I finally focused on her, and our gazes connected.

"Please, help me."

Like I haven't heard that one before.

"Just be quiet, okay?"

"Help me," she said, but her tone took on an aggressive, deeper tone. "Or I'll scream so loud every living *or* dead person will come running."

If there was one thing I didn't stand for anymore it was being played. "So? I just watched a guy get eaten."

Nearby, maybe only two shanties away, clattering sounded, like pots clanking against one another. Both of us stopped speaking, but once no further noises came she continued.

"I don't know you," she said, wiggling her fingers and squinting. "Who are you?"

I didn't reply and she didn't seem to care, because she confessed to me anyway.

"Minister Encler hid the keys to the gate three days ago. Some of us got away right after the dead took over, but then the storm came. Fence's too slippery to get over, too many of *them*. People are coming out of their hiding spots to try again. Eddy…"

"Fine, I got it. Why didn't you just climb over and escape yourself?"

"My arm is…hurt"

That was an immediate red flag. Usually when someone said 'hurt,' it meant they'd been bitten. It was painfully predictable. But if I didn't help her, she'd give me away. I decided not to think of it as her playing me. We'd earn mutual benefits from the deal.

"I'm going to come over. Just get up one or two planks and I'll pull you up."

I holstered my gun and, despite the pain in my leg, got to the top and straddled the fence. Over the roof of the shanty, two more shabby buildings came into view, and beyond that an open courtyard. Bodies were strewn around and the Zs shambling to them.

I bent down, pressing my stomach into the edge of the fence. The girl did as I said, awkwardly maneuvering until she reached her good arm up and grasped my hand. She was already cold and sweaty. She weighed next to nothing, and even in my weakened state I was able to help haul her up.

She mirrored my position, wobbling to keep her balance. I didn't wait for a thank you, but instead brought my other leg over, getting ready to climb onto the shanty roof.

As I set one knee onto the roof, I heard her gasp. She must've lost her balance. She hurdled toward me, head connecting with the roof, which made her neck twist at an odd angle. She fell back into the narrow alley, her impact sending out a loud, echoing bang.

The howl of a runner preceded a chorus of groans.

That's what I get for trying to help someone. As usual.

"Eddy?"

I was surprised she wasn't dead, but I wasn't going to stick around. I pushed myself off the fence and spread my weight evenly over the tin roof of the shanty.

Their vocalizations escalated. They must've seen her. I twisted until I could peek over the edge. Her body was completely paralyzed, but she blinked furiously and her lips quivered. She was looking beyond me, into the sky. I'd seen that look before, when someone knew it was the end.

A painfully thin runner darted into the alley and pounced on her. Blood sprayed the fence as the runner tore into her neck like a rabid dog feasting on its catch.

I shimmied up the slanted roof until I could see farther out. Sure enough, at least ten slows and a handful of runners were making their way from the courtyard I'd seen earlier.

Directly in front of me was another shanty, within jumping distance. While I waited for the Zs to clear away below, I reassessed the two story building and the area around it.

Each shanty was about fifteen to twenty feet wide and there were six to my left, spanning to the other side of the enclosure. The shanties were built to circle the two story, with a large expanse of space between the two. The second story was smaller than the first, creating a tower on the left side. The rest was flat roof. Three double doors and windows on the first story. A painted white cross on most of the doors.

I should've realized it was some type of church.

Veins of red traveled through the mud, and it took me a moment to realize this came from the church. Thinner, crimson paths trailed from the bodies strewn all around the courtyard. Blood from the initial slaughter three days ago, I imagined, mixed with storm water and today's fresh kills. It trickled down the slight incline towards the beach.

I took a breath and shifted backwards, laying my cheek on my hand. The church was where I had to go. It had to be. Blaze was in a cage somewhere, according to that girl, and I doubted it was in one of the shanties. Where else would prisoners, especially a witch, be held captive?

The feast grew louder as more zombies gathered. I looked out again. No more came from the immediate area. Mentally cursing at every squeak my boots made against the roof, I crouched, then stood.

Another deep breath. I jumped to the next roof. My bad leg buckled and I came down to one knee. Ended up laying down. It wasn't even a jump. More of a big step.

In the shanty underneath me I heard shuffling, but it stopped right away. Probably a living person, hiding and alarmed by noises on their roof.

I needed to speed up. I ejected the Glock's clip and counted a total of 12 rounds, including one in the chamber. If I kept my calm, I could make it out of there on 12 shots. I'd been in worse situations before. I slammed the clip back.

My clothes were stiff from the cold. Little ice crystals brushed against my hand as I reached into my pocket and withdrew the bottle of Oxycodone Dr. Banks gave me. The traction on the fingertips of my gloves made pressing and turning the childproof cap easy. I took one and waited. It would take at least 10 minutes to kick in, so I wanted to give it a head start.

I felt the sharp edge of the locket box when I put the pills back. Dr. Banks would never know if I delivered it or not. Whether I delivered it or not wouldn't make a difference. After seeing what a mess Fort Christian was, it was safe to assume her sister was dead.

I crawled to each side of the shanty to find the best way down, and found a lean-to built on one side. It didn't look stable enough to hold my weight, but it would at least break some of the fall.

The feast quieted. It was only a matter of time before zombies began to disperse, making my goal a hell of a lot harder. With one deep breath, I sat on the edge of the roof, planted my feet on the lean-to, and climbed down. It protested at the weight, and as I dropped down I saw it was no more than a plank of wood propped up with two flimsy metal poles.

Getting out is going to be harder than getting in.

My body felt loose as the Oxy took effect. The pain in my leg fuzzed and I felt warmer.

I tightened my grip on the Glock and stayed towards the middle of the narrow streets, between the shanties. All of the windows and doors were cutouts without any coverings. Only some showed curtains, while most were gaping, black holes.

Feeling confident, I began walking faster, glancing down each alley as I went. I stayed away from the courtyard and got as close as I could to the church.

Drugged up and armed, I clenched my jaw and made a run for the double doors. Death followed right behind me, chasing my coattails.

Chapter 25

Hands grabbed at me. Mouths opened and closed, dripping bile and rot. Light from outside illuminated every fucked up sight in the congregation room, every zombie that wanted to eat me.

Me. The only living thing in sight.

The doors weren't locked, but I wish they had been. The Plexiglas windows were spray painted white, so I couldn't check inside before I entered. I might've tried to do things differently, had I been forced to reconsider my idiotic frontal assault.

Regrets were useless. There were at least twenty Zs in the room. Though there could've been more.

Most were near the back of the building, huddling together in their usual unspeaking, clueless horde. Some of the poor corpses were entangled in overturned chairs and tables. Others were maimed so badly that they could do no more than wiggle their torsos and snap their jaws.

And the smell? Every bodily fluid that can be produced by a human was plastered, splattered, or pooling on the walls and floor.

I wanted to puke, but couldn't spare the time. A handful were close to the doors when I opened them. They lunged at me. The Oxy made my body feel good, but it didn't help my aim. I fired a round into a teenage boy's neck, knocking him back.

A burly older woman grabbed my arm, yanking me to her like I weighed nothing. Her bite would've broken skin, but my layers of soggy clothes gave me just enough protection. Lucky for me, the round I fired hit its mark. Gooey brain matter splattered onto the wall, blending into the collage of other fluids.

The boy came at me again. Over his shoulder, I saw another Z. Another teenage boy. A segment of femur had torn through his leg. The jagged whiteness was speckled with blood and pressed through ribbons of rotted flesh. His broken leg dragged behind him, his boot scraping against the wood floor.

Behind them was the only open door in the area. Inside the room beyond, a ladder reached up out of sight. Other than that, the area was small. I would've seen any undead lurking within. There were none, so instead of wasting bullets on the unmanageable horde, I burst past the two between me and the door, knocking them to the ground.

Shredded fingertips grazed me. I held my breath and hurdled into the room, pulling the door shut behind me. A zombie toddler got caught between the frame and wood just as I slammed it shut. His pudgy gray skin burst and thick blood oozed down the center of his face. I removed him with one swift kick, yanking the door shut completely.

A heavy wooden plank leaned against the wall to my right. I shoved my gun back in its holster and hefted the beam, dropping it into slots on either side of the door.

The thunderous pounding of fists against wood came a moment after.

I allowed myself a minute to catch my breath. A quick check assured me that the old woman's bite hadn't broken through. My pulse raced in time with the beating on the door. It was the only sound I could hear, and it threatened to overwhelm me.

The room was void of body parts. Only smears or small pools of blood marked anything out of place. In its center, a metal ladder went up to a closed wooden door. I brought my gun back out, but after two attempts of climbing one handed I gave up and stowed it again.

When I reached the top, I tried to listen for motion on the next level. Even if there were ten of them up there, I wouldn't have heard it. The Zs outside were louder than ever. I could picture them pressing against each other as hard as they could, ignoring the existence of their fellow undead.

There was no latch or handle, but I pressed the entrance upward with the palm of my hand. It gave way then stopped, as though caught on something.

Loops of rope connected the top of the hatch to a metal ring fixed into the ground. I used my free hand and retrieved my knife, sawing at it until it broke free.

Now wasn't the time to hesitate. I pushed it open completely, eyes darting about the room.

Three beams of light sliced through the darkness of the tower's second story. The brightness filtered through shotgun holes in a wall opposite a gun jerry-rigged to the top of a desk.

I made it halfway through when something shifted in the tower.

Her midsection and most of her ribs were obliterated. I'd seen wounds like that before. The girl must have escaped the slaughter downstairs by going into the tower and tying the hatch shut. Living threats wouldn't have been able to open it, runners would never have the patience to use their dexterity to climb the ladder, and slows were just too dumb. If it wasn't for the knife, I wouldn't have been able to force it open.

As for the bloody craters in her torso? She made it up, but tripped the shotgun trap. Too bad for her.

She wobbled over from the corner, fingers outstretched and grasping. I scrambled, sliding across a slick pool of blood as I crawled out of the way.

I turned onto my back and found she'd made faster progress than I would've liked. She was in front of the hatch, awkwardly bending down to grab at my foot.

Why waste bullets? I kicked, aiming for her chest and hoping I'd knock her down into the first story. But my lack of success was embarrassing. My boot crunched and dug deep into her ribs. When I tried to yank it back, it only brought her closer to me.

My foot was stuck.

She was small, maybe about fifteen before she died, but despite her light weight I couldn't shake her off. Globules of congealed blood and chunky bile pumped out of her mouth each time I tried to dislodge her.

Using my other foot, I gave her ribs another firm kick. This time she flew off. My boot came free with an audible sucking noise. Down the gaping hole in the floor she went.

I crawled across the small distance to the door. After pulling it shut, I tied it with a piece of the rope I'd cut off.

There wasn't time to revel in the close call. Once I looked about the room and saw what I'd just risked my life for, an overwhelming sense of grief took hold of my entire body.

There was a desk, a cot, and a bureau. On the domed ceiling and walls, countless white crosses were spray painted, mocking me with their crazy, feverous design.

What wasn't there was a cage with Blaze in it.

That dominant, snide part of me chided the emotional, desperate side. *Did you really think you'd find a cage with her in it? You're so fucking stupid.*

My other side rebutted. *It's not over yet. She's here somewhere.*

You lead him on a wild goose chase, you idiot. We're both *going to die now.*

"That's enough!"

I bit my chapped, quivering lip and squeezed my eyes shut. The rhythmic pounding of the undead downstairs faded into one obnoxious blur. That fuzzy feeling the Oxy gave me dimmed.

Another one won't hurt, I thought as I popped a pill into my mouth. *Isn't this what* normal *people do? Make it all go away with a pill?*

I wasn't crazy. I was just having an inner dialogue, not hearing voices. I just needed to regroup.

But how? This was supposed to be it. The final destination. End all be all. Every time I *regrouped* I had a clear plan, and usually a backup plan. But most of the time my plans were half-assed at best. I needed to level with myself. Had I been flying by the seat of my pants the whole time? What was I supposed to do now? Even if I had come up with an alternative, the situation was beyond control.

My only exit was packed with zombies. I was freezing and in pain.

It all hit me at once. I *was* fucking stupid. Who goes that far to try and have a chance at that obscure, useless concept called "love." What was I thinking? Every justification I made along the way was for naught. There was no point in trying anymore. The spark of determination and conviction that got me to the beach was overwhelmed by the cruel hand of reality.

Blaze wasn't here.

Instead of regrouping, re-justifying, or giving myself a pep talk, I laid on the sticky wood floor, ready to let the hypothermia take me.

Chapter 26

Beatrice Wright had gotten used to the smell of cooked human flesh. After a while, she learned to block it out. When she blew up Fort Christian's propane tanks, the fatty, oily scent was nothing more than another fact of apocalyptic life.

The explosions were a last ditch effort to get the undead out of the church and courtyard. Minister Encler kept all the weapons and boat keys in the bureau upstairs, far out of the reach of his "disciples." All Blaze had to do was get them coming in her direction and she could loop around, get inside, and Rambo the fuck out of that place.

Many zombies caught fire, but not nearly enough. Blaze climbed rooftops and darted around shanties until she had a clear view of the church. She tightened her grip around the crowbar she'd scrounged up from somewhere.

Of course the doors had to be shut. *Of course* the undead were too stupid to get them open. They weren't even locked for fuck's sake! The damned things were still shambling around inside the church instead of coming to the barbeque.

Then she saw something happen she never expected. A figure with fiery red hair came out of nowhere, limp-running to the church doors. Was he on drugs? Did he have any *clue* what was in there? What kind of idiot…

It hit her. The one and only, fucked-her-over-big-time, Cyrus V. Sinclair. She recognized his face before he disappeared inside. What was *he* doing on the island?

Cyrus V. Sinclair. If anyone asked Blaze, the V stood for vile.

Months ago, when she woke up alone in the middle of nowhere, she was confused and hurt. She barely knew who she was, let alone *why* she was. After a day of wandering through a fucked up town called Goldbar, she remembered who helped her get that concussion. Blaze went back down the highway to the broken bridge, only to find her prized Mustang wrecked and flooded on the side of the riverbank.

No Sinclair in sight.

She'd have gone to Frank's cabin, but she had no clue where it was. She gave up without trying to find it, and spent a couple weeks in a farmhouse off the side of Highway 2, not far from the bridge. She used the time to let her head heal and build strength for the journey, reverting to her original plan from back in Monroe. Lay low out East near the mountains then go to the island.

When she felt the slight chill of fall, she began her trip to Samish Island. It didn't take her long to raid Goldbar for supplies and a couple guns, get a vehicle, and reach her destination, even though she'd been abducted by the groups of Cannibal Crazies (as she liked to call them).

The whole journey, she rode on the hope that she'd find her brother. It was silly, sure, but it was something. She knew if he was alive, that's where he'd be headed.

Then the incident with Minister Encler almost ruined her. He abducted her at Samish, effectively turning every Fort Christian inhabitant against her by claiming she was a witch. Something about how the first frost of fall happened the night she showed up. Later, it was obvious that the minister was trying to reunify the group. His control over them had already slipped.

Being kidnapped was bad, but nothing she couldn't handle. Getting to the island and finding out it was taken over...that was harder to take. It meant Beau wasn't there, or if he was he would be captured, too.

The whole thing *almost* did her in, but not quite. She knew to wait until the time was right to escape. After that she planned on killing every single motherfucker who'd even *looked* at her the wrong way since she got there.

Three days ago, before the unspoken restlessness of the colony ran its logical course and the people rebelled, she escaped The Cage.

Blaze laughed under her breath. The Cage was their term for lockdown in one of the smaller, windowless shanties. There were three of them, used for Encler's disciples who misbehaved. Blaze was a permanent resident in one.

It was a classy place to stay compared to the trucks the Cannibal Crazies had put her in. Food and church once a day, a roof over her head, and hey, no attempted rape. Encler was a lunatic but he taught them sex of any type, if it wasn't with him, was a mortal sin.

That was wrong, she guessed, but it worked to her advantage. The only thing she didn't prefer were the beatings she'd get three or four times a week.

She banished the memories and focused back on the present.

Cyrus.

In her short time with him, she'd noticed his inability to follow through. He thought he was strong and calculated, but he was just as bipolar as any other person she'd met. And the pet ferret? What the hell? Did he think he was in a Disney movie?

She exhaled slowly, taking her eyes away from the church and leaning against the shanty at her back. Blaze would kill for a cigarette. She'd gone cold turkey since she been there, but it wasn't enough to break the deep rooted need.

A flash of regret swept over her. Then as quickly as it came it was gone.

Blaze took her time circling the church once more, running past the slows and killing the runners. When she saw an opening, she wasted no time. She darted across the courtyard.

Chapter 27

Since when could a zombie climb? Were the undead changing? The fingers and boots jamming into the shotgun holes in the wall were fast. Not clumsy at all. I lay on my side, shivering, as the tip of a crowbar shot through one of the holes. The curved end jerked the wooden panel off.

I couldn't muster up the energy to move. The second Oxy was in full force, making me feel light headed and apathetic. It would make my death a lot easier.

Another plank clattered away. Bright sunlight poured into the room. I squeezed my eyes shut and flopped onto my back.

I readied myself to die. But instead of ragged screams and grasping hands tearing me apart, I heard steps. Then nothing.

"Well, well, look who it is. The cocksucking fucker who left me for dead. And I thought we were buddies, Cyrus."

Great, I thought. *There she is again.*

"Get away from me, zombie Blaze. I'm not in the mood."

"Are you on drugs, you dumbass? Do I look like a zombie? Can zombies climb walls?"

There she was, hovering over me. She scowled. That ragged scar down her left cheek blended into a new scar on her forehead. Dirt and smears of blood coated her skin. Her hair had grown longer, but still shot off in different directions.

It had been so long since I saw the woman, I'd forgotten what she looked like. The photo I stole from Beau portrayed a Blaze that no longer existed. The one standing over me was the survivor on overdrive I met months ago. A feral insanity dwelled behind her dark eyes.

This wasn't the zombie Blaze that haunted my dreams. That woman was a fabrication my subconscious cooked up to confuse me, to more effectively guilt-trip me. But then again, the person in the room with me…I wasn't sure I knew her either. From the brief time I spent with her, something captivated me. Was that same callous, practical, and cool woman still within her?

Snap out of it, Cyrus. Are you a romantic now? You can't decide she's changed based on the look in her eyes.

I sat up. My head swam. All I could think to say was, "I came to find you. To rescue you."

"Rescue me?" Blaze didn't wait for another response. She turned on her heel, marching over to the bureaus I'd seen earlier. Under her breath she muttered, "Fucking idiot. I'm rescuing him!"

So much for riding in on a white horse to save her.

My name is Cyrus V. Sinclair. I wished the V stood for valiant, but it was more like valueless in that moment.

She rammed her crowbar between the bureau doors, breaking it open. Weapons of all types were packed in rows in the small space. Blaze repeated the process on the other bureau, with similar results. An old .22 rifle fell over, crashing onto the ground. A bullet whizzed by me. My ears rang.

"Be a little more careful—"

"Hey!" she cut me off. "I don't want to hear a *word* from you."

"What's the problem?" I pushed myself to my feet. "What the hell did I do? I came all this way to save you."

She took a deep, long breath then turned to face me. That wildness was gone. Cold, calculating Blaze seemed to be in control again. "Let's resolve this right here, right now. I'm not getting any younger and I want to get the hell off this island."

"Okay."

"You left me for dead back in Startup."

I took a step towards her, but stopped when I saw her fists tighten.

"That's not true," I said. "I woke up and you were gone. I looked for hours and couldn't find you. I swear."

"Yeah? You didn't look hard enough. We shouldn't have been in that situation to begin with. If you'd been paying attention, you wouldn't have driven off that bridge."

The scene came back to me as though it happened only moments ago. Golden sunlight caressing her face. My gaze catching hers. Not being able to look away when I realized I *felt* something for her.

"When I met you, I changed. I—"

Her hand came up to silence me. "I changed my mind. I didn't know you were going to get so fucking heavy on me. I thought this was going to be fast. We're not on movie time here, Cyrus. This is real life. A minute is a minute. With every one you waste, more undead gather outside."

I felt so stupid. That was happening an awful lot lately.

She saved me from having to say anything more. "Are you able to shoot?"

"Yes," I said.

"There are plenty of guns in here, but the problem is ammunition. The nutjobs weren't into conserving ammo, so we can't stay and just pick them off from up here." She surveyed the contents of the bureaus. "Help me sort what's left. We take whatever gun has the most rounds."

I helped her, trying desperately to act sober and focus on the task. A bone-shaking shiver coursed through me. My knees almost buckled.

Instead of sympathetic words, Blaze looked at me and asked, "What's your problem? Can you climb?"

If she was going to be a jerk, so was I. I mustered up some fire and spat back, "Does it look like it? I'm fucking freezing to death."

"What? Did you swim here?" She turned away and yanked open the lower drawers on the bureau. Miscellaneous papers and other junk flew as she dug through them. She finally came up with bunches of clothing and tossed them at me. "Get your act together. It would be nice to have another trigger finger to help out, but I can get out of here on my own if I have to."

I bent down, snatching up the heap of clothes. Two pairs of dusty jeans and an obnoxious green sweater were all I had to choose from. I moved away from her and peeled off my cold, stiff garments. My skin erupted into gooseflesh when the cold air hit. I wasn't going to look stylish, and what I did have wasn't that warm, but it was better than the chilly alternative.

My vest wasn't too saturated with water, so I pulled that back on after I shook it out as best I could. It felt better to have *something* protective on instead of walking around in plain clothes.

"You take this shotgun," Blaze said. "We've got thirty rounds. Here's ammo for that Glock. Can you climb?"

I glanced at the jagged hole she'd created in the side of the tower. A crisp, cold breeze came through. Beyond the shanties, the bright daylight filtered between the evergreens.

Then the pounding downstairs reached its crescendo, followed by a loud bang. It had to be the door downstairs. Enough persistence seemed to get the undead anywhere. Any thought I had of trying to get Blaze to Rambo it down the tower and through the church vanished.

"Yes," I said, though I meant, *I don't have a choice.*

"It's not hard," she said, stating it more than reassuring me. "There are support planks about a foot apart around the entire building."

A chorus of clinking caught my attention. I peered around Blaze in time to see her shoving key chains in her coat pockets. There were many sets. Most were wooden bobs, or anything that would float. Definitely the keys to the boats I'd seen on the beach.

I fit the last shotgun shell into my vest and jeans pocket. It took every bit of extra mental power I had to block the thunderous waves of embarrassment flooding me.

Blaze wasn't interested in waiting. She had an assault rifle slung across her back and a satchel that bulged with ammo boxes. She went first, turning around and picking her footholds carefully.

I came over once the top of her head disappeared from sight. Directly below the tower was the roof of the congregation area and the horde of Zs. She scaled down the wall and gingerly dropped down onto the roof, not turning to see my progress. Blaze crouched and went to the edge of the building.

Unlike her, I didn't have a shoulder strap on my gun. I called out to let her know I'd have to drop it. Finally ready to co-operate, she caught it when I tossed it down.

No one liked getting left behind. I kicked it into high gear and began climbing. Adrenaline pumped through me, my thoughts of suicide fading by the second. My leg still felt good from the Oxy as I wedged my boot onto the thin protrusions and climbed down. A couple of minutes later, I was on the roof with Blaze.

They were everywhere.

Whatever had distracted the undead—probably the explosion I'd heard earlier—wasn't enough to keep them away from the church.

Some had probably seen Blaze, but the gunshots alone were enough to draw them. The whole town was there.

I'd seen movies like this before. Almost anything that had *of the dead* at the end had a scene that described our situation. Slows pressed up against each other and the building, five deep. Runners paced on the outskirts, some hitting each other or growing frantic at the sight of us, blood spewing from their mouths as they howled. How many times had I seen this in the theaters? End of the flick and the last characters were surrounded.

"Not many behind the church. They're trying to get in through the front doors," Blaze said.

I gingerly crossed the roof, painfully aware of the creaking boards underneath me. Sure enough, there were less on the other side.

One of them looked up at me, raised a gnawed hand, and groaned. The rest followed.

I jumped when I heard a gunshot and turned in time to see Blaze aim again. Another shot cracked.

"I'll take out the runners. Figure out a way to draw the ones behind us to the front," she ordered. "Trust me. I've got a plan. Just do it."

The authority in her voice let me know the plan wasn't up for debate. I didn't need to have every detail explained, but a basic overview would've been nice.

There were sixty, maybe more, in front of the church. Behind that there were fifteen at most. We couldn't just climb down. They'd see us right away and make it over before we could get to the ground, even though they were slow.

I didn't need to think about what to do. It happened naturally. As I stood there, they congregated around my area, moving in from the sides. I moved a couple feet to the right. Sure enough, the Zs followed me, as though they had a chance of magically levitating upward.

That was all it took. I took a few steps to the right and led the group around the corner. Blaze's gunfire excited them, too, and seemed to encourage them. It took a while, longer than I wanted, but after she stopped firing eventually they joined the mass in front. If I could gather them far away from the side we were going to climb down on, Blaze would have a clean exit on the opposite side. Once I left their sight, they'd disperse and try to follow me back, but in the time it took them to get around the building I'd be climbing down then booking it out of there.

"Huh," I mused aloud. "Easier than I thought it would be."

"We're not in the clear yet," Blaze said, shooting down my optimism. "They won't focus on us for long. I'll go first. Toss your gun to me then get your ass moving."

I gave her a minute head start to climb down the back of the building, shouting and waving my gun around to keep the Zs interested, then crossed the roof. A loud splitting made my heart sink. My foot dropped through the roof, all the way to the knee.

"Blaze! I'm stuck!" I grunted as I tried pulling it out. My wiggling dropped me farther in, all the way to the hip. My left knee was bent hard. I tried to push myself up and out. "Wait, come back!"

I strained to hear her over the wild moans of the undead, but there was nothing. Something brushed up against the tip of my boot. I knew what was beneath me. What was waiting to drag me down. I visualized them getting a hold of me, pulling hard enough that my entire body broke through the roof, snapping in places it shouldn't…

If Blaze was coming back, she'd be here by now. I strained upward as far as I could to see over the edge of the flat roof. In the distance, Blaze came into view as she dodged between two shanties towards the beach. Once there, she'd use one of those boat keys to get off the island. Far, far away from me.

Panic overtook me. I used every bit of strength I had and planted my hands on either side of the roof then pushed.

When I was a kid, my grandma told me stories of women lifting cars to save their babies, or men being capable of extreme acts of strength in order to save someone. *It's fight or flight, Cyrus*, she would say. *If they decided they had nothing to live for, or nothing to fight for, they'd run away and regret it their whole lives.*

I didn't believe women lifted cars to save babies because, hell, why would they *ever* need to lift a car off a baby, but the main idea was what stuck with me. At some points in life, you have to decide if you are going to whimper like a little bitch and die, or—in the words of my selfish, abandoning friend Blaze—cowboy the fuck up.

Exposed nails and sharp pieces of ply-board tore through my pants, scraping me from hip to knee. As my leg came free and I looked down the gaping hole, a mass of undead clawed at each other trying to get me, arms outstretched.

I wanted to yell in happiness, or spit in their faces, but my body pumped endorphins into my bloodstream so fast I felt disoriented. I went on auto pilot and staggered to the edge of the roof, tossing the shotgun into the mud as far away as I could before I climbed down.

Slows lurched around the corners of the church and came from the alleys between the shanties. They were closing in on me fast, so if I didn't make a run for it now, I'd die.

Flight or fight, Cyrus.

I felt warm blood soaking my jeans where the cuts were particularly bad. I gritted my teeth, accepting the pain, and jumped the last couple feet to the ground.

When I turned to run for my gun, I bumped into two of them. They'd closed in on me faster than I predicted.

One was a woman in a soiled dress, dead longer than most. Her lips were chewed off. Teeth were broken or missing. Next to her was a man, his arms torn off at the elbows and half his body burnt to a crisp.

The lady was slow, so I wasn't sure how she'd gotten to me so quickly, but the man was fast. His reflexes were twitchy, and since he had no arms he flung himself at me, head first, and snapped his jaws.

I barreled between the two and lunged for my shotgun, nearly tripping over myself as I lifted it and turned. I fell flat on my ass, but facing the oncoming undead. I pulled the trigger. Nothing happened.

Stupid, stupid! Pump the gun!

I shivered with delight then I aimed, pressing the butt of the shotgun into my shoulder, and pulled again. The top of burnt man's head exploded. The area from his eyes up disappeared. Brain and blood splattered onto the church wall behind him. He fell to his knees, unmoving.

More flooded in from the front of the church. I got to my feet, saving my shells and choosing to run, or rather jog with a limp, into the shantytown.

But they really were everywhere. A handful of them closed in from the sides, coming around the corners of the little huts. They clogged the alley I planned on going down. I raised my shotgun and mowed them down, aiming for heads, but sometimes only hitting bodies.

Blood and gore sprayed the mud. Chunks of flesh blew off torsos and extremities, spattering other undead and buildings. Those who I didn't put down permanently got knocked over by the body shots. Four pumps of the shotgun later, I stepped over dead bodies and kept going in the direction Blaze went.

Nothing had ever been so clear. Regardless of what happened so far, in that moment I knew exactly what I needed to do. Fight my way through the onslaught of zombies and get to the docks. Take Dr. Bank's boat and leave. With or without Blaze. After that, I didn't give a fuck.

I rounded a corner and came face to face with two slows. They took me by surprise. I managed to get off one shot, which obliterated the Zs face in a flourish of red. Its companion grabbed the shotgun and stepped in closer, the other hand stretching towards my throat.

I pulled the trigger, since the Z had pulled the barrel towards his body. The round left a gaping hole in his stomach, pushing him back. His grip was too strong, though. Maggots and chunks of who knows what plopped out of his mouth as he opened it to groan.

I released my hold on the gun and used one hand to keep him at bay, my hand planted firmly on his chest. It was risky, but I didn't have a better idea. The bastard was heavy. I withdrew the Glock and brought it under his chin.

Boom.

A fountain of brain spewed from the exit wound. He dropped. I put the Glock away and pried the shotgun out of his iron grip.

From close by came a loud metal-on-metal squeak. It echoed through the town, undoubtedly drawing the attention of any zombie in the area. Down the street, a shanty door flung open and a very alive family of three dashed out.

The gate, I thought. *Blaze got it open.*

I continued jogging, occasionally glancing back to see the oncoming horde squeezing through the alley. Blaze hadn't taken out every runner, and they were trying to push their way through the thicket of slows in front of them.

A minute later I cleared the shantytown and came upon the gate. It was huge, made of welded steel, and was slid to the side.

The family I'd seen struggled with two Zs just outside the gate. The dead would win that battle. They'd already taken down the mother, and the father was trying to pull the feasting undead off her. Redness spread from his neck down his shirt. He'd already been bitten. The little boy stood still, watching the scene hopelessly.

But it wasn't my problem. They were gone. I rushed past them and cleared the gate.

***

In front of me was nothing but trees, and through them I saw the Puget Sound glistening in the midday winter sun. The fresh scent of pine and the saltiness of an ocean breeze replaced the nasty rot of Fort Christian.

The vegetation grew thinner on this side as I followed a path to the beach. Grass and dirt gave way to rocks and pebbles. In the distance were the docks. Yachts and motorboats bobbed in the water, all safely roped down.

Queen Banks, I thought as I trekked through the sand. *That's the boat I'm looking for. And where's Blaze?*

My boots thudded against the wooden dock. I stopped and strained to listen. Under the sound of the water and boats bumping against each other was a familiar sound. Pulleys. Wind in sails.

There was movement at the end of the makeshift dock. I moved low and quiet until I could see.

Sure enough, it was Blaze. She prepped a sail boat for launch. I'd killed two birds with one stone, since the boat she was on was *Queen Banks*. Dr. Banks said it would be a sailboat and that was the only one around. Blaze had the keys to all the other boats, but I could see why she chose this one. When it ran out of gas, she'd have no issue traveling by wind.

I had the upper hand this time. So why was *I* sneaking around when *she* was the one who'd left me behind? Blaze didn't make any effort to save me, whereas when she got lost I at least tried.

I stopped hiding and straightened up, walking straight for her.

Fight or flight, Cyrus.

Blaze saw me right away. Dropping the rope in her hand, she drew her assault rifle. "You made it, huh?"

I aimed the shotgun at her, taking every step slowly as I went to the plank. "That was low, Blaze. I thought we had something."

"Listen, you cocksucker, it's kill or be killed. How many people have *you* left behind to survive? To get a few extra seconds?"

Many, many people, I thought, *including your brother.*

I came up the walkway. We were mere steps from each other. I watched as her eyes shifted to my side, towards the beach.

"They're coming out of the forest," she said, refocusing on me. "If we're going to—"

Now *I* got to cut her off. "I've got the keys to this boat. Truce for now. Let's get out of here."

It took her a second, but she lowered her assault rifle and stepped aside. "Truce. Welcome aboard, Captain Cyrus."

Chapter 28

Dawn of the Dead remake, I thought as I watched the undead crowd the docks. *That's what this reminds me of.*

We'd worked together to get the boat going. It had some gas, so we pulled out of the dock and cleared the area in no time. I could still hear the zombies' desperate calls. The splash when they accidentally pushed one another—or simply walked—off the dock and into the icy depths of the sound.

Neither of us spoke as she studied a map we found in the main cabin. Inside was the truly dead body of none other than Dr. Banks sister, Melinda. It was a suicide. The yellow sticky note said *"I'm sorry I didn't listen -Melinda."* Dried blood trickled down her chest from the ragged bite mark on her neck. Suicide instead of zombification. I'd seen it before.

The body wasn't old. She must've escaped with the bite when the onslaught first began. In her right hand was a measly .22 pistol. Enough to get the job done, nothing more. I checked the gun and it was empty. She had one shot and made it count.

She laid on the floor between the kitchen nook and benches. Sticky, dark blood pooled around her head, traveling downward and under the door that led to the living quarters in the back of the boat.

When I realized who it was, I placed the locket around her neck. Blaze didn't ask, and I didn't explain. We dragged her body onto the deck and tossed it overboard. Who knew? Maybe it would float to Samish and Dr. Banks would find her. See that? I did her favor. I didn't let her down after all.

After we found a course to take, an awkward tension grew between us. I kept my side towards her, so I could see if she was going to pull anything, but found myself getting distracted watching Fort Christian grow smaller in the distance.

The engine gave a soft hum as Blaze turned it down. I watched her from the corner of my eye as she walked closer to me to pick up her satchel.

The first punch hit my cheekbone and hurt like hell. As my hands came up to block her, her other fist connected with my jaw.

"You useless, lazy motherfucker!" she shouted, grabbing my forearm and swinging one of her legs under mine, bringing me to my knees in one swift motion. "You think *I'm* the bad guy? Well fuck you!"

It took me a second to reorient, but once I did my aggression came out in one long, powerful wave. I grabbed her fist as she tried to punch me in the head and pulled her down, using her own momentum to send her flat on her stomach. I clenched that hand and brought it behind her back, twisting it upward.

"I'm sick of you, Blaze! I came all this way for a coldhearted bitc—"

Every bit of animosity she'd been carrying for me over the past months surfaced as mine did. She flung her body to the side and my grip loosened. A hard kick landed in my stomach, knocking me backward. My head hit the railing on the side of the boat.

She got to her knees and lunged. Both her hands wrapped around my throat and she squeezed.

This was serious. She really wanted to kill me.

"You can't go around trying to change people," she snapped as I clawed at her hands. "People don't change, you dumbass! You knew exactly what I was before you went gallivanting off to find me. What made you think I wouldn't be a coldhearted bitch now?"

I struck the crook of her straightened elbow with as much force as my position allowed. Her arm buckled and she was knocked off balance. She caught herself, came in again, but I reacted faster and hit her face. Blood dribbled from her lip as she looked back at me. I stood.

"*You* changed *me*."

Blaze's chest heaved. She ran her tongue over her teeth. I felt warm liquid stream from my nose. I tasted blood.

"I'm not telling you who to be, Blaze," I said, my voice lower. "But I'm not going to pretend I don't feel something for you. And when you've never felt anything for *anyone* in your life, it's a big fucking deal when you do."

When she didn't even blink, I kept going.

"I've had nothing but the determination to find you keeping me alive. I didn't know what I'd say to you if and when I found you, but I *knew* if I found you I'd figure it all out. And here I am, figuring it out."

Silence.

"There's something wrong with you. There's something wrong with everyone. But that isn't going to stop me from trying to make something out of this. You can tell me you don't feel anything for me, and I won't care. You can tell me you want me to fuck off and die. I won't care. If you told me you're going to kill me, I'd tell you I'll sleep with one eye open every night. I—"

"Shut the fuck up!" preceded her next blow. Her fist acquainted itself with my nose. More blood.

I couldn't take it. The pain of everything—her rejection, my body shutting down—made me crumple to my knees.

Blaze was on top of me again, her hands on my shoulders. She pulled me up and slammed me back onto the deck. My skull hit the wood.

Blackness.

Chapter 29

"She didn't run away."

Waves. Splashes. Salt water.

Where am I?

"You left her."

Blood and snot in my nose. Dryness in my throat. Pain in my wrists and ankles.

I opened my eyes. We were in the cabin of the boat. Blaze was laying on the bench in the window nook, feet propped up and back against the wall. Dim light shone through the open cabin door and port windows. A tiny red dot brightened and dimmed as she inhaled her cigarette. Shadows cast one side of her face in darkness.

Where did she get that cigarette?

She tapped the ash onto me while I looked up at her. How much of Melinda's blood and brains had rubbed into my sweater? For that matter, how did I get here in the first place?

I coughed then gagged. A wad of cloth was stuffed in my mouth, held there with another band of fabric around my head.

"We all left her."

I tried to speak, but all that came out was garbled. Unfortunate. I had a hell of a lot of questions. Why was I tied up? Where was my stuff?

"Are you listening?"

She brought her legs down and kicked my side. A spasm shot through me. I tried to curl around the pain in my ribs, but she stopped me with her boot.

Listen to her, Cyrus. That's what she wants.

I inhaled through my nose. The junk in there sucked back and dribbled down my throat, but at least I could breathe.

"I'm going to kill you. If you care so much about me, you'll answer my questions. Understand?"

I nodded.

"Your little friend Gabe, remember her?"

I nodded again. I pictured the Gabe I remembered now. Enrobed in white, being protected by cannibals.

"She didn't run away." Smoke billowed from her nostrils. She looked like a demon when the embers of the cigarette reflected in her eyes. "I went into her room while you and Frank were sleeping. I sedated her. I dragged her out of the house and put her in the shed in the backyard. Sedated her again just to be sure.

"You and Frank fell for my lie. Because you *wanted* to. Deep down you both knew she was useless. That's why you didn't question me. All I had to say was that she left. I let you do your half-assed check of her room, but then we left. We *all* left."

Did I tell her Gabe was alive? It was the only card I had that I could hurt her with. But I wasn't in any position to talk back. She wasn't bluffing. I was on the edge of death. One wrong word and she'd kill me.

"What do you think of that, huh?"

It made sense. It did. Gabe would never leave—*you're so fucking stupid, you knew that, Cyrus*—she'd never run off to be on her own. Blaze deceived me. She used me. Lied to me. Got rid of Gabe because it made things a little easier for her.

So many sensations bombarded me that I went supernova.

The truth I always suspected was confirmed. But now what? What did Blaze want?

"You don't feel good, do you, Cyrus? You feel fucked over. You feel how I feel right now."

She moved fast, putting her arms under my pits and dragging me out of the cabin. My ass thumped against the handful of stairs. She dropped me and I shifted onto my side. It was lighter outside, not quite sunset. The sun was a raging shade of orange. Purples and reds brushed across the sky, gradiating into inky blackness.

There's my stuff, I thought as I focused on the heap of items in front of me. My gun, my vest. Everything was scattered across the deck. Everything but—

Blaze flipped me onto my back and stood over me. She leaned down and shoved something in my face.

And there it was. Blaze Wright's smiling face looked back at me from the photo, her brother missing from her side.

"Where the fuck did you get this?"

She wasn't smiling now.

In fact, once she took the photo from my sight, all I saw was the barrel of a gun.

Epilogue

Blaze and Cyrus huddled around a campfire deep in the woods of the Pacific Northwest, fending off the unusual summer night chill. Their packs were nearby, rifles within reach.

They hadn't been settled in one spot for years. The transitory feel of the scene was familiar. Comfortable.

"The Brotherhood massacred an agro settlement ten miles north of Valtown. Every time they take out a survivor's settlement they become more confident. They're the biggest group of crazies we could ever imagine killing and the most deserving of death. We need to do this, Blaze. It's what we've wanted to do since we started." Cyrus smirked. "Besides, Valtown's leader is desperate for us to help him."

"*You* started this. I should've shot you when I had the chance."

"You're still sore about something that happened five years ago? Give me a fucking break."

She scowled. The light from the campfire shone in her dark eyes. The ragged scars on her face deepened before they were obscured by an exhale of cigarette smoke.

"Besides, you know if Beau is alive he might be there," Cyrus reasoned. "Every time we go on a hunt, I see the hope on your face."

"And how about the fucking depression when he isn't?"

"That, too."

Blaze kicked the edge of the fire with the heel of her boot, sending sparks flying towards Cyrus. He shielded his face and brushed them off as they landed on his clothes.

He knew she wouldn't hurt him. Not really.

"We're running out of supplies. Valtown, Surville, and Brickston have raided every city within a hundred miles. We can't squat in a house or salvage anything useful from the suburbs anymore."

"And who helped them raid? We did. It's our own fault we rely on them for supplies. We help the survivor's colonies find supply hoarders, untapped cities, and neighborhoods. All the gung-ho, guns blazin' bullshit you talked about? We never do that anymore."

She was right. Cyrus had convinced her they should kill every crazy they could find and she had liked the idea. It kept them together, and they did just that in the beginning; slaughter cannibals and raiders.

But after a few years, survivors with good intentions started securing and colonizing cities, specifically easily fortifiable storage unit facilities. They scavenged supplies closest to them first, but their population and need for resources spiraled outward continuously until Cyrus and Blaze had no choice but to deal with them for ammunition, guns, and other necessary supplies. Blaze wouldn't leave the northwest corner of Washington because that's where Beau could be. It was both of their faults. Cyrus wouldn't say it out loud.

Cyrus tore the top off his last red Pixy Stix and sprinkled half on his tongue, savoring the sweetness. Even candy was a commodity. *Everything* was a commodity. The survivors colonies had every-fucking-thing. Knowing this next sugar fix might be his last made him appreciate each morsel even more. That's why they *needed* to kill The Brotherhood. If they did, every town would owe them. Talk about bargaining power. They'd never want for anything again.

Plus The Brotherhood, if their clan descended from Kevin as Cyrus suspected, were the people who seized Beau. Cyrus believed him to be dead. How could someone be captured by cannibals and still be alive five years later? But it was all that kept Blaze and him together.

Blaze squeezed her eyes shut. "Fine."

"I knew you'd agree," Cyrus said. "This will be it. I can feel it. We'll find Beau. We'll kill them all."

Blaze stubbed out the cigarette butt and flicked it aside. He watched her and couldn't quite hide the smug, self-satisfied smile that played at the corner of his mouth.

Cyrus V. Sinclair.

The V stands for fucking vigilante of the apocalypse.

Acknowledgments

As I write this sentence, I'm filled with profound anxiety, because I'm worried that when my beta reader and first editor Tamara Biediger reads it she'll cringe at the grammar and wonder if all her help was for naught. I would like to assure her that her efforts have made me a better writer. Her editing and commentary taught me more than any of my English classes ever did.

Tamara, your editing hurts so good. Thank you.

For Evan and Matt who have proven to be a kickass fan through thick and thin.

And of course, I thank my group of fans (you know who you are!) who take the time to contact me and share their thoughts on my work.

About Eloise J. Knapp

Eloise J. Knapp resides in Seattle, Washington. She never complains about the rain and rolls her eyes at those who do. She enjoys graphic design and attempts to fend off writer's block so that she might enjoy writing, too.

The Undead Haze is Knapp's second novel. For more on Knapp visit www.eloisejknapp.com

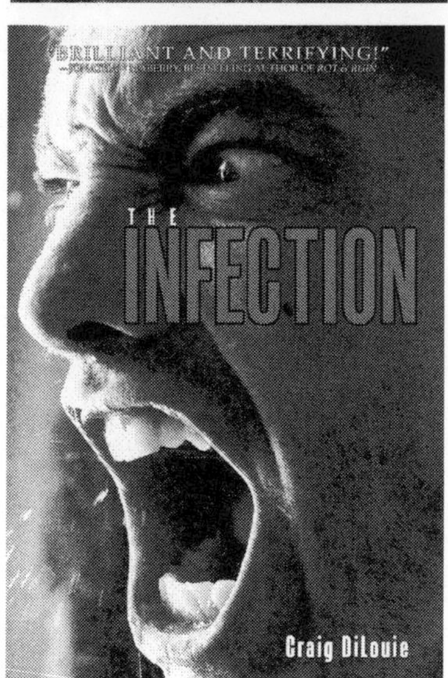

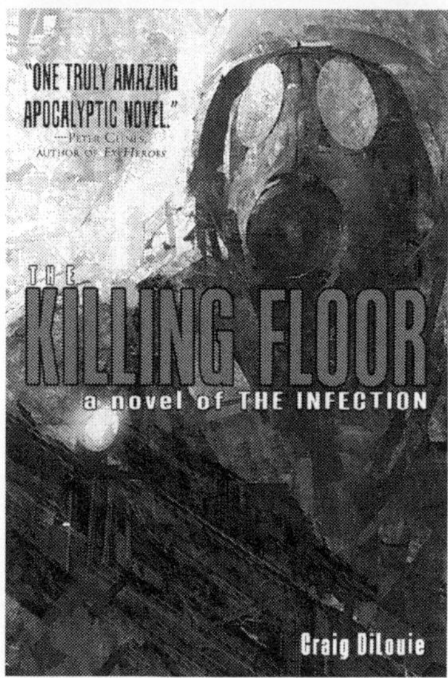

MORE DETAILS, EXCERPTS, AND PURCHASE INFORMATION AT

www.permutedpress.com

Made in the USA
Charleston, SC
28 April 2013